Willow Ashwood:
The Girl Who Danced
with Dragons

EVA ELIZABETH REA

Dragons' House

First published in Great Britain in 2019 by
DRAGONS' HOUSE

A CIP catalogue record for this book is available from the British Library.

ISBN: 978-1-9993707-0-1

In partnership with:

Charity Registration 1132883

Some of the profits from this book will be donated to All Dogs Matter

Dragons' House

This book is dedicated to
kids and grown-ups who didn't do well
in the parent lottery.

About the Author

Eva Elizabeth Rea, B.Sc. M.Sc. Dip. Psych. Dip. Hyp. Dip. Couns. CPsychol. AFBPsS, is a psychologist with lots of experience working in private practice and the NHS. What she loves doing best is helping kids and grown-ups to let go of the ghosts of the past and achieve their goals.

Her work brought her in close contact with the stigma monster that has been intimidating humans of all ages into keeping emotional difficulties under wraps. This book is her contribution to defeating that controlling fiend.

Willow Ashwood, a lonely teenager, triumphs after freeing herself from the sticky claws of the stigma monster.

A note from Eva Rea

I love re-homing rescued pooches; it's a wonderful feeling turning around the life of a homeless mutt. I got my current dog, a Chihuahua, from All Dogs Matter. I'll be eternally grateful to them for letting me have an amazing furry friend. I hope to repay their generosity by donating some of the profits from this book.

My rescued dog is called Pepe. He came with an interesting story that I'd like to share with you. A dog warden captured Pepe when he was living on the streets of London. He had a skin condition and was destined to be put to sleep. A kind-hearted woman rescued him and at a later date placed him for adoption with All Dogs Matter.

He has a Maltese microchip, but the police couldn't identify any travel documents, so they concluded that Pepe was trafficked to the UK.

When Pepe joined my family, he was too scared to go outdoors and didn't make a sound. I didn't want to have a mute hound, so together with my husband, we taught Pepe how to bark. He is now a confident little dog and tells everyone that he's the rightful owner of our house and the pavement in front of it.

If you think about getting a dog, please spare a thought for homeless hounds. I can tell you that they repay the love and care you give them with a huge interest.

Pepe

Contents

CHAPTER ONE

The Voice from Nowhere

Sometimes I really hate my mum. At work, she's a psychologist; at home, a bully. Mum always says all the right things – in a soft and fluffy voice – to anyone who's not family. The way she talks to my dad and me is totally different; more often than not, she uses cross and harsh words. It beats me as to why she's so angry with us.

Why does she turn every little tiff into a battle? She's like an erupting volcano, frustrated sighs bubbling into spiteful words, bursting into waves of molten malice. This afternoon she was in the kitchen, quarrelling with my dad over flour. Can you imagine anything more stupid? I don't know how anyone can argue about flour, but you can always trust my mum to find a way.

'Why did you buy self-raising flour?' she shouted. 'If I've told you once, I've told you a million times: buy plain flour!'

I was upstairs in my bedroom trying to read about the history of peaceful Asian dragons, but I could still hear them both clearly. We live in a very run-down Georgian house, so voices travel freely from one room to another.

'Don't lose your rag over nothing. You know how busy I am at work. I can't remember everything you tell me.'

'I was counting on you to buy it!' hissed Mum, sounding like a volcano just before it erupts.

'If you need plain flour so urgently,' Dad answered back,

'why won't you go and get it yourself?'

The angry voices fuddled my brain, and the words about the friendly oriental dragons jiggled about on the page and wouldn't make sense.

'You're useless!' yelled Mum – the eruption was quite high on the volcanic index. 'You can't even buy the right flour! Is there *anything* you can do?'

Shrinking into myself, I put my hands over my ears and waited for things to blow themselves out.

'How *dare* you! Look at the state of this kitchen, it's a complete mess! One more word from you –'

'If you so much as lay a finger on me, I'll call the police. Do you get that?'

'Don't you threaten me! That's what you always say.'

'This time, I mean it – just you wait and see!' spat Mum. 'I couldn't care less if you lose your job.'

'You watch it –'

That was it – a massive volcanic eruption. I closed my book, jumped up and ran downstairs. I was opening the front door when Mum turned on me.

'And where do you think *you're* going?' she demanded. 'Lunch is almost ready.'

'I'm not hungry,' I said, opening the door. 'I'm going out.'

Mum slammed the door shut, glowering at me. 'You're not going anywhere. You're staying here for lunch.'

No way could I eat anything – I felt as though I was just about to throw up. 'Mum, I feel sick. I want to go out for a walk.'

'You can do that *after* lunch,' she snarled. 'Right now, you're staying here! Do you hear me?'

'I hear *you* alright. The trouble is, you never hear me.' I felt resentment surging inside me. 'All you do is boss everyone around!'

'Eleanor,' said Dad, 'let her go. You know she can't eat when she's upset.' He then turned to me. 'Willow, you can go out, I'll talk to your mother.'

Mum turned her back on me and faced Dad, her blue

eyes blazing. 'Stop contradicting me! Willow behaves like a spoilt brat because you allow her to do whatever she wants.'

Mum is of average height and quite slim, but her small figure can produce a loud and scary racket when she's furious. My poor dad is tall and fit, but his shouting is no match for Mum's bad-tempered outbursts.

Mum was glaring at Dad as though she'd like to kill him – I seized the opportunity, opened the door and shot out of the house, charging forward at lightning speed. A passing car swerved to miss me, the driver sounding its horn and shouting at me to look where I was going.

It didn't take long to reach Hampstead Heath – I carried on running. In my head, a film clip of Mum and Dad yelling at each other played over and over again. My legs moved faster.

After a while, the picture show in my mind changed into a marvellous movie about flying dragons. With every step, my body became lighter. The spectacular loops and cartwheels of these wonderful creatures made the angry voices and nasty film snippets disappear.

I didn't notice the grass beneath my feet; I didn't notice anything at all. The fabulous creatures drove me on. I left the shouting voices behind. I felt a wave of ease and calm throughout my entire body.

The dragons – with their fearless eyes, shiny scales, powerful wings and arrowheads at the end of their strong tails – soared up into the sky and then dived back down. Orange and yellow flames surged from their great open mouths and thick smoke coiled from their nostrils.

Apart from the dragons and the movement of my legs, the world had ceased to exist. Gradually the beating of their wings synchronised with the thudding of my feet. I was at one with the dragons. I was free.

When I reached my favourite weeping willow tree on Hampstead Heath, I collapsed on the grass under its shady enclosure of sweeping branches that almost touched the ground.

I love willow trees and their abundant, trailing foliage; inside their green canopies, I feel kind of sheltered and safe. The only thing I like about myself is my name – it's really cool to be named after a seriously awesome tree.

Inhaling the earthy scent of the ground, I listened to the long, slender leaves as they rustled in the breeze. An inquisitive squirrel stopped to look at me, then scurried up the tree trunk.

'Hey, squirrel, don't be afraid. I'm a big friend. If you come down, I'll bring you nuts next time.' I so wanted to have a little furry buddy, but the squirrel – from his perch on a high branch – looked at me without moving a muscle. 'Please come down,' I begged. The squirrel ignored my invite, turned around and disappeared.

Then, to my surprise and delight, a large brown dog with long, droopy ears padded over and sat down right next to me. He was mostly chocolate brown, save for a white bib on his chest and three dirty white socks. His shaggy fur was matted in places and a bit smelly. He looked at me with doleful eyes. *Poor thing*, I thought. *He must be homeless.*

I would've loved to have given him a good wash and brush, and lots and lots of food, but for now, I just stroked him, looking into his sad amber eyes and loving him even more for being homeless. The hound's coat sent waves of warmth from my fingertips to every muscle in my body.

The caressing movements of my hand slowed down as I became more and more relaxed. My furry pal stretched out and positioned himself close to me. He looked at me, sighed, and then closed his eyes. Both of us knew we could trust each other.

If only I could cuddle him every time Mum had a go at Dad or said mean words to me. This shaggy mutt could shield me from awful things, and, believe me, I have heaps of horrible stuff in my life.

When dusk fell, I embraced my canine chum and whispered in his ear, 'Sorry, I've got to go home now. Next time I'll bring you something to eat, and that's a promise.'

Having given him one final hug, I ran home.

From the outside, my house looked pretty neglected and uncared for, like the homeless dog in the park. But I loved it all the more because it hadn't seen a paintbrush for a long time. Yet it appeared graceful and proud, even in its dilapidated state.

I opened the front door quietly, crept upstairs to my room and switched on the small reading lamp above my bed. It seemed that Mum had stopped spoiling for a fight, but the sound of my parents stomping about downstairs and slamming doors told me they still hadn't made up.

The curtains in my room were old – only their hem retained some of the original bottle-green colour. Decades of dust and soot from the fireplace had painted the rest varying shades of grey and black. The rail drooped in the middle and a few hooks were missing. I reached up and drew them as best I could.

Lying in bed, I gazed at the flaking wallpaper on the shabby walls and the damp patch on the ceiling. I didn't feel like doing anything with Mum and Dad still hostile to each other, so I turned to my favourite pastime of picturing.

I imagined going into Mum's hospital and telling the receptionist that I'm Dr Ashwood's daughter and that she's a horrible mother. But the receptionist insisted that what I'd said couldn't be right because Dr Ashwood only ever says nice things.

My imaginary visit to Mum's hospital ended abruptly with the slamming of the front door: Dad was on his way to the pub to see his mates – that's what he does after a fight with Mum.

I bet he has lots of friends in our local because he can be very jolly – I love the way he jokes with people. My mum has only a couple of friends, but I rarely see them. Neither of my parents ever invite anyone to our house.

My parents are also at odds with each other when it comes to their appearance. Dad is pretty laid-back – his brown hair tends to do its own thing, and it looks a bit wild because he often runs a hand through his shock of curls. Mum only irons her own clothes and Dad's ironing skills are hugely underdeveloped. So semi-ironed shirts and unruly hair make Dad look casual and very different to Mum who spends ages getting ready to go out.

A little while later, I heard Mum leaving the house, too.

I was alone.

Or so I thought.

Just then, I heard a weird, raspy man's voice say, 'A good day to you, Miss Ashwood. I am heartily glad to talk to you. How do you do?'

I went cold deep inside, feeling totally stunned. It was the strangest thing that had ever happened to me. The voice was cracked and hoarse and the pitch was low, like a double bass. I'd never heard anyone talk like this, not even ancient men with very sore throats.

'Miss Ashwood,' said the Voice again.

I couldn't tell if the Voice had come from outside my room, upstairs, downstairs, or if it was just inside my head. My heart started thumping so hard that it felt like it was going to thump its way right out of my ribcage.

I again heard that bizarre Voice say: 'I am truly sorry, Miss Ashwood, it was not my intention to frighten you.'

My jaw had gone stiff – I couldn't say anything. After a massive pause, I gabbled, 'Who's there?'

The Voice croaked, 'My identity will be revealed in due course. If you please, Miss Ashwood, I would like to speak to you.'

Where was the owner of that spooky Voice? I listened carefully, but all I could hear was my thundering heart and blood pumping in my veins. Inhaling deeply, I told myself to calm down, but my trembling body refused to obey.

A lot of questions whizzed in my head like an electrical surge: *What's going on? What was that deep, creepy Voice? How come he speaks in such a weird way? Did I imagine it all?* There were so many thoughts that they didn't fit inside my overloaded brain – I was convinced that one more would cause my head to blow a fuse.

I jumped out of bed and ran to the door. My shaking hand fumbled with the handle. I opened the door, but there was no one on the staircase. Running back, I scanned every corner in my room, but couldn't find anyone.

'Who are you?' I whispered.

'Miss Ashwood, I am a friend. You can trust me.'

'I ... I ... don't understand ...'

'I assure you that I am a friend, and I am very happy to converse with you.' I heard long, deep and joyful laughter reverberating around the room.

'How ... can you be ... a friend?' I stuttered. 'I never met you. I don't know who you are –'

'You will find out when the time is ripe, Miss Ashwood. Or would you prefer I called you Willow? When I was young, everyone was addressed by their surname unless they were well acquainted.'

Thoughts again raced in my head: *He must be really, really old. Perhaps he's some grandpa who's lost his memory and can't find his way home. But then how does he know my name? How did he get in?* 'Who are you?' I muttered. 'Tell me.'

'You will find out shortly. For now, let me just say that my intentions are honourable.'

Somehow, I found within myself a little bit of strength I didn't know I had. 'I don't have invisible friends. Where are you?'

'I am unable to elaborate on this at present,' replied the Voice. Then I heard a deep groan. 'Oh, my joints ache.'

It wasn't the groan of a human being, at least not that of an ordinary human.

'Can I help?' I asked, desperate to find out more.

'Perhaps one day you will be able to help me. I implore you to trust me.'

'It's easy for you to say that. You can see me, but I can't see you. It's not every day I hear voices from nowhere.'

'Oh, I would not say that. In fact, I am closer to you than you think.'

I looked around my room again, but still couldn't see anyone. 'Come out and show yourself then,' I blurted out. And, before I could stop myself, I went on, 'Stop scaring me! You're freaking me out.'

'Is that the right way to talk to your elders? Show me some respect, Miss Ashwood. Young people these days.'

He's an ancient museum piece! 'Alright, I get it. If I ask nicely, will you turn up?'

'Not yet,' said the Voice firmly. 'It is imperative that you do not divulge anything about our conversation to anyone, especially not to your parents. They would not understand. This is our secret.'

'Even if I did, they wouldn't believe me.'

'I insist upon you maintaining silence. Talking about me will spoil the plans I have for you.'

'Plans?' I gasped, shivering in disbelief. 'You've *plans for me*?'

'Miss Ashwood, as I intimated earlier, all will be revealed at the right time. Patience is a virtue.'

'Please tell me just a little bit,' I begged. 'What plans?'

'Upon my honour, they are good plans. I will send you to a special place.'

'What d'you mean?' I mumbled, my whole body trembling. 'This is my home. I'm not going anywhere.'

'But you are not happy here. Are you?'

'No, I'm not, but I'm still staying here.'

'You will thank me for instructing you to go there. I say no more than the truth.'

'Can I at least tell my dad about you?' I pleaded, feeling too frightened to keep it all to myself.

'Absolutely not! I forbid you from doing such a thing.'

'Alright, alright, I'll keep it a secret.' I was now ever so desperate for the Voice to go away. 'I promise.'

'Heed well my words, Miss Ashwood. I bid you farewell.'

CHAPTER TWO

Family Secrets

At night, mean intruders interrupted my sleep. I dreamed of ghosts chasing me around the house and materialising in every room I escaped into. I dreamed of trolls taunting and laughing at me from every computer screen I looked at. I dreamed of kids bullying me at school. I couldn't stop thinking about that weird Voice. Most of the time, it didn't feel real. *Did it happen?* I kept asking myself.

Mum had always grumbled that I was different from other girls; she'd asked me lots of times, *"Why can't you be like other girls your age?"* After my encounter with that wacky Voice, maybe she and the kids in my class were right; perhaps I was a hopeless weirdo who imagines things.

'Get up,' Mum snapped in the morning. 'How many times do I have to tell you?'

'Give me a break,' I mumbled, 'I'm dead right now; I didn't sleep well.' My body sagged down into the bed; it refused to be vertical.

'Get out of bed *now*,' Mum demanded irritably, pulling the duvet off me. 'You'll make me late for work.' She was ready to leave the house, dressed in a black pencil skirt and an impeccably ironed white blouse.

I curled my lanky body into a small ball. *Why can't she get it that I'm a pillow lover and a morning hater?* I asked myself, but out loud I said, 'If you leave me alone, I'll –'

'Get up *NOW*, you lazy bones!' she shouted, grabbing hold of my shoulder and shaking me. 'Right now! Do you hear me? And, just for once, brush that hair of yours. You look a right mess.'

When my mum goes to work, her curls are thoroughly combed, pulled back tightly into a neat bun, and every hair is firmly fixed in its place with an extravagant amount of hairspray.

'I like my hair exactly as it is. I'm thirteen, so I can be a mess if I want to.' *She should know by now that the more she drones on and on about my seriously tangled mass of tight curls, the more determined I become to never ever touch a comb.*

'You don't brush your hair just to annoy me,' she hissed.

For once we understand each other, I thought. I saw anger flash across her face. Mum always lost her rag pretty quickly, but recently it had become worse. *Is it because she'll be forty next year? Whatever the reason, I'd better make a move before she explodes.*

I dragged myself out of bed and staggered into the kitchen, thinking about the Voice from Nowhere. *If only I could tell someone. Mum wouldn't understand – she never has. Dad would listen to me, though it's unlikely that he'd find all that weird stuff credible. Or perhaps, I could tell Sophie, my best and only friend, but she might think that living in a creepy house, turned me into a freak.*

A number of times Sophie had accompanied me to my front door and she'd told me that even from the outside my home looked spooky. Sophie had never been inside my house – Mum doesn't allow me to bring friends home because it's such a run-down dump.

Let me tell you a little about my four-storey Georgian terraced house. It has high ceilings and tall windows. It is situated south of London's Hampstead Heath, so the locality where I live isn't as posh as other neighbourhoods surrounding the heath.

Dad inherited my home from his grandparents before I was born. He said that he'd had lots and lots of plans for restoring it to its former glory, but my parents couldn't agree on how to do it. Mum wanted a modern interior because she hates anything old, while Dad wanted Georgian *décor* on the inside to match the outside. The end result was no improvement whatsoever.

'A penny for your thoughts,' said Dad, handing me beans on toast. 'You've been looking pretty serious lately. Anything on your mind?'

I wanted to tell him about the Voice from Nowhere. At the same time, I remembered I'd been warned against telling anyone. Yet, not being able to keep what had happened to myself, I mumbled, 'I ... I just don't know if I should bother you.'

'Go on, tell me,' he said. 'A problem shared is a problem halved.'

'Do you really want to know?'

'I do,' replied Dad while shifting his weight forward and focusing his light-brown eyes on me.

'It's sort of loopy, perhaps the kind of things you hear from the kids you work with.' Dad is a teacher in a special school for teens with all kinds of problems.

'Listen, Willow. You can tell me whatever you want. Even very wacky stuff.' He smiled and I relaxed a little.

'Well ... if you really want to know ... I hear strange things. I don't know if that's for real or just in my head.'

Dad got up and put his arm around my shoulders. 'Let's have a chat,' he said gently. 'You can be late to school for once.'

I looked into his serious eyes and immediately felt bad – he had enough problems with Mum without me talking about demented things. It might be best not to tell him about the Voice from Nowhere. 'Actually, not right now. I don't want to be late today. Perhaps after school.'

'Alright then,' he agreed reluctantly. 'I won't pressure you. We'll talk this evening. I'll be on my way now.'

After school, I knuckled down to my homework. The English teacher had asked us to write about a book we had enjoyed reading in primary school. It took me one second to decide that my literary hero was Tolkien. The only trouble was I didn't have a clue where I could find my copies of his books.

The lower ground floor had been a dumping ground for many years. I decided that that would be a good starting place. I walked down the stairs carefully, trying to avoid the junk on the steps.

The basement was full of old clutter; tools, tins of paint, rolls of antique wallpaper, broken toys and whatnots. One wall was covered with ancient wine racks and there were boxes everywhere, some empty and some full of old stuff. I walked to a worn-out bookcase with all kinds of things propped on the shelves – even books!

I noticed an old, yellowish envelope between two paint tins. The crumpled envelope intrigued me – I picked it up and found inside some old photos. I recognised Mum's blue eyes and curly brown hair. There were snaps of her at different ages – perhaps from the age of five to fourteen. I decided to abandon the search for the book and get it from the library.

Mum never talks about her childhood. I'd learned way back that asking questions about her family would get her into a real mood, so I'd given up a long time ago. I studied the photos carefully; in a number of them, she was with various different women. I looked at a close-up of her face and shuddered when I noticed that she was smiling only with her lips; her eyes were blank.

In another photo, the camera captured her upper body and head. I was surprised to see Mum behind solid metal bars with fear in her eyes. In that snap, she looked about ten. *Why was she there? Had she done something terrible?* I took the envelope with the photos upstairs.

Unlike Mum, my dad happily talks about his childhood and lots of other things. I can say without any hesitation whatsoever that he has a thing about books. He told me that he'd always enjoyed literature and poetry; a love that drove him to study English at university and become an English teacher. He would often say, *"There's nothing like a good book to take your mind off things and make you feel better."*

My special moments with my dad had been around books. From as early as I could remember, he'd taken me to libraries to choose books that he later read to me. He taught me how to read before starting school and I soon became independent in my reading.

Sitting on the sofa, I buried myself in a book while he read one of his favourite authors. Whenever I came across a word I didn't know, he would explain its meaning. He loves it when I use a new big word – his eyes light up and this makes me learn more.

Using my parents' long, complicated vocabulary and showing off to my dad had turned out to be a game, and that's how I became good with words. Needless to say, Dad introduced me to Tolkien, fantasy and mythology.

When Dad comes home from work, he looks tired but he's always willing to discuss a novel or a poem. I was hoping to distract him from our unfinished "I heard strange voices" conversation by talking about the book I'd chosen for my homework assignment.

My ploy worked during the evening meal. But after supper, Dad said, 'Now Willow, tell me about the strange stuff you mentioned this morning.'

'What strange stuff?' Mum asked, looking at me with her psychologist face on.

'Oh, that,' I said casually, doing my best to sound cool. 'I'm no longer bothered by it. Mum, I found photos of you in the basement.' I handed the envelope to her.

She looked dismayed and then angry. 'You should ask permission before you look at personal things that don't belong to you!'

'Sorry,' I said, taken aback. 'I came across them when I was looking for a book. Why were you behind bars? Who are the women in the photos?'

'It's none of your business!' Mum shouted. 'You know perfectly well I don't like talking about the past.'

'Eleanor, be reasonable,' Dad intervened. 'Willow didn't mean any harm. It's only natural that she wants to know more about your childhood.'

'Why won't you support *me* for once?' Mum snapped. 'Oh, shut up the two of you!'

'Just tell me about the women in the photos,' I insisted, 'and then I'll shut up.'

'Now you listen to me! When I say no, it means no. So drop it now!'

'Stop this idiotic behaviour,' Dad said irritably. 'You're making a mountain out of a molehill.'

I noticed that he was trying to control himself. I'm telling you, my dad's calm most of the time, but when faced with sudden, stupid outbursts, he can lose his cool. That's not surprising, because my mum could turn a saint into a serial killer.

'Alex, what do you know?' she shouted. 'You, with your silver-spooned family.'

'Hardly, my grandparents bought this house when property prices in London were dirt cheap.' he said, pacing around the room. 'Why do you always throw this in my face?'

I felt awful – it was all my fault; I shouldn't have asked about the photos. 'Why do you argue all the time?' I cried. 'Why can't you talk like normal parents do?'

'You spoilt little brat!' spat Mum. 'Don't you dare to teach *me* what's normal.'

As a psychologist, Mum behaves as if she knows everything about normal people and those that are barking. 'It's a real pity they didn't teach you how to talk to your family on your stupid psychology course,' I said, getting up and pacing like Dad.

'The two of you are just as bad as each other!' yelled Mum.

Escaping out of the room, I quickly put on my trainers and a hoodie, and shot out of the house. I knew that unless I ran, my brain was in grave danger of a massive overload and a total breakdown. Jogging on the heath calmed me down, but I still didn't want to go home. I called Sophie – it was a huge relief when she answered.

'I've got a mega-cool new computer game,' she said. 'If you like, we could play.'

'Not sure about playing right now.'

'Has something happened? You sound weird.'

'It all got a bit hairy at home. You know, the usual stuff of my mum getting angry with the whole world. I can never get it right. I desperately need a break from her.'

'Aww, then come to visit me. Get a move on.'

I ran all the way to Sophie's home. She opened the front door and invited me into her room. She has a beautiful dog that's a long-haired, mostly black, Chihuahua. The pooch has tan markings around her muzzle and on the inside of her fabulously big ears. She also has two tan spots above her eyes and matching socks. The dog welcomed me and jumped onto my lap. Stroking her soft fur relaxed me somewhat.

'I've seen a top that I'd like to buy,' Sophie gushed. 'You know what? I think you'd look great in it – a perfect match with your I-can't-stand-combs hairdo.'

Sophie, the chatterbox, is the complete opposite to me. She loves clothes and looking after herself. She's utterly gorgeous: long, blonde hair, blue eyes, and a perfect figure – whatever she wears looks great on her.

And if that wasn't enough, Sophie also has a natural artistic talent for animal portraits. It all had started with her posting online a painting of her seriously stunning Chihuahua. After that, she received lots of offers to paint other people's pets – she actually makes money from doing something she loves.

Sophie's parents are massively proud of her, and the art teacher treats her like a special whizz-kid. So, Sophie has two great parents, a Chihuahua, good looks, natural talent and lots and lots of friends.

You probably wonder why Sophie has any time for

someone like me. I thought about that a great deal and concluded that she made friends with me because:

1. My looks, or utter lack of them, show off her lovely figure – a kind of beauty and the beast situation.
2. She likes anything strange, including weird kids.
3. I look miserable most of the time. Sophie's mum is the caring type and that's why she's kind to me and encourages Sophie to invite me to their home. Sophie puts up with me to please her mum.

Listening to Sophie was difficult with the Voice from Nowhere playing in my head over and over again. She nudged me with her hand. 'Hey, I'm talking to you. I don't think you've heard a single word I've said.'

'Sorry, Sophie, can I tell you something loopy?'

'I love hearing strange stuff. Normal things are so boooring.' She flipped her long hair back and looked at me expectantly. The Chihuahua pricked up her big ears.

'Promise not to laugh. Well ... erm ... last week, after school ... when I was home alone ... I heard a really bizarre voice talking to me.'

'What do you mean?' asked Sophie, looking baffled. 'Who was talking to you? Am I missing something?'

'That's the trouble, I couldn't see anyone. It feels kind of dreamlike.'

'Perhaps that's what happens when your mum's a psychologist and your dad teaches problematic kids. Nothing like this has never happened to me, but mind you, I have a stay-at-home mum and my dad works with computers.'

'Do you think I'm barking?'

'Don't ask me. I haven't got a clue. Why don't you talk to your mum?'

'No way, she never understands. I don't know what to do. The words play in my head all the time, just like a song on a repeat.'

'I've never heard about voices that belong to no one. Hey, wait a minute! Perhaps you've got a ghost trapped in your house – a tormented soul that can't find peace. I always tell you that your house looks spooky enough for a resident ghost. Wow, that's really exciting.'

'Hardly,' I said. 'Actually, it's quite scary.'

'Let's talk about something different then. Do you want to go shopping tomorrow?'

Shopping is hardly inviting when you're the miserable owner of an unsightly body like mine. I've matchstick arms and legs – clothes never fit; they hang on me. With my wild, tangled hair to boot, some kids at school call me a scarecrow. 'Perhaps another day. I think I'll go now.' All of a sudden, I wanted to be alone.

'But you've only just got here! I haven't even shown you my new computer game. It's very special. You can create your own characters.'

That was the last thing I needed; I had too many in my head already. What I did need was a good jog. 'Sorry, not now. I've got to go now.'

I said goodbye to Sophie and her Chihuahua. The moment I was outside, I sprinted into a run – gradually the movement of my legs freed me from the words playing in my head. Then the dragons turned up and accompanied me home.

I was surprised to find my home completely unlit. After opening the door with my key, I called into the gloomy darkness, 'Mum, Dad, where are you?'

There was no reply. The intense silence frightened me. I switched the lights on, but couldn't find anyone on the ground floor. Dread hit me when I heard stifled sounds. *What is it this time? Is it the Voice from Nowhere?*

CHAPTER THREE

Bonzo

I tried my hardest to silence my thundering heart and figure out the whereabouts of the muffled sounds. Even though I was listening really intently, I couldn't detect their location; they could have come from anywhere in the house. I again checked every room on the ground floor, then crept upstairs to the first floor.

Having tiptoed across the landing, I opened the door of my parents' bedroom – there was no one there. I slunk to my room – it was empty and dead silent.

Just as I was going past the bathroom door, the sound of quiet sobbing made me shudder because all at once I knew what had happened. I pushed the handle down, but the door was locked on the inside.

'Mum? Open the door!'

'Go away. I don't want to talk to you.'

The pressure in my chest and head became unbearable. I can, however, put up with this crushing sensation when I picture a macaque monkey jumping onto my shoulder and then playfully taunting me.

The creature also helps in another way; when my head is seriously overloaded with dreadful words and thoughts, I picture handing the worst ones to the monkey. So right then, to prevent a brain meltdown, I imagined a macaque chatter in my ear: *Now look what you've done, you horrid silly brat!* I'm telling you, it helps because monkeys are funny and cute and mischievous, so mean words and thoughts hurt less this way.

'Mum, open the door! Let me in,' I begged, pushing the

door handle down again. I want to be with you.'

'I told you to leave me alone.'

The grasshoppers in my stomach turned into a quivering mass. 'Mum, please open the door.'

'Stop it. You're getting on my nerves, scat.'

I sunk onto the stairs outside the bathroom, waiting for Mum to come out. I knew that my head would start playing a nasty film clip without the protection of a powerful friend. I tried to picture Lightning, my favourite air dragon, but I couldn't conjure him up and, instead of Lightning, an annoying snippet of Mum and Dad shouting at each other showed up.

When dragons refuse to rescue me, as they do sometimes, I then picture the snow-covered mountains of my school holiday in Switzerland. It worked; the awesome Alps stopped the uninvited picture show.

The sound of the bathroom lock turning startled me, sending shivers down my spine. Mum walked out of the bathroom with a tear-stained face. I trembled when I noticed a red bruise on her left arm. I stood up and put my arms around her.

'I don't want you near me,' she snapped, pushing me away. 'Right now, I want to be alone.'

'I'm really sorry. I shouldn't have gone out.' Dad never hits Mum in front of me – believe me, I'm an excellent human shield.

'It's *your* fault I'm still with that idiot,' she said crossly. 'You're just a horrible mistake! I wish you'd never been born.'

Those words hit me like a volcanic lava bomb. Closing my eyes, I pictured a macaque jumping on me again and saying comically: *A horrible mistake! Your parents are together because of you.*

We stood there without saying anything, just looking at each other. The silence was scary. Thoughts whirred around in my head like a tornado: *Dad does want me – that's what he himself has said.* At that moment, other unwelcome thoughts sneaked in: *You've heard all kinds of untrue things; people call them white lies. Was this one of Dad's well-intentioned fibs?*

When Mum says I'm a horrible mistake, panic threatens to shut down my brain. To make myself feel a little better, I remind myself of two fundamental things:

1. It's difficult to even like a horrid brat like me.
2. Because I'm so hateful, it's not my mum's fault that she can't love me.

After re-connecting with these two elementary truths that I sometimes forget, I feel sorry for my mum; she deserved a kid she could love and be proud of. Poor Mum: her mother didn't want her; my dad hits her; and she has me for a daughter. Life is so unfair.

'Willow,' she said, looking miserable, 'I'm sorry. You know I don't mean what I say when I'm angry.'

So that's how it goes: Mum picks a quarrel with Dad – he hits her, and she wounds me with cutting words. Afterwards my dad looks very unhappy and slinks off to the pub. My mum isn't the forgiving type, so she resumes fighting after his return. It all leaves me feeling deflated and totally fed up.

'I'll go to my room now,' I said, yawning. 'I'm dog-tired. I'm sure glad, it's Saturday tomorrow.'

I fell asleep the second my head touched the pillow and woke up early with an unhappy taste in my mouth. Yesterday's events unfolded like a picture show. I wanted to forget my parents' never-ending epic battles; I wanted to forget I existed; I wanted to forget the world existed. But I knew I had to get Mum out of the house before she resumed yesterday's fight.

Having dragged myself out of bed, I picked up my clothes from the floor and put them on. Knowing that Dad normally sleeps on the sofa in the reception room after a quarrel, I walked quietly to my parents' bedroom, hoping

CHAPTER FOUR

My Friend George

Looking at Dad's angry eyes gave me a massive bout of the heebie-jeebies. To calm myself down, I invoked images of the picnic with Mum and stroking Bonzo on Hampstead Heath. It didn't work – Dad's fury blocked any cool stuff.

'Where did you go?' he demanded.

I could hear my own shallow, rapid breathing. 'We went on the heath. I wanted to go there. Honestly, Dad, it was my idea.'

'How could she do this to me?' he snapped, pacing around the room angrily.

I couldn't stop my body from quivering. 'What ... what are you talking about?'

'Last night, your mother sent emails about me to a number of people,' he thundered. 'She'll be the death of me. And then she went out with you as if nothing had happened.'

'Are you ... are you also in a rage with me?'

'No, I'm not,' Dad said wearily, his voice no longer cross. He sank into the sofa and buried his head in his hands. 'Sorry, I shouldn't be so angry in front of you.'

'I ... I thought ...,' I mumbled.

'Look, Willow, I'm truly sorry. All this mess must be very hard for you.'

He had cooled off – the good Dad had returned. I tell you, my dad cares about me, only sometimes he can't control himself. 'Please, don't fight with Mum.'

'I'll be calm. I promise ... I'm sorry.' He stood up and

put his arm around my shoulders. 'Come and sit down. I don't like to see you so upset.'

Looking at my dad's sad eyes, I felt guilty that my parents had to be together because of me. 'Please don't say anything to Mum,' I begged, plopping down. 'Let me tell you something special. We met a super lovely dog on the heath. I named him Bonzo. Poor hound, I'm pretty sure he's homeless.'

'Are you trying to tell me something?'

'Mum has already said that I can't have a pet, but could we go to the heath with some food, just in case we bump into him?'

'If you're not talking about dragons,' Dad sighed, 'then it's dogs.'

'Talking about fire-breathing creatures and canine friends,' I said, hoping to distract him from thinking about Mum, 'I've written a new poem about a Chihuahua and a vegetarian dragon making friends.'

'I love the concept of a little lap dog and a fire-spitting beast forming an alliance,' he remarked, looking a little bit more chilled out.

I breathed freely again. 'I'm going to call it "Chiquita and the Dragon",' I said, feeling relieved that the bait had produced the intended results 'Would you like to hear it?'

'I'd love to. Run upstairs and fetch it.'

'There's no need; I know it by heart. Tell me what you think.'

'It would be great if the kids in my class would take a leaf from your book. I'm all ears. Go ahead.'

I recited:

'Chiquita left her home and stood by the gate,
Looking everywhere for a cool playmate.
A squirrel looked friendly and lots of fun,
"Hi there, red squirrel, come down for a run."
The squirrel said, "Little dog, go away,
I'm in a real hurry, I've no time to play."

On went Chiquita, further from her place,
Still hoping to find a welcoming face.
A rabbit looked friendly and lots of fun,
"Hi there, rabbit, shall we go for a run?"
The rabbit said, "I must hide straight away,
Strange things have happened around here today."

Oh, what's that strange noise high up in the sky?
That creature may want a Chihuahua pie.
I must run away; I must quickly hide.
"Oh, please someone help me," Chiquita cried.
There isn't a hole at the foot of the tree.
My legs are too short for me to flee.

Going away was such a huge blunder.
Oh, why did I do it? I now wonder.
The noise was getting louder and nearer,
The sound of flapping wings became clearer.
Chiquita made herself very small and round.
She closed her eyes and didn't breathe a sound.

Chiquita felt hot air on her little head.
She tried to run, but her legs were like lead.
"Little dog, little dog, don't be afraid,
I'm a true friend and I came to your aid."
"You could be like the wolf in tales I've heard,
To me you look like a scary fire-bird."

"I love little dogs. I love playing best.
So please come out and put me to the test.
My magic mirror on my den's red wall,
Said Chihuahuas are the cutest of them all."
"How do I know what you tell me is real?
I don't want to be a dragon's roast meal."

"I don't eat animals. No, not at all,
I've been vegetarian since I was small.

You're really safe with me as a friend,
We'll have lots of fun, we'll play without end."
The fantastic dragon played many tricks.
Chiquita ran around fetching small sticks.

Chiquita, the dragon did hugely admire,
When he roasted chestnuts with his hot fire.
Together they went for amazing flights,
High in the sky, seeing wonderful sights.
Back at her home, Chiquita opened the gate,
Enter the dragon, her best ever playmate.'

'I love it,' exclaimed Dad. 'Print me a copy. I'll show your poem to my pupils and ask them for feedback.'

'Hey, not so fast. It's only the first draft – I'll let you have a copy after it's finished. Please, Dad, don't argue with Mum.'

'I've promised already. I'll keep my word.'

I wanted Dad to go out – he and Mum needed more time to cool off. 'Why won't you go for a walk on the heath? I always feel better after a run there.'

'I think you might have a point. You know what? I'll do just that. If you want, you can come with me. We may meet that dog of yours.'

We walked on Hampstead Heath, but we couldn't find Bonzo anywhere. 'Shall we look for your homeless mutt tomorrow?' asked Dad. 'Don't worry, strays know how to look after themselves.'

'I just want to see him. There's something about him that I really like.'

'Finding a path into our affections,' Dad laughed, 'is what they do best.'

On our way back home, we went to an ice-cream parlour. I had the most scrummy vanilla sundae with fresh strawberries, topped with melted chocolate.

* * *

Having woken up early on Sunday, I lay in bed wondering what the morning had in store for me. I really wanted to go to the heath with Dad and look for Bonzo again. This thought helped me to get up and face the day.

I walked to the window to check the weather. After pushing the lower sash up, I noticed the inner sill – only remnants of paint showed in places. 'You poor house,' I remarked, 'nobody has any time for you.'

When I was in Year One, Dad told me that our home had been built during the Georgian era; a time when four kings called George reigned. So it seemed right to name my home George. He also had said that King George III was mad. A loopy monarch is cooler than a royal who follows the expected protocol and does all the proper things.

For me, George's windows were his eyes and the panelled shutters were the eyelids. The shutters had lost their handles and most of the paint a very long time ago.

I started talking to George after the first time I'd overheard my mum saying that I was a horrible mistake. Since that time, when I was home alone, I'd let him know about my parents' fights and the cutting words Mum says when she's angry. Sophie tells Chiquita, her gorgeous Chihuahua, all kinds of things, but I'm not allowed to have a pet, so why shouldn't I talk to my house?

Over the years, George became a good friend and that's why I decided to share with him the freaky Voice from Nowhere. I just had to tell someone who wouldn't think I was nuts. I returned to my bed and turned my head to his wall.

'George, something totally weird happened last Sunday. I heard the most bizarre voice talking to me. I just can't stop thinking about the strange words and the old-time way that voice spoke.'

I didn't expect an answer because I always did all the talking; George just listened. When I heard laughter, I jumped off my bed and looked around. *Is it happening all over again?* I asked myself.

It was the same eerie laughter I'd heard before, only this time it was much quieter. I could recognise it in my sleep because it had played in my head so many times.

Thoughts raced in my head: *At least someone, a spooky house or a creepy ghost, is enjoying this barmy stuff. But perhaps demented things are more likely to happen in a house built at the reign of a mad king.*

'What ... what d'you want?' I mumbled.

'Miss Ashwood,' the Voice said, 'fear not. I solemnly promise that my intentions are full of integrity.'

I remembered that the Voice liked politeness. 'Please tell me, who are you?'

'Firstly, let me say that I am aware that you have almost divulged our secret to your father, but in the end you have courageously refrained from that course of action. So now I am in a position to disclose my identity: I am George, your home.'

'Houses don't talk. Are you ... are you a ghost?'

'I am certainly not. I assure you, I am your house.'

My jumbled-up head was spinning as if someone had whacked it with a tennis ball. 'Who are you for real?'

'I am George, your home. I implore you to believe me.'

The more I thought about my home talking to me, the more muddled my head got. 'Oh ... it's so confusing. Is it you for real, or am I losing it?'

'You are fine, you merely need some time to get accustomed to us conversing.'

'I just can't get my head around you talking to me.'

'All buildings have a life force. Over the years they mature until they develop their own personality and an ability to communicate – some people call it a character or a soul. This happens after they have had enough experience. It may take a long, long time, up to one hundred years or so.'

'You've got to be kidding me!'

'I am not,' said the Voice firmly.

'I didn't expect in a million years that you would say anything back to me. Is it really you, George?' I asked, still not knowing what to make of it all.

'I swear upon my honour that I am George, your home. You have been speaking to me for many a year, so it is high time I returned the compliment. When I was built, courtesy and social etiquette were held in high esteem.'

Perhaps life would be more interesting with a talking home, I thought. 'If what you tell me is true, then you must know lots and lots of things about me and other people who have lived here.'

'Over the years,' said George in his deep, croaky voice, 'I have been privy to some joyous events, though other events nearly broke my beams. What you have been telling me has weighed heavily upon my frame, and for this reason I decided to talk to you.'

'So you know all about my parents' never-ending war.' It was a huge relief that another entity witnessed what had been happening in my family.

George was silent for a little while. 'I have beheld all of their quarrels and –'

'Can you talk to them?' I blurted out, desperately hoping that George would *do* something. 'Can you tell them how much I hate their stupid fights?'

'I can only converse with people who are ready to hear me.'

'That's, like, so unfair. I've told you many times that after their rows, horrible thoughts and pictures haunt me, and I mean it; they won't leave me alone. Only dragons can stand up to them, especially my favourite dragon. His name is Lightning. He's utterly awesome.'

'I could not but notice how many hours you spend with them. If it is not reading books or writing poems about them, then it is sitting in front of that strange light box with your fingers dancing on the letter board, in search of something new about these magnificent creatures.'

'I love them and their strength. I know they're good. They help me when I'm down.'

'I am glad you have discovered kind dragons. I like them, too. Some of them are my friends.'

'That's cool,' I said and then a thought struck me: *George and the dragon – a talking house called George who loves dragons?* I couldn't help laughing.

'If you please, young lady, what amuses you so?'

'I named you George, and you tell me that you like dragons. I thought that George was a dragon slayer, not a dragon enthusiast.'

'I will be delighted to recount to you one day the true story of George and the Dragon. George did not slay the dragon. However, at this moment, time is of the essence. I must tell you something of the utmost importance. I have some very particular friends who will help you. Did you notice a stray brown dog on the heath?'

'A large chocolate hound with droopy ears and a white bib?'

'That is the one.'

'He sat next to me on the heath yesterday. I named him Bonzo. Hang on, how do *you* know about him? Don't tell me that, as well as talking, you go for walks on the heath for a bit of fresh air!'

'I wish I could,' George laughed. 'I know about the dog because I sent him to find you. He goes by the name of Billie. He is a member of the Order of the Custodians.'

'Order of the Custodians? I've never heard of them. Who are they?'

'They are the holders of loving kindness. At the present moment though, let me tell you about Billie, or if you prefer, Bonzo. He will take you to a place where you will be helped.'

'No way,' I cried, a shudder running down my spine. All the good feelings from laughing with George evaporated in an instant. 'I'm not going anywhere.'

'I entreat you to trust me. You will be happy there. It is a sanctuary for youngsters who belong to the Nobodies' Club for Kids with Sad Eyes.'

'I've never heard of that club. I'm not part of it.'

'Every unloved child who did badly in the parent lottery is a member.'

'What will my mum and dad say?'

'I will take care of that,' replied George firmly. 'If you please, hear me out and heed every word carefully.'

'I'm staying here,' I said resolutely.

'I insist upon you following my instructions. You will spend the entire school summer holidays in a very special place.'

'I have plans already. I'll be going with Sophie –'

'Now listen to me,' cut in George. 'You must obey my orders to the letter. Prepare to bring with you a powerful torch, batteries for the torch and a change of clothing. Tomorrow morning, precisely at ten, you will go to the lower ground floor. To the left of the bookcase where you found your mother's photographs, count five bricks up from the floor. Look for a loose one and take it out. After doing that, you will see a lever. Press it, and then a section of the wall will open. Billie will be waiting for you.'

'I'm afraid ... of going somewhere unknown ...' I hummed and hawed for a while, and then asked, 'Are you sure Billie will be there?'

'I give you my sincere pledge that he will be waiting for you. Billie will take you to a place where you will meet the most unusual creature you have ever beheld. His face resembles a Chihuahua's muzzle. He has very special, long rotating ears that can pick up sounds from a long distance. His name is Radar and, like me, he can talk. He will take you to a place where dragons dwell. Heed my words, Miss Ashwood. Your father is presently behind my front door with the Sunday papers. I bid you farewell.'

I heard Dad entering the house. My legs were shaking as I staggered downstairs.

'Willow, you're so pale,' said Dad. 'Are you alright? Has anything happened?'

'I'm ... I'm fine. I really am ... just a bit tired.'

CHAPTER FIVE

Radar

I kept waking up at night, tossing and turning, with my head full of the previous week's totally weird events. The Voice from Nowhere turned out to be George, my house. And if that wasn't enough, George had told me to leave my home for the entire summer holidays and meet a creature called Radar. The thought of an exceptional animal with a Chihuahua-like head and very long ears was hugely intriguing, but curiosity was mixed with lots of fear. In the end, I decided to obey George, after all, he had been a good friend for many years.

Early on Monday morning, I found Mum and Dad in the kitchen having breakfast and getting ready for work. It was a big relief to hear them talk to each other, making my decision to follow George's instructions somewhat easier.

'Morning, Willow,' Dad said, smiling. 'You're up early on your first day off school.'

'I couldn't sleep last night and just got fed up lying in bed.'

'That's new,' remarked Mum. 'Normally, I can't get you up. Will you see Sophie today?'

'Possibly … not sure,' I replied, trying to be vague about my plans for the day.

After my parents had gone to work, I stared at the time on my mobile. At five to ten, I walked to the door of the basement, carrying in my backpack the things George had told me to bring: a torch, batteries and a change of clothes. Just then, my dread and doubts increased massively, making my heart beat like a drum.

I stood in front of the door of the lower ground floor, hesitating. Eventually, I took a deep breath, opened the door and walked downstairs. On my way to the bookcase where I had found Mum's photos, I replayed every single word George had said to me.

Standing by the bookcase, I told myself that I could trust my house. The inviting promise of seeing Billie, Radar and dragons was shrouded in fear; I was scared of what else might lay behind the wall. Despite my dread, I decided to push on.

Crouching down on the dusty floor, I counted five bricks up and located the loose one George had told me about, but I couldn't prise it out with my fingers. Searching around, I found a rusty old screwdriver in an ancient tool box and, after a few attempts, managed to tease the brick out.

My heart missed a beat when I found the lever George had mentioned and froze. Uncertainty took over: If something happened, then Mum and Dad wouldn't know where to look for me. I wavered for a while between going back and pushing the lever down.

A few deep breaths helped me to become more resolute. I got my torch out and switched it on. *So here goes!* I thought and pressed the lever. I quivered when a small section of the wall started to open up quietly. To my immense relief, Billie was waiting for me with a furiously wagging tail. Another deep breath helped me to walk through the narrow opening. I reassured myself: *I'm safe with Billie; he won't let me down.*

It was comforting to be next to my furry friend. I buried my head in his neck. 'I don't care that you smell, it's so good to see you.'

My four-legged guide placed a paw on a lever and the opening in the wall closed silently behind us. I shuddered at the sight of a derelict, damp tunnel, feeling the gloomy passageways closing in on me. The stuffy air increased my fear of being trapped. I wanted to turn back and escape from that ominous place.

Billie grabbed hold of my right sleeve with his teeth and tugged hard. He then bounded a few metres ahead, turned around, looked at me and barked softly. I wanted to remain with him, but I was scared of walking into the unknown.

The hound fixed his eyes on mine, commanding me to follow. I felt as if there was an invisible chain keeping us together. I put my trust in Billie and took a few steps into the tunnel.

At that moment, any courage I'd had evaporated in an instant, giving way to overwhelming fear and daunting thoughts: *We could get lost and no one would find us. Best to get out before it's too late.* I froze. Billie turned around, jumped on me and licked my face, plastering it with his slobber.

'Go away,' I said, wiping my face. '*I washed my face this morning, but tha*nks anyway.'

Suddenly, totally unexpected thoughts gatecrashed my mind: *We must hurry. Radar's waiting for us.* Where did these thoughts come from? I was sure that they didn't belong to me. I followed Billie along the creepy opening. When I looked at him, another thought zapped through my brain: *We must walk quickly.*

'What's going on?' I asked Billie out loud. I stopped and grabbed hold of his large head. 'You impish dog, are you planting thoughts in my mind, or am I going nuts?'

I quivered when a mute reply showed up in my head. *I'm talking to you without words. And there's no need to worry; you're absolutely fine.*

The dark tunnel and Billie's unspoken words had completely unnerved me. I stopped and said, 'I've changed my mind. I'm going back home.'

Other thoughts quickly tumbled into my mind. *You won't regret letting me lead you through these passageways. When we're out of this maze, you'll meet Radar and he will take you to a place where dragons dwell.*

'Right now, I've had enough of this horrible place.'

Billie turned around and darted behind me, blocking my way back home with a determined look in his eyes. Once again, he grabbed hold of my sleeve and pulled hard. A command entered my head: *We must speed it up; there is no time to waste.*

I had to stay with Billie – knowing full well that I wouldn't be able to cope in that awful tunnel on my own. I walked briskly, with my four-legged guide bounding ahead of me. All I had to do was to follow him. Now and then he turned his head back in my direction. In some places, water dripped from the ceiling and there was an overpowering smell of dampness. The dark, gloomy underground labyrinth gave me the willies.

At times, I was terrified, thinking that someone was lurking in the shadows. We walked for a long time and, despite my daily runs on the heath, my well-exercised legs started to ache. I desperately wanted to see daylight and breathe fresh air. I wished that all that spooky stuff that felt like a dream, but wasn't one, would end.

Feeling dizzy, I stopped walking. Billie turned around, nudged me with his nose and transmitted another message: We're nearly there. Come on. Even though I was feeling unsteady on my feet, I continued to move. At long last, we reached a door. Billie lowered his nose to a crack between the door and the floor and sniffed for some time. Eventually, he conveyed a message through my head: *It's safe for us to get out now.*

Billie placed a paw on a handle and the door opened. When we were on the other side, the hound pressed a well-camouflaged lever and the door closed quietly behind us.

We climbed up a flight of stairs with streaks of daylight breaking in. The exit was concealed with freshly cut small branches covered in green leaves. Billie pushed them to one side with his strong head and we got out. He helped me to replace the cover by lifting one branch at a time with his mouth until the exit was hidden from view.

We were in the middle of a forest. I hadn't a clue where

it was, but was utterly relieved to see natural daylight. It was wonderful to breathe fresh air after the long walk along the stuffy tunnels. I inhaled lungfuls of forest smells while looking at the bright blue sky.

Suddenly, a magnificent reddish-brown animal appeared from nowhere. I stood completely still and looked in breathless wonder.

The creature had stunningly large green eyes and the biggest ears I had ever seen. He had the body of a reindeer with a white underbelly. I trembled with excitement when I realised that I was looking at Radar – electricity was charging through every fibre of my body. George was right: Radar's head did look like that of a Chihuahua, only a hundred times larger. Billie ran to Radar, wagging his tail and then lowered his body to the ground.

Everyone tells me that I'm tall for my age, so it was pretty cool to have Radar's nose almost touching my face and his ears towering over me. George had described Radar's long, rotating ears. I'd pictured their movements many times, but seeing them swivel in front of me was truly awesome.

Dad had told me that it's rude to stare, but I couldn't help it. Radar was the most incredible being ever. He was totally extraordinary and unbelievably strange. He had the eyes of an old man; I wondered how old he was, but how could I guess his age when any possible wrinkles were covered with fur?

'Welcome, Willow, I'm Radar. I know that your house has told you about me.'

Despite knowing that Radar communicated in words, I was surprised to hear his deep and measured voice. And then I thought: *I should have got used to the idea that it's not only humans that talk after conversing with my house!*

It took me a while to reply, 'He did. Only ... I'm bowled over to see and hear you.'

'You'll get used to me pretty quickly,' said Radar, and then he turned to Billie. 'Thank you for bringing Willow.

You are free to go now.'

My canine friend walked to me. I hugged him and murmured in his ear, 'I hope to see you soon.' I looked at him when he went on his way, feeling sad.

'There's nothing for you to worry about,' said Radar. 'I'll take you to the Custodians' Sanctuary where you'll meet our dragons.'

'Is Radar your real name?' I asked, wanting to know more about him.

'It is. I was named after my big ears. They can pick up sounds and energies from a radius of several kilometres.'

Radar spoke in a confident manner, making me feel calm and secure. 'Do you live in this forest?'

'I'll tell you more when we've time to talk,' he replied. 'Right now, we must hurry to the sanctuary where you'll be safe.'

'Why? Are we in any danger? This place looks so peaceful.'

'Appearances can be misleading. It isn't safe, especially for new arrivals like yourself.'

'What d'you mean? Why would anyone want to harm me?'

'Not so much harm, as trap you. The Nastorians would love to make you one of their own.'

'Who are the Nastorians?' I asked, feeling completely confused. 'Why would they want me to join them?'

'Unfortunately, they like recruiting new members when they're young. By boosting their numbers, they gain more power and dominance.'

'Not so fast,' I begged. 'First, tell me who they are.'

'Time to make an urgent move,' said Radar abruptly, cutting off my questions. 'We must reach the Custodians' Sanctuary without delay.'

CHAPTER SIX

The Custodians' Sanctuary

Radar saying that we were in danger gave me the heebie-jeebies – yet at the same time, I was exploding with curiosity. I really wanted to find out more about the extraordinary Radar with his rotating ears and the Nastorians.

There was no need to ask any questions; Radar read me like a Wikipedia page. 'Be patient, Willow. Right now, we must be on the lookout for any Nastorians in disguise.'

'What do I look for? Tell me just a little about them.'

'You're a persistent young person,' said Radar, sighing. 'Very well. I'll tell you while we're walking. The Nastorians are openly evil; they take pleasure in being unkind, which is why it's easy to recognise them.'

'Wow. Are there any of them around here?' I asked, struggling to keep up with Radar's rapid pace.

'Unfortunately, yes. At least with them, you'll know your enemy and you'll be able to protect yourself. Some Nastorians pretend to be kind and caring and that's why we call them Pretenders. They're masters of trickery and deception and have a great ability to mislead. You must be very careful because of their ability to masquerade as Custodians. I'd rather face an overtly malicious being than a hidden one.'

Listening to Radar made me grow edgier – doubts about leaving home crept into my head again. 'I'm not sure I like the sound of this ...'

'You can prevent Nastorians from detecting you by

creating in your heart and your mind feelings of loving kindness. When you do that, you generate good energy and compassionate vibes. The Nastorians are unable to detect these frequencies; love can't resonate in their stony hearts. When you're having unhelpful thoughts and create bad energy, they'll track you down.'

'So kindness will protect me. Is there anything else I can do?'

'Friendliness, goodwill and understanding others are equally helpful. In effect, any thoughts, feelings or behaviour driven by good intentions will safeguard you.'

'Alright then, I think I know how to protect myself from the openly malicious beings. But what do I do about the con artists?'

'That's much harder because they can mask their malice with fake good deeds and false kindness. It takes a long training and much experience to detect the true nature of the more sophisticated impostors.'

'So how will I know when I come across one?' I couldn't get a grip on lots of fearful thoughts whirring in my head.

'Let's begin by practising how to keep the nasty ones at bay. Concentrate on sending loving thoughts to those you care about, be it an adult, a child or an animal.'

'I love my parents, but at times they drive me up the wall. Sophie and her mum are nice to me, and I absolutely adore Sophie's little Chihuahua.'

'Generate good feelings towards them,' said Radar firmly. 'You don't have to do it perfectly, just don't allow any destructive thoughts to take over.'

I had sent good energy to Sophie, her Chihuahua and Billie, aka Bonzo. But then, a movie show of my parents quarrelling played in my head for quite some time.

My thoughts were suddenly interrupted by a loud, heart-wrenching yelp. Looking around, I saw Billie limping on three paws. He had a terrible gaping wound on his head. Seeing him seriously injured struck me like volcanic bomb – I could feel my throat closing up and my eyes welling up with tears.

'Billie, what happened to you?' I cried, running to him.

Radar blocked my way. Billie yelped again, staring at me with pleading eyes.

'Let me go to him! Can't you see that someone's attacked him?' I tried to move forward, but the maddening Radar again obstructed me.

'Stay where you are,' he commanded sternly.

'What are you doing?' I shouted. 'Are you blind or something? I must help Billie.'

'This is *not* Billie, but a trickster. You've had dark thoughts and the Pretenders have detected those vibes. Now that they know where we are, they'll pursue us.'

'He's not a cheat; he *is* Billie! Can't you see?'

'I've warned you that the Pretenders would use any underhand deceit to trap you. That dog is an impostor. Trust me, I've been living here for very many years.'

'But he looks exactly like Billie,' I insisted, still not convinced.

'This isn't our friend! Together we'll focus on sending our love to the real Billie, and then you'll see the true colours of the hound in front of you. The deceiver you're looking at won't withstand our combined energies.'

I invoked the memory of stroking Billie on Hampstead Heath; picturing him lying close to me. When I looked at the injured dog, he appeared to be unhappy.

'Don't look into his eyes,' commanded Radar. 'He'll try to break your concentration and draw you into his negative energy field.'

Gazing down, I connected with my friend Sophie and her Chihuahua. I then heard the wounded dog growling and the thudding of paws. Looking up, I saw him running away on all four paws. Once he'd disappeared from view, Radar heaved a sigh of relief.

'Did someone injure that dog so that I'd feel sorry for him?' I asked angrily. 'No animal should be harmed, no matter what.'

'The Nastorians and the Pretenders would never, ever hurt one of their own. They show exceptional loyalty to each other. They've used make-up to create the injuries.'

'I'm glad he isn't wounded. I adore dogs.'

'I've noticed! Many unloved kids turn to animals. Right, we must be on our way. The Nastorians will do whatever they can to capture you.'

'Believe me, I'm exhausted. I think I've had enough for one day – this is way more than I bargained for.'

'We're not far from the sanctuary,' said Radar. 'I now have to summon back-up. We must hurry because the Nastorians know where you are.' He tapped his right hoof on the ground and produced an unusual rhythm. 'Other Custodians, like birds and forest animals, will relay my message to the sanctuary and they'll send fast-footed helpers to assist us.'

Fear and doubts about continuing with the journey grew stronger with every step, but then, I heard the thunder of hooves. Turning my head, I saw two red horses racing towards us. As they drew nearer, I stared at them in disbelief. They didn't have horses' heads, they had dragons' heads! I could neither breathe nor move; their strength and beauty chained me to the ground.

Having recalled reading on the internet that some dragons didn't have wings, I was pretty certain that the charging creatures were dragon horses. Pastel-coloured vapours poured out of their mouths and nostrils. I was totally mesmerised by them. This was the most amazing moment of my entire life. Now I definitely didn't want to go home!

'Are they dragon horses?' I asked in a whisper.

'They are,' Radar said. 'They'll take you to our camp.'

The dragons reached us. One of them lay down on the ground. 'Jump onto my back,' he ordered. 'Hurry up.'

I obeyed without any hesitation. In no time at all, he was on his feet and we were on our way. Holding tightly to his long mane, I felt a rush of energy sweeping into every muscle of my body.

At times I feared falling off, but somehow managed to hang on to the galloping dragon. *We're running away from a pack of bullies of the worst kind, and yet I feel excited and buzzy,* I thought.

Radar and the dragon horses stopped in front of a wooden fence with a gate. After Radar had tapped a rhythm on the ground three-and-a-half times, the portal slowly opened and we entered the camp. I dismounted the dragon and walked to the heavily panting Radar.

'I don't know why I feel so great,' I said.

'There's a great deal of loving-kindness energy here. You're mostly safe inside the camp. However, you still have to be vigilant because the Nastorians and the Pretenders keep trying to enter our grounds. You can go for walks in the sanctuary's forest but, should you come across a stranger, don't talk to them, and report this immediately to me. Also, if you notice anything untoward, no matter how small, let me know right away. After your cleansing ritual, you will be ready to join us.'

'A cleansing ritual?' I asked. 'What's that?'

'It'll remove the negative energy you've brought with you from your home and the encounter with the impostor. It's vital to have more good than bad energy, as there's always a risk that the destructive force might take over.'

We walked to a big clearing in the forest. In its centre, on a black pedestal and base, stood a large green marble bowl with wooden steps on two sides. Standing there, I saw a large, black and white hound running towards me.

'This is Winter,' said Radar. 'He's a Siberian Husky. He is very strong and very loving. Be careful, his love may knock you over.'

As if on cue, Winter jumped up and licked my face. I had to steady myself when he placed his front paws on my shoulders, yet I enjoyed every moment of his unrestrained greeting. He looked at me with his piercing blue eyes, and I knew that I had a friend for life.

Suddenly, I heard voices – looking around, I saw children and teenagers walking in our direction. 'Who are they?' I asked Radar.

'They're orphans or youngsters with parents who don't know how to love them. They all belong to the Nobodies' Club for Kids with Sad Eyes.'

A number of grown-ups joined us. A kind-looking old man told us to make a circle around the green bowl. I immediately liked his calm voice and warm eyes. The shoulder-length grey hair complemented the crimson robe and the white sash he was wearing. He approached me, smiling, and immediately, I felt chilled out. I sensed that I could trust him.

'My name is Chris Light,' he said. 'Welcome to our camp, Willow. We'll talk after your meeting with the practical helper.'

Before I had a chance to ask any questions, Chris called, 'Cooee! Can I have your attention? Listen everyone, we're starting by washing our faces with the ceremonial water.'

The girl standing next to me whispered, 'I'm Tania. You're gonna share my room.'

She appeared to be about twelve or thirteen, but her voice sounded much older. I noticed deep sadness in her big brown eyes. The unsightly feature of matchsticks for arms and legs was common to both of us, but we differed hugely when it came to our hair. Tania's black tresses were straight and neatly combed back into a ponytail. In comparison, my unruly corkscrew curls looked wild and completely out of control.

'I'm Willow,' I whispered back.

'The water we wash in comes from an uber-special lake with loads of good energy,' said Tania in a hushed voice. 'It protects us from bad stuff. A sea serpent guards it from the nasties. The bowl for the water is super-cool. It was made by an awesome artist.'

The moment I touched the water, calmness spread throughout my mind and body. The face-washing brought back good memories and made me feel completely at ease. Small children used the wooden steps to reach the top of the marble bowl. It was great to see the sun coming out on their faces when they put their hands into the big bowl.

A pair of green dragon horses joined the two red ones that had transported me to the camp. They stood facing north, east, south and west. Now I had a chance to have a closer look. They appeared gentle, but I sensed they could be fierce. Each had alert eyes, two small orange antlers and a long, thick mane. Their legs displayed trailing tufts of fur resembling red flames.

'Ten steps back, everyone,' called Chris. 'Make space for our dragon horses.'

We all moved back. The dragon horses trotted into the centre. One by one, they dipped their mouths in the marble bowl and then emitted soft, pastel-coloured steam from their mouths and nostrils. Afterwards, the four dragons produced a captivating fire display.

'Do you wanna know what the colour of dragons' fire mean?' asked Tania.

'Sure thing,' I replied.

'The colour and strength of their breath, like, shows how they feel. Pale colours mean everything's good in the hood, get me? But when they get mean, their flames are wicked, ultra-strong red.'

The sound of flapping wings made me look up; I stared in disbelief at four air dragons. I'd been picturing running with airborne dragons for a very long time – I just couldn't grasp that they were in the sky and not in my head. It was a weird sensation; I was in a spooky zone where my secret film clips were available to everyone.

I stood completely still, glued to every detail of an amazing aerial display. One dragon was green, while the other three were sky-blue, red and brown. Their tails were long with a white triangle at the end. Seeing their large wings open in full flight was spellbinding.

They were flying above us; I assumed they were on the

lookout for any danger. The dragon horses returned to their guards' posts outside the circle. Then, one by one, the air dragons briefly descended and dipped their mouths in the ceremonial bowl.

'The air dragons ain't ever gonna come down together,' Tania went on. 'They're afraid that if they all fly down at the same time, we may get jumped.'

'And now,' Chris announced, 'we'll be having fun! Let's begin with drumming and after that you'll sit back and enjoy a wonderful canine show.'

Chris gave everyone a drum and we jammed. Those who were musical introduced variations of their own, creating a rich tapestry of patterns. Some of the rhythms were very complex, all of which culminated in a fast and furious crescendo. After the drumming had finished, an adult with two black and white Border Collies joined us.

'These dogs can do really cool things,' Tania continued with her running commentary. 'They're trained by Alfie Doggard, our dog whisperer.'

The dog trainer looked the sporty type. He wore a white T-shirt and black tracksuit bottoms. *Lucky guy,* I thought, *he probably goes for runs with the hounds.* The dog whisperer, as well as his two canine charges, had brown, alert eyes.

The Border Collies performed a well-synchronised dance. Watching them reminded me of Radar; I looked around and saw him with his long ears constantly moving. The expression on his face was serious and focused. He suddenly raised his head and looked up at the sky. I did the same and saw two dragons, one navy and the other grey. *Where did they come from?*

'Everyone, run to Emerald halls!' shouted Radar.

'Run under the cover of trees,' bellowed Chris. 'Run. Run. Run as fast as you can!'

CHAPTER SEVEN

The Battle

I ran with everyone else, dread choking my throat. My worst fears had been confirmed; we were being attacked by what I assumed were air dragons belonging to the Nastorians on my very first day in the Custodians' Sanctuary.

We did what Chris had told us and kept off the long, wide path leading to Emerald halls. While running in the forest, I had to dodge low-hanging tree branches and massive roots. In some places, beneath thick canopies, the wood was quite dark; I bumped into stinging bushes and nearly tripped.

Having noticed a little boy – looking about five or six – trailing behind, I grabbed hold of his hand. The terror in his eyes made me fearful too, but I did my best not to show it. Two red dragon horses charged behind us. I slowed down and let them reach us. Using all my strength, I swiftly lifted the boy onto the back of the smaller dragon.

'Hang on to the dragon's mane,' I shouted. 'Hang on for dear life.'

The mounted dragon horse slowed down. I tried to run alongside the boy and keep an eye on him, but the other dragon nudged me with his head. 'Run for safety,' he ordered, 'we're guarding from the rear.'

The boy will be okay with them, I reassured myself and turned attention to the ground ahead of me, trying to avoid prickly shrubs and prominent tree roots. Suddenly, I heard the beating of powerful wings above us.

Chris was at the tail end of the stream of kids. 'Thunder

is ready to face the Nastorians,' he shouted. 'Run as fast as you can! The battle is commencing!'

We reached Emerald halls, gasping for air. I helped the boy to dismount the dragon horse. Keeping him in my arms, I ran indoors. He buried his head in my shoulder. He didn't make a sound, but his chest heaved and, at times, his shoulders quivered. I tightened my embrace.

Everyone rushed to the windows overlooking the path between the halls and the forest clearing. At that moment, Tania joined me. I saw the red dragon horses race back to the glade. Where we stood, I had a good view of the unfolding combat.

The attacking air dragons were navy and grey. I was relieved that I could easily distinguish them from our mid-green Thunder.

'Look,' shouted Tania, grabbing hold of my shoulder, 'the Nastorians are on either side of Thunder, ain't that just awful!'

They flew towards Thunder, aiming their breaths of fire at his flanks. Thunder suddenly dived down, and the Nastorians partly hit each other with their own flames. Shrieks of pain and anger filled the air.

'Willow,' cried Tania in nervous excitement, 'Thunder's stopped them from getting closer to us. The Nastorians wanna torch our hall and force us all out. Then, they'll grab you and the other newbies.'

Tania's words made me shudder. With panic taking over, I could hardly think. But after a few incredibly long seconds, I shook my head and then decided that I had to believe in Thunder winning.

Agitated kids cried, 'Come on, Thunder! Get them! You can beat them!'

Thunder's determination was apparent in his sharp and resolute moves. He was smaller than the Nastorians, but he was very fast and nimble. The navy air dragon flew up above Thunder while the grey Nastorian dived down. I held my breath. It appeared that Thunder knew what to do; with swift and constantly changing moves, he sped horizontally and suddenly plunged down, aiming a fireball at the grey dragon. To my huge disappointment, the enemy managed to avoid his fire.

'Why don't other Custodians help?' I asked, fear spiralling through me. I trembled at the thought of Thunder sustaining an injury.

'We can't use all our air dragons in the battle – the other three must guard the sanctuary from other Nastorians,' replied Tania. 'Thunder's our best defender. He's never gonna let them get close to our buildings and burn them down.'

The aerial fight was raging above the glade. A fireball just missed Thunder. Our dragon flew down with the attackers in scorching pursuit. My legs were shaking. Touching the wooden window frame steadied me a little.

Tania went on, 'Thunder's tryin' to keep the Nastorians as close to the ground as possible, waitin' for our dragon horses to join in the scrap – they can't breathe fire very far, so they ain't gonna be of much use if the Nastorians fly high up.'

Thunder flew in loops and zigzags, dodging attacks from the navy and grey air dragons. But then, to my horror, Thunder's left wing was hit directly by enemy fire. He shuddered, lost his balance and was forced to dive down.

I heard cries of alarm and frustration. Seeing him injured felt like a body blow, as if someone punched me really hard in my stomach. When I dared to look out of the window, Thunder was flying horizontally a few metres above the ground.

'You vile beasts,' called angrily a tall, blond boy standing next to me. 'I'll kill you. Chris, can we go out to help?'

'Absolutely not,' commanded Chris. 'Our dragon horses are waiting for them.'

'The small red dragon horse is called Lava and the bigger one Volcano,' said Tania. 'They're gonna help Thunder from the ground. The three of them make a fantastic team.

Other dragon horses from the pavilion are gonna arrive soon.'

Just then, Lava and Volcano charged from beneath the trees with their heads raised and their manes flowing behind them. They aimed breaths of crimson fire at the Nastorians. The attackers, realising that Thunder was injured, turned on Lava; the navy Nastorian shot a fireball, hitting her on the back. The grey air dragon aimed at Lava, too, but to my huge relief, he missed.

I was shocked to see the grey Nastorian diving towards Lava with his talons spread out in front of him, lunging at her head and striking it. Seeing her raise her head and open her mouth in agony, was heart-wrenching.

The little boy who rode Lava to the halls, was standing on a chair next to me. 'They're going to kill her,' he cried. 'I'm sure she'll die.'

Volcano charged towards the grey dragon. I was astounded by the huge fireball he shot at him. And then something incredible happened: Thunder, with his injured left wing, flew lop-sided above the grey dragon and scorched him with his fire. The Nastorian shrieked in pain and let go of Lava's head.

For a few moments, the grey dragon appeared disoriented. Volcano reared up on his hind legs and zapped the enemy's chest while Thunder struck the top of his head. The Nastorian flew to the left of Lava, but Volcano moved in the same direction and shot a fireball at him. The grey dragon then unsteadily flew higher and disappeared from view.

'One Nastorian down,' said Chris, 'but there's still the navy one to take care of.'

Fear and tiredness had now evaporated; a rush of energy pulsated in my entire body. I knew what I had to do. Closing my eyes, I willed Thunder and Volcano to victory, trying not to look at Lava lying motionless on the ground.

Thunder was leaning heavily to one side, each flap of his left wing seemed increasingly laboured. But, even so, he flew towards the navy intruder and launched a co-ordinated attack with Volcano; both hitting the Nastorian at the same time.

'Get him!' the kids shouted. 'Get that Nastorian!'

Tania perked up a little. 'Volcano is Lava's partner. Right now, he's kinda really, really mad. When dragons are driven by fury, they can produce these insane flames.' Turning away from me, she called, 'C'mon, Volcano.'

The dragon horse didn't need any encouragement. He charged after the navy dragon, aiming massive shots at him. He was crazed by rage. I looked at Thunder and my heart skipped a beat; he was gradually losing height. His breaths of fire appeared smaller and weaker.

The Nastorian flew higher and Volcano's fire could no longer reach him. Thunder tried to follow the enemy, but his left wing could hardly flap. He lost height and plunged down to the ground, breaking the fall with his strong talons. It was an immense relief to see the navy Nastorian fly out of view.

'We must get the injured dragons out of the clearing!' hollered Chris. 'They're far too exposed and might be attacked again. I want all the adults and teenagers to come out with me.'

I hurried out with Tania and the others. When we reached Thunder, he was breathing heavily, taking in strangled gulps of air.

Chris leaned over him, 'You must get into the forest! You're too visible here.'

'Don't worry ... about me,' faltered Thunder. 'I'll be okay ... look after Lava ...'

I saw grown-ups rushing to the glade with a large, two-wheeled cart. They tipped its rear end in front of the injured dragon horse. Chris and a middle-aged woman with short grey hair forced Lava's mouth open and poured a potion down her throat. I heard the woman say, 'You must wake up! Do you hear me?'

'She's a body healer,' whispered Tania. 'Her name of

Ophelia Leech.'

Lava raised her head slowly and looked at us with blank eyes.

'You'll have to get onto the cart,' said Chris firmly.

Just then, I saw around a dozen dragon horses of varying colours charging into the clearing and positioning themselves around us.

'They're Custodians,' said Tania, looking relieved. 'They'll block any fire aimed at us.'

A teenage boy shouted, 'The Nastorian is back!'

Looking up, I saw the navy air dragon flying towards us. Thunder positioned himself over Lava.

'Thunder is protecting Lava,' said Tania. 'He'd do anything for anyone. I'm telling ya, he's the kindest dragon you're ever gonna meet.'

I held my breath when a sky-blue air dragon appeared and hovered over us. 'This is Gale,' cried Tania excitedly, jumping up and down. 'She's a Custodian. I guess Radar sent her to defend us, instead of patrolling the airspace beyond the camp.'

The Nastorian air dragon shot a breath of fire at the dragon horses. They didn't flinch; working as a team, they repelled the fireball in mid-air. The enemy dived down and aimed his fire at Thunder.

'That vile Nastorian is after Thunder because he's injured and can't fight back,' cried the blond teenage boy angrily. 'What a horrid wimp!'

Lava tried to raise herself off the ground in vain; on her second attempt, many hands helped her to steady herself. Slowly, she managed to get onto the cart and lay down in it. Two broad-shouldered men fastened their hands to the poles in front of the cart and pulled it towards the trees around the glade. Other grown-ups helped by pushing the rear of the cart. Thunder walked alongside Lava's cart while Volcano galloped around it.

The navy Nastorian again descended towards us. Volcano's furious eyes were fixated on him and he zapped the enemy with an enormous fireball. The intruder flew higher and Volcano's fire could no longer reach him.

The dragon horses accompanied us to the edge of the clearing. They positioned themselves on the border of the glade, their focused eyes scanning the skies. Volcano walked with us until we arrived at a dense canopy created by branches and foliage – at long last Lava and Thunder were sheltered.

Chris turned to the woman who gave Lava the potion. 'Ophelia, start treating them here. I'll take Volcano and Willow to the lake to trap the navy dragon.' Then he told me, 'Willow, run back to Emerald halls and fetch a chalice. You'll find one on the table in the front hall. Fresh water from the lake will help our wounded dragons.'

I raced to Emerald halls, grabbed hold of the chalice and charged back to the canopy. Immediately after my return, Chris, Volcano and I walked briskly to the lake.

'You'll see our sea serpent,' said Chris. 'Her name is Nessie. No prizes for guessing how she got that name. She guards our ceremonial water from the Nastorians, stopping them from ruining it with their malice. The Nastorians can't tolerate loving kindness, so contact with the water makes them ill for a little while.'

The lake was about fifteen minutes' walk from the canopy where we'd left the dragons. Having arrived, we stood beneath a tree and Chris bellowed, 'Nessie, come out.' We waited for a while, and then he hollered again, 'Nessie, we need you.'

Ripples appeared in the middle of the lake – as they drew nearer, I saw several humps moving swiftly in the water. Soon afterwards an aquamarine sea serpent's head with four webbed horns on each side emerged. I was totally captivated by the astounding creature.

'Nessie, I'd like you to help us defeat a Nastorian air dragon,' Chris called out, and then he turned to Volcano. 'We have to lure the navy dragon down. Make yourself visible. Shoot fireballs.'

Volcano emerged from beneath the tree we stood under and produced enormous flames. After a while, I noticed the Nastorian circling above the lake at a safe distance from Volcano. Then, the dragon horse turned and slowly walked back towards the trees.

The Nastorian plunged down. When he was a short distance above the lake, he shot flames at Volcano.

'Watch out,' shouted Chris.

Volcano moved swiftly sideways and the fireball missed him. At that moment, Nessie raised her head and spat water at the navy air dragon, hitting his head and making him shriek. Disoriented, the Nastorian dropped down. Nessie rose higher and sunk her teeth into his right leg.

The sea serpent dragged the navy air dragon down into the water, making him flap his wings frantically. She half submerged the squealing Nastorian and after a while let him go. The enemy rose out of the lake and flew upwards unsteadily. It was great to see Gale, our sky-blue air dragon, chasing him away.

'I think we're safe for the time being,' said Chris, and then he hollered across the water, 'Nessie, are you okay?'

'I'm fine,' roared Nessie. 'I'm always happy to help. Is there anything else I can do?'

'Not right now. Thank you,' bellowed Chris. 'We'll be off now.' He turned to me, saying, 'Willow, get some water. We must hurry.'

I filled the chalice. Chris took it from me and we walked as fast as we could to the thick canopy where Lava lay motionless in the cart. Thunder was sprawled on the ground with the body healer kneeling by his side.

I looked at Ophelia's face and knew immediately that their condition was serious – her anguish and fear were visible to everyone.

'Are they alright?' I whispered to Tania.

'I ... I dunno,' she stammered. 'It doesn't look ... good.'

CHAPTER EIGHT

Emerald Halls

Before I'd had a chance to ask any questions about the injured dragons, Chris said firmly, 'I want everyone to gather in Emerald halls.' I knew I had to obey; right then, he had lots to deal with – my being co-operative would make his work somewhat easier.

On our way to the halls, I inhaled deeply the scents of the forest – hoping that trees and plants would help me to chill out. When we arrived, Chris guided the kids into the main meeting room and asked us to sit in a circle on the cushions on the floor. The emerald green cushions and the matching curtains reminded me of rolling grass-covered countryside.

It was only now that I'd had any chance of having a close look at the interior – the inside mirrored the outside. I loved the bare, uneven wooden pieces on the walls, each had a unique shape with some retaining their tree forms. *A carpenter must have had lots of fun working on this building.*

The large windows allowed remnants of fading light to enter the room. The leaded stained-glass windows depicted forests and animals. Looking at them, I felt a little better, but my eyes kept closing as I fought off overwhelming fatigue. I couldn't help but notice how unhappy some of the kids were; they looked defeated.

'Trust our dragons' fighting spirit,' said Chris calmly. 'We're all going to help them now. Close your eyes and focus on sending them loving thoughts. See them becoming strong and healthy.'

Chris believes that the dragons will be okay, so I will do the same, I told myself. I pictured George, the house, Radar with his rotating ears and Billie, the dog. The three of them helped me to centre my thoughts on the injured dragons; I willed Lava, the brave dragon horse, and Thunder, the selfless air protector, to recovery. I knew I had to create heaps of healing energy. We sat in silence for some time.

'You can open your eyes now,' said Chris. 'Do not allow fear to triumph. I ask you to continue to believe in the power of loving kindness and compassion. And now let's welcome Willow, our newcomer. She was sent to us by her Georgian house.'

Unexpectedly I felt very shy. Shrinking into myself, I gazed at the floor. Eventually, I looked up and managed a smile.

'The kids and the grown-ups in this place didn't have a happy childhood,' said Chris, looking at me. 'I'll tell you briefly about myself. From the age of seven, I stayed in a boarding school. Both my parents had demanding careers, but very little time for me. Everyone thinks you've a privileged life as a boarder in a private school, but in reality, there's bullying and homesickness and no one to turn to. I felt lonely most of the time despite sharing a dormitory with nine other boys. Willow, tell us about your family.'

Chris openly talking about his childhood helped me, but I couldn't bring myself to tell everyone about my mum saying that I was a horrible mistake and my dad hitting her. Staring at my hands, I tried to think what to say – suddenly, I felt a wet tongue on my face. Looking up, I saw Winter, the blue-eyed Husky, standing right in front of me with his tail wagging. I hugged him, muttering, 'I didn't see you coming, you hound!'

Winter took up residence on my lap – despite his size and weight, it was good to have him close to me. He kind of shielded me, creating a barrier between me and everyone else. 'My parents don't get on well,' I uttered. 'When my mum is mad with my dad, she says that they're together because of me. Dad is alright most of the time.'

Other kids talked about their families and how they'd arrived at the Sanctuary. The little boy whom I'd helped in the forest faltered, 'I'm Ollie ... I'm seven years old. My mum and dad ... died in a car crash last year ... My aunt takes care of me now, but she works long hours ... so other family and neighbours also look after me ... I wish I had a brother or sister.'

I flinched when I saw his brown eyes welling up with tears. *Perhaps, I should be grateful for having a mum at all, even if she says horrible things to me.*

A teenage girl with short curly ginger hair and blue eyes introduced herself, 'My name is Kayla. I'm fourteen and it's my third year here. My dad took his own life, and after his death my mum couldn't cope. A number of foster families brought me up. I think that things are okay with the foster family I've now because of me coming here during every school holiday.'

With exhaustion taking over, I could hardly keep my eyes open. It had been the most eventful day of my entire life, but all I could think about was lying down. Despite my weariness, I tried to remain awake until we received news about the injured dragons.

After what seemed to be a very long time, a grown-up entered our room. 'Lava is stable,' he stated in a sombre voice, 'but Thunder is still critical.'

'The healers will take good care of them,' said Chris in a calm and confident voice. 'Right now, I'd like everyone to go to sleep. Willow, you'll share Tania's bedroom in Moonstone halls.'

I gave Winter another hug and told him that I'd see him soon. When we got outside, it was good to see around half a dozen dragon horses waiting for us – I felt safe walking with them to the halls. As we were approaching the building, I noted that it was also built of timber. There were lots of questions I wanted to ask, but I was too tired to say anything.

'You'll love my room,' said Tania. 'It has mega-special furniture with no straight lines. Wow, you look totally gone.'

After entering Tania's room, I muttered, 'Can I lie down for a little while?'

'Of course,' she replied. 'The bed by the window is yours.'

*　*　*

I heard someone saying, 'Mornin', Willow.'

Looking around, at first I didn't know where I was. *What's going on?* I wondered. I couldn't remember how I'd got there. Then, all at once, yesterday's events flooded into my mind. 'Morning, Tania,' I replied, taking in my surroundings.

The bedroom I slept in was totally amazing; it had the coolest furniture in the history of free design. All appeared to be hand-crafted, each piece unique with natural, curvy, flowing contours. None resembled any bed or chest of drawers I'd ever seen before. My bed was oval-shaped and the bedding was leaf-green in colour.

'I love all these rounded edges,' I chortled while running my fingers along the undulating top of my bedstead. 'They make me think about plants and trees. Actually, I feel, like, I'm in a forest.'

'You're right on the money. That's what our carpenter wanted to achieve. He'd love to hear what you've just said.'

I saw a number of large crystals on top of Tania's chest of drawers. I got up and walked to have a closer look. 'This one is so beautiful,' I remarked, touching a pink crystal with a slightly rough surface.

'It's rose quartz. It kinda means love and harmony. Chris gave it to me when I was down in the dumps after my parents had decided to place me in a children's home.'

'Did it help?'

'I think so,' Tania sighed, trying to look cheerful. 'Cool minerals make you feel better.'

'Why didn't your parents want you to live at –'

'I'll tell ya another time,' she cut in abruptly. 'I'm not in the mood to talk about my family. Not first thing in the morning.'

'Sorry, I shouldn't have asked.'

'No worries. After the mornin' ritual, I'm gonna go to Emerald halls and I'll talk to my trust restorer about my lovely family.'

'Trust restorer? What do you mean?'

'They're therapists. They try to convince you that, despite everything, humans are alright.'

I looked at Tania – her face showed that she'd been a fully paid up member of the Nobodies' Club for Kids with Sad Eyes for many years.

'My house told me that I'd stay here throughout the summer holidays, but what about my parents?'

'The practical helper will take care of that. Right now, we gotta get ready. In the bathroom in the top drawer to the left of the basin, you'll find a toothbrush, toothpaste, comb, soap and shampoo. You can use the red towel. It was all prepared for a new arrival, so now it's yours.'

I quickly washed and cleaned my teeth. Then thoroughly combed my tangled mop of curls and threaded them into a ponytail; my hair now looked tame. At home, I hardly ever brushed my corkscrew curls; I think my mum would've been seriously shocked to have seen me so well-groomed.

Tania and I walked to the dining hall. Like the other buildings, it was built of wood on the inside and outside, making it blend with the trees and plants around it. The back wall, though, had large panes of glass that allowed lots of light in. It was good to see well-tended flowers. I could almost smell the scent of roses and hyacinths.

'This place is called Pumpkin Hall,' said Tania. 'The head cook, Coriander Meadows, has a passion for growing huge pumpkins and cooking them. Her cooking is out of this world – totally and utterly yummy. By the way, she's a veggie.'

'So am I,' I laughed.

'Then you're in the right place. You'll love her scrummy meals. I always die for her pumpkin soup. She even bakes pumpkin cakes – believe you me, they're really something. Behind her back we call her Miss Pumpkin.'

Long tables were laden with heaps of food. I sat next to a tall, lanky teenager with unkempt brown hair. I liked his dimples – they made him look different in a nice way.

Tania introduced us, telling me that his name was Liam. When he looked at me, I was taken aback by the unhappiness in his blue eyes. 'Is this your first time here?' I asked.

'Second year,' he replied. 'You?'

'I've just arrived.'

'You'll like it here. I'm forever hungry, so right now I'm gonna focus on the food in front of me. My mum moans that I eat her out of house and home.'

We helped ourselves to breakfast cereals with fresh raspberries. On the table were three large jugs – I thought that one looked like a smoothie, while the other two appeared to be juices.

'What's exactly inside these jugs?' I asked.

'Our morning drinks,' replied Tania. 'They're prepared in the kitchen of this hall. Miss Pumpkin can't stick anything commercial. She wants us to drink only natural, fresh stuff. The green is a mixture of banana, cucumber and avocado, and it's really good. The red is beetroot juice with a bit of lemon. The orangey one is a blend of apple and carrot.'

I trusted Tania's taste buds and tried the green smoothie. I liked the creamy banana and avocado texture. 'Wow, it's delicious.'

'According to Miss Pumpkin, the green smoothie is an energy restorer. We get different juices or smoothies every day. Life is never dull here.'

'I bet, that's the first time I'd had an avocado drink and

heard of pumpkin cakes.'

After the cereals, we'd muffins with home-made apricot jam and Dragon Well tea. I loved the name of that tea, its delicate yellow-green colour and the gentle, sweet taste.

'What kind of tea is it?' I asked.

'It's green tea,' said Tania, 'we get it quite often 'cause Miss Pumpkin reckons that it's gonna keep us healthy and happy.'

'I like it too,' said Liam, 'Don't know about the healthy and happy bit, but it tastes pretty good.'

I wanted to find out more about the food and drinks, but the bell sounded and we had to go to the morning ceremony. On our way to the glade in the forest, I asked Tania whether the morning ritual would be similar to the one I took part in yesterday.

'The washing of our faces in the special water is gonna be the same. Yesterday afternoon though, it was an extra one to welcome you. In the morning, we're having the whole shebang – almost everyone's gonna be there.'

'How do you know all that?'

'I've been coming here during every school holiday for ages. I love this camp – it's my real home. I'm telling you, I belong here.'

We reached the clearing where dragon horses were waiting. I was thrilled to see Radar and stared again at his long, rotating ears. Billie, aka Bonzo, aka kid rescuer, and Winter were playing with other dogs, wolves and foxes. The sight of all kinds of birds on trees surrounding the glade was awesome.

I walked to Billie, crouched down by his side and stroked his head. 'Thank you for bringing me here,' I whispered in his ear. 'I'll be eternally grateful. I owe you a biscuit.'

Billie responded by planting a thought in my mind: *Better make it a packet!*

After the cleansing ceremony, Chris handed all the humans a drum and introduced the daily rhythm. We all – including animals and dragons – practised for a while:

the kids drummed; the dragon horses tapped their hooves; the air dragons rapped their talons; the birds sang; the dogs barked and the wolves howled. Soon we all knew the daily beat and were able to perform it together.

'You know,' said Tania, 'this is the code that opens the gates of the camp.'

'What would happen if a Nastorian or a Pretender overhears us, learns the code and tries to get in?' I asked.

'That has been taken care of by Radar. What's important is the number of times you repeat the daily rhythm. Sometimes we use only part of the beat. Only very trusted humans, dragons or animals know how many times to reproduce it, and the code is changed regularly.'

'But is it safe?'

'Honestly, you gotta stop worrying so much. Radar uses the number of repetitions as a way of finding out who is a true Custodian and who is an impostor. Get it?'

After the morning ritual, Tania said, 'I'll come with ya to Ruby halls where you'll meet the practical helper.'

'What does she do?'

'She helps with things like real-life problems and staying here. She's totally brilliant when it comes to convincin' parents, guardians or social workers that the sanctuary is good for kids.'

'I know for sure that I'll not be allowed to stay here for the whole summer holidays.'

'You gotta give Elena a chance,' Tania grinned. 'You'll be surprised to see what she can do.'

'There's nothing I want more than to remain here. It's better than anything I've ever imagined. I never expected, not even in my wildest dreams, to be with a flight of dragons.'

'Though I stayed here lots of times, during the first day of each visit, I still find the dragons utterly awesome. It's almost – I dunno – as if I discover them all over again.'

'Wow, lucky you! How do you get to come here so frequently?'

'Elena, like, persuaded my social worker to let me come here during every school break. To be honest, I think that everyone is happy to have me off their hands for a while.'

A sense of foreboding invaded my belly when I saw Chris approaching me with a serious expression on his face. 'Willow,' he said, 'you'd better hurry to Ruby halls and see Elena Howell, our practical helper. You'd have met her yesterday, but the attack by the Nastorians delayed your meeting. Unfortunately, your parents and the police are looking for you.'

CHAPTER NINE

The Grand Order of Healers and Helpers

The words, "Your parents and the police are looking for you" felt like a cricket ball striking my head and making me dizzy. Just then, a film clip of my mum and dad quarrelling showed up – it was a while before I could steady myself and say, 'I don't want to go back.'

'We'll do whatever we can to keep you here throughout the summer holidays,' Chris reassured me. 'It all depends on our practical helper convincing your parents that you're safe here. You must hurry now. Tania will take you to Elena.'

'C'mon,' called Tania, tugging at my arm. 'We gotta shift it.'

On our way to Ruby halls, I said, 'Tell me a bit more about trust restorers and practical helpers.'

'Well, they're members of the Grand Order of Healers and Helpers. The order has body healers, trust restorers, a creativity guide, an activities organiser and a practical helper.'

'Wow, that's a list and a half! What do they all do?'

'I'd told ya already what trust restorers and practical helpers do. Body healers look after anything that moves. A creativity guide explores your interests with you – and becomes thrilled when you do something original.'

'Okay, got it, and the activities organiser?'

'Things like dragon horse riding. The best thing she's in charge of is the Custodians' Festival during which dragons and animals show off what they do best.'

'What do –?'

'I'll tell you another time, right now, you need to talk to Elena.'

We entered Ruby halls. It was good to see Billie running towards us and then going through his usual enthusiastic welcoming routine.

'Nice to see you too,' Tania said to the prancing mutt. 'Comin' to Elena's room?'

The hound followed us with his tail wagging, but we couldn't find Elena in her room.

'Billie,' said Tania, 'take us to Elena.' The pooch obliged by bounding happily in front of us. Tania then turned to me. 'I'll take you to the Dragon Horses' Pavilion after your meeting with Chris. I'll wait for you in the front garden of Emerald halls.'

We reached a beautiful garden at the back of the building. A middle-aged woman of middling height, smiled when she noticed us. She was wearing loose, comfortable- looking grey trousers and a blue t-shirt. I liked her immediately, especially her friendly, warm dark-brown eyes. Her black tresses were pulled into an untidy bun with curly strands floating down her neck. She was standing amongst plants and small trees.

'Hello, good to see you both,' she greeted us cheerfully, and then she turned to me. 'I assume you're Willow. Chris told me you'd be coming to see me. I'm Elena.'

I loved her voice; it was soft and welcoming, almost like hot chocolate. 'Nice to meet you,' I chuckled.

'I'm off now,' said Tania. 'Cheerio.'

'This place is really amazing. Can you help me to remain here?'

'I'll do my very best,' replied Elena. 'I hope your parents will let you stay here until you're ready to go back home.'

'Believe me, right now, I'm definitely not ready!'

'Well then, let's go to my chamber and deal with the business in hand.'

'Can Billie join us?'

'I don't see why not. What number shall I call?' Elena asked, after we'd reached her room.

I gave Elena my mum's mobile number. 'I hope she'll pick up. I can hardly ever get hold of her.'

Mum answered almost immediately. The practical helper spoke to her in a calm, gentle voice. 'Mrs Ashwood, my name is Elena Howell. I'd like to talk to you about your daughter, Willow. I'm with her now.'

I could hear what my mum was saying because Elena put her mobile on speaker. 'What's happened? Is Willow alright? Is she in a hospital?'

'I assure you she's safe and well. She's in an organisation that helps children and teenagers when they go through a difficult time.'

'Who are you?' Mum demanded prissily. 'I don't know what you're talking about. Why do you think my daughter needs you? How come she's with you? There must be a misunderstanding.'

'I don't mean to upset you. May I tell you a little about us and what we do?'

'I'm not interested! You crossed a red line when you allowed Willow to stay overnight without obtaining my prior permission. I want my daughter back home immediately. Do you hear me? Give me your address and I'll come and fetch her. I'd like to inform you that the police are searching for her.'

'I know that, kindly let me explain. We're a registered charity and we've an excellent track record that can be verified.'

Mum put her psychologist voice on. 'Ms Howell, my daughter does NOT need your help. She's part of an intact family and loved and cared for by her parents. If you won't tell me where Willow is, I'll call the police!'

'There's no need for that. In the case that you and your

husband will not permit Willow to stay with us, I'll bring her home immediately. Please let me make it clear that I'm not implying anything negative about either you or your partner; kids might have problems because of social media bullying or difficulties at school.'

'I guess, you've got a point,' said Mum, her voice somewhat softer. 'In my work as a psychologist, I come across teenagers who are unhappy for all sorts of reasons.'

'We seem to be on the same page. As you know, hormonal changes in a growing body can also cause misery.'

'Has Willow told you what's upset her? At home, she keeps her thoughts and feelings to herself.'

'Lots of kids do. Actually, as yet she hasn't had a chance to do so; I've only just met her. I've phoned you as soon as possible to let you know that your daughter is safe.'

'I really appreciate that. Waiting for Willow to come home or call was agonising. Can I talk to her?'

'Of course,' replied Elena, passing her mobile to me.

'Willow, why didn't you call me? Both your father and I have been ever so worried. I can't let you stay where you are without first checking the place out. You've got to come back home.'

'I'm sorry, but my mobile was flat and I couldn't charge it. Where I'm is a wonderful activity centre in the countryside. The fresh air has already worked miracles; you won't believe it, but I've actually combed my hair and tied it back in a ponytail. I look tidy and respectable.'

'That's quite something,' Mum muttered nervously, 'but I can't let you stay in a place I've never heard of. Let me talk to this Elena person again. I need to find out more about that organisation.'

I gave the phone back to Elena. 'As I told you,' she said, 'we're a registered charity – you can check us out. We're listed under The Woodland Activity Club for Children and Teenagers. I'll give Willow a charger and will ask her to call you every two hours. If you prefer, you can talk to Willow via Skype, then you could also see her.'

'I need time to make enquiries and talk to my husband before I commit to anything. Now, can I talk to Willow again?' Elena handed her mobile back to me.

'I really, really love it here, I promise to call you every two hours. Please, Mum, let me stay.'

'I don't think that's a good idea. Appearances can be misleading.'

'There are lots of great activities here. Please, believe me, I'm happy here. You make your enquiries and if you find anything suspicious, then ask Elena to drive me home. I've already made a friend. Her name is Tania – she's cool.'

'I don't know what to say ...'

'Some of the kids have been coming here for years. I promise you, it's very safe.'

'I can't let you stay in a strange place.'

'Please, just a little longer. I spent the night here and you can hear from my voice that I'm fine. I'm telling you, it's great to be busy during school holidays. I don't have time to get bored.'

'Alright then,' said Mum hesitantly, 'you can stay 'till this evening. I'll talk to your father and together we'll decide what'll happen after that. We may still ask Ms Howell to drive you back home.'

I breathed a sigh of relief; Mum had melted a few degrees. 'Thanks a million.'

'If I can't answer my mobile, send me a text message. I've got to go now. You must make contact every two hours, or you're coming home right away.'

'I promise to do that. Bye for now.' I hung up and handed the mobile back to Elena.

'So, Willow, for now you're allowed to stay with us. Here's a charger. You must remember to call your mum every two hours. Billie will take you to the Amber Chamber in Emerald halls where Chris is waiting for you.'

The hound jumped to his feet and led me to another wooden building in close proximity to Ruby halls. He located the room, sat by the door and scratched it with his right paw. I heard Chris say, 'Come in.'

I entered with Billie. 'Make yourself comfortable,' Chris welcomed me warmly.

He was wearing a white robe with a green sash. On his desk stood a Tiffany style lamp – the shade was made of yellow-orange-brown stones.

'Wow, this lamp is so special. Are the stones real amber?' I asked.

'They are. Amber has gentle, welcoming energy and that's why my room was named after it. This lamp was given to me by a woman who'd been coming here most of her teenage years and later became very successful.'

Amber undoubtedly suited him – he, too, had gentle and welcoming vibes about him.

'Good to know that she did so well. But is there any chance of charging my mobile in your room? I must call my mum every two hours.'

'Of course.' Chris took the charger from me and plugged it to a power point. 'How are you finding this place?'

I heaved a sigh of relief when I connected my mobile to the charger. 'It's totally awesome. I love it.'

'I'm happy to hear that. After your return home, you'll keep in touch with other Custodians. Your Georgian house is one of us.'

'I guessed as much because he sent me to you. By the way, I call him George. I wish I could live here all the time. At home, I feel so alone.'

'Now that the two of you talk to each other, you won't be so lonely. I know George well – he's a good Custodian.'

'I can always rely on him. How my mum behaves depends on her mood.'

'Can you tell me a little bit more about your parents?'

'Mum's a psychologist and my dad's a teacher in a school for problematic teens.'

'How are you getting on with them?'

'I don't have any problems with my dad. But my mum loses her rag at the drop of a hat and then she says horrible things.'

'Do you feel ready to talk about this?'

Looking into Chris's sincere and caring eyes, I knew I could tell him everything. 'She says that ... I'm a ... horrible mistake ... and ... and that ... I shouldn't have been born ...'

'I'm sorry to hear that. Do you know anything about your mother's childhood?'

'All I know is that her mum didn't bring her up. She goes ballistic when I ask about her family. It seems she doesn't have any relations to speak of – or at least, I've never met any of them. I only know my dad's family.'

'Perhaps she hasn't worked through her own unhappy experiences, so history repeats itself.'

'It's so unfair. What happened to her wasn't my fault. Sometimes, she's also horrible to my dad; she presses his buttons until he hits her.'

'The Americans say that bad things roll down hill: father hits mother, she, in turn, beats her child, who kicks the dog.'

'I'd never ever hurt any living creature. When I'm miserable, I want to look after homeless animals and neglected houses.'

'It's heartening to know that. What drove me to work with kids was my inability to help when I heard boys secretly crying at night in the dormitory of the boarding school.'

'Why doesn't she do the same? After all, she's a psychologist – isn't she supposed to be kind?'

'Your mother is probably disconnected from her own feelings and that's why it's difficult for her to love you. It's quite likely that she has a poor opinion of herself.'

'I'm not so sure about that. She can be very scathing about other people.'

'It may be that placing herself above others helps her to disregard her low self-esteem. Now, let's talk about you. What do you do when you're unhappy?'

'I run with imaginary dragons, read or write poems

about them. George also has been helpful. Even before he started talking to me, I would tell him lots of things.'

'You seem to do good things Can I ask about your stay here? What did Elena arrange with your parents?'

'Right now, I'm allowed to stay only until this evening.'

'If you get permission to remain longer, you'll see a trust restorer and a creativity guide. You'll also spend some time with our activities organiser. She's responsible for the dragon horses and arranges riding lessons. She has extensive knowledge of dragons.'

'I'd love to meet her and talk about all things dragon. I'm okay about seeing the creativity guide, but not so sure about the trust restorer.'

'I fully understand your love of dragons. At the same time, it's important that you see a trust restorer. I've asked Edgar Houghton to work with you.'

'Can that wait for a little while? I don't think I'm ready.'

'Every kid at the sanctuary has a trust restorer, and that's why you'll have to see Edgar. You're welcome to talk to me whenever you want, especially, if something upsets you.'

I said goodbye to Chris and left clutching my mobile and the charger Elena had given me. Billie then accompanied me to Emerald halls' front garden where Tania was waiting for me. I thanked Billie for being a wonderful guide and let him go on his way.

CHAPTER TEN

The Dragon Horses' Pavilion

Tania and I walked briskly to the Dragon Horses' Pavilion. Mum allowing me to stay in the camp until the evening was terrific. I kept reminding myself to call her every two hours – I was bent on keeping my side of the deal so that I could remain longer.

Breathing in the smell of trees and wild plants energised me. As we got closer to the pavilion, I saw a statue of a dragon horse on top of the building's sloping roof. The undulating timber walls were covered with carvings of dragons. I ran my fingers on the curved wall, enjoying the contact with the wooden panels.

'Now, Willow, I'll tell ya about our festival. There's, like, four teams made up of dragon horses and riders that are named after the colours: green, blue, brown and red. Hey, are you listenin' to me, or am I talkin' to myself?' asked Tania, waving her hand in front of my eyes.

'Sorry, I was thinking about my mum; I must 'phone her now. Let me make that call and then I'll hear every single word you say to me.' Mum didn't answer, so I left a message telling her that I was well and feeling great.

We entered the pavilion. I stopped dead in my tracks; the sight of a herd of dragon horses stunned me – all I could do was stand there and admire them in silent wonder. There were around twenty of these superb beings moving freely around the great hall. Before that moment, only in my happy daydreams had I found myself in the company of so many enchanting creatures. I felt a big buzz of excitement in every atom of my body.

I loved everything about their appearance. I was completely at one with them; for the first time ever, I fully connected with dragons without running. A pleasant sensation of softness and comfort enveloped me; right now only the dragons mattered. I closed my eyes, wanting to remember that moment forever.

'They're just out of this world,' I sighed cheerily. 'I'm so glad they've got different coloured scales; it's easier to recognise them that way.'

'Just like you, I was hooked when I came here for the first time. I'll never ever forget that moment.'

A crimson dragon horse approached us. Tania introduced him, 'This is Fireball, he's super-cool.'

'I'm Willow, I'm thrilled to meet you.'

'Welcome to the pavilion,' said Fireball, nudging me with his head.

'Thank you,' I murmured, stroking his neck; his scales made my hand tingle. I sensed immediately that he was loyal and reliable. 'You're so friendly. I feel great just standing next to you.'

'Well,' said Fireball, 'I love kids and what I like best is protecting them.'

'Why?' I asked, feeling massively intrigued.

'Because I know how it feels to be unhappy. When I was very young, I was bullied by Nastorians. First their dragons killed my mother and then they wanted me to be one of them. I was afraid of them, but I refused to join.'

'So what did you do?' I asked.

'I spent a lot of time running and making myself strong. I also practised my fire-breathing and became good at shooting huge flames. My real name is Elmo, so now you know why everyone calls me Fireball. I learned early in life that you have to stand up to bullies. They are cowards, believe me, they only pick up on those who wouldn't retaliate.'

'I tell you, we've plenty in common,' I chortled. 'I'm

into running too, and kids at school call me a weirdo –'

'Now, Willow,' Tania chimed in, 'we gotta make a move. There's lots of things I wanna show you.'

'You can always come and visit me anytime you want,' said Fireball.

'I'll take you up on that,' I laughed. 'Believe me, I don't need a second invite. I'll see you very soon.'

We spent some time in the company of other dragon horses. 'I'll show you now the riders' four changing rooms, each has its own lockers and benches.'

Tania led the way to the first one. The walls retained the natural hues of their wooden panels. Sport shirts and long capes hung on the walls. I liked the embroidered oak tree on the garments; the dark chocolate colour of the tree trunk and the emerald green of the leaves contrasted well with the light-brown colour of the outfits. Large numbers from one to five were stitched beneath each tree emblem.

'Just in case you hadn't worked it out,' Tania chuckled, 'this one belongs to the Brown Team. We call them Browns. The best rider and dragon horse are together number one.'

From there we moved to a room where the walls were covered with bluish horizontal wooden planks. The garments were in azure with an embroidered pink lotus on the shirts and capes with a number beneath each flower.

'The wall cladding is made of Blue Mahoe timber imported from Puerto Rico,' Tania went on. 'As you can see, the room belongs to the Blue Team.'

In the adjacent room, the wall panels were reddish-brown. The embroidery on the red kits depicted a flame in varying shades of yellow with strands of orange.

'The panels are made of wild cherry trees,' Tania continued, 'and no prizes for guessing that this room belongs to the Red Team.'

The next changing room had light green walls, shirts and capes. A large leaf in mid green was embroidered on the outfits. The leaf was outlined in brown while its veins were highlighted in creamy-white. 'This broad leaf belongs to the sycamore tree,' said Tania. 'It has, like, five lobes and pointed tips. I like reading about all kinds of trees.'

We wandered around the different parts of the pavilion. 'This place is terrific,' I declared. 'I love it. There's something very special about it.'

'Buildings must have more good energy than bad. Believe it or not, even a building can become a Nestorian and attack us.'

'That's really strange. How would they do that?'

'They could drop their joists or panelling on us,' Tania explained. 'But there's no need for you to worry right now. You're safe here with so many dragon horses.'

I glanced at the time on my mobile and realised I had to 'phone my mum again, 'Sorry, just give me a couple of minutes to make a call.'

'You can do that on our way to the Calcite Healing Retreat. It's really awesome.'

While walking to the retreat, I 'phoned my mum – she didn't pick up. I left her another message and also texted her.

'Well, Tania, what's so special about the retreat?'

'You'll find out yourself very soon,' she replied, smiling broadly.

Tania was right, the retreat was utterly amazing, especially the stained-glass windows depicting all kinds of dragons and animals.

I immediately connected with the beautiful crystals in the reception area. I'd have loved to have stayed there to admire them, but Tania tugged at my arm. 'Now Willow, I'm gonna show you something you'll never forget.'

Tania and I walked to an enclosure at the back of the building. I looked around and, to begin with, I couldn't see anything interesting. Then I noticed in the far-left corner a newly hatched, all-white air dragon. 'Am I dreaming?' I whispered.

'You're not. It's a real baby dragon. If you don't believe me, get closer and see for yourself.'

Just then, the hatchling's mother returned. The baby dragon snuggled up to her and she enveloped it with her sky-blue wings. 'Wow!' I laughed. 'That's soooo special. Perhaps it might be best not to disturb them.'

'C'mon, then, let's go to the next den. Another surprise is waiting for you there.'

We entered a pen where a green air dragon was crouching on lots of straw. 'Well, what's the surprise?'

'What do you think the dragon is doing?' Tania asked.

'Haven't a clue. Tell me.'

'She's keeping her egg warm. We're expecting a baby dragon to show up soon.'

'It'll be amazing to see a brand-new tiny dragon. Now I want time to pass quickly.'

'Likewise. I just can't wait for it to hatch.'

'I hope she doesn't mind our visit.'

'She likes kids entering her den. Our dragons aren't only protective of their young; they also guard us. They treat us kinda like their own family.'

'So I have lots of parents.' I gushed, and then had a fit of giggles. 'How cool is that! I adore the idea that I'm a member of a huge family, and that soon I'll have a newly hatched brother or sister.'

'Honestly, we're one big family 'cause that's how they see us. They really care about those who belong to the Nobodies' Club for Kids with Sad Eyes.'

My curiosity was again aroused. 'Why is that?'

'Just like Fireball, they want to help us 'cause of their own suffering. In the past Europeans killed and wounded many dragons. Some retaliated and turned on both enemy and friend. But the good ones weren't like that; they were totally kind and their descendants like helping others, especially unhappy kids. You can always count on them.'

'It looks that way, they risked their lives to protect us. I can't stop thinking about Lava and Thunder.'

'We can see Lava and Thunder in the Dragons' Hall of Recovery. You gotta do your best to send them tons of healing thoughts and love.'

While walking to the hall, I braced myself for seeing the wounded dragons. The hall had lots of exotic plants growing in big pots and boxes. It also had large crystals – I couldn't stop looking at one of them. 'That big purple one is truly exceptional,' I said, 'totally unique.'

'It's a geode,' said Tania.

'What's that? I'd never heard that word.'

'It's a small cavity in a rock lined with crystals. The one in front of you has amethysts. You'll learn a great deal about semi-precious stones in this place. They're used for healing and for building good energy.'

'They do have something very special; I feel better just looking at them. I also love the brownish-orange and yellowish colours of the one next to the geode.'

'That's a fire agate crystal. It belongs to the Quartz family. It helps you to connect with the earth and this makes you strong and safe. Creativity guides swear that it helps with originality and is particularly good when it comes to overcoming artistic blocks.'

'Thank you, I think you'd make an excellent commentator on documentaries.'

'Sweet,' Tania laughed, 'I'd love to do that.'

The floor of the Dragons' Hall of Recovery was covered with straw. I looked around and my heart plummeted when I saw Lava lying motionless in a shadowy corner. Thunder lay not far from her. 'Are they okay?' I whispered.

'I do hope so. It looks like they're asleep right now. Let's send them tons of love.'

We stood there for a while channelling healing energy to the dragons. I pictured them making full recovery and becoming strong and active again.

Afterwards, Tania took me to the apothecary where Ophelia Leech, the body healer, was working on what I assumed were remedies. The wall behind her had shelves filled with jars and bottles all the way up to the ceiling. Ophelia raised her head when she noticed us. 'Hello, girls, did you come to ask after the dragons?'

'We did,' replied Tania.

'I'm certain that Lava is on the mend,' said Ophelia. 'It may take a while, but she'll pull through. However, Thunder is still critical. He was previously strong and fit, so let's hope he'll recover. Right now, I'm preparing a potion that he urgently needs.'

'We better get out your way then,' said Tania.

'That's thoughtful of you,' said Ophelia, dashing past us. 'I must attend to Thunder right now.'

Ophelia's urgent tone made my blood stop in its veins. After a few agonising seconds Tania said, 'Let's make a move.'

Just as we were passing by the Dragons' Hall of Recovery, I heard Ophelia shouting, 'Oh, no! Thunder isn't breathing!'

Her panic-stricken words felt as if the earth was shaking and my new world crumbling around me. *Why Thunder? Why has this happened to such a kind dragon?*

We entered the dragons' hall. I felt a cold wave of dread and froze when I saw Ophelia trying frantically to revive Thunder. She hurriedly fetched another potion, forced open Thunder's mouth and poured it down his throat. She looked at us – her blue eyes clouded by anguish and fear.

'All we can do now is wait and see whether the most potent elixir I have, would help him,' she said, mopping her brow. 'Please, don't tell anyone about Thunder's condition; despair won't help him. Focus on sending loving thoughts to him. Everyone in the camp will have to create an awful lot of healing energy.'

I looked Ophelia in the eye, 'Will Thunder survive?'

Her sadness was tangible when she replied, 'I really don't know … only time will tell.'

CHAPTER ELEVEN

Unloved Kids

After leaving the Calcite Healing Retreat, Thunder totally occupied my mind. I couldn't stop thinking about him, switching between believing he would recover and having a gut-wrenching fear that he might die.

Glancing at my mobile, I made a mental note to call my mum in twenty minutes. I kept checking the time and 'phoned her exactly two hours after my last message. This time Mum answered.

'Hi,' I said, doing my best to sound cheerful, 'have you enquired about the club?'

'I have, and you'll be glad to know that so far all the information I've obtained is positive. Elena called me and I think I can trust her. Do you still want to remain there?'

'Absolutely! I said, heaving a sigh of relief. 'Can I?'

'Possibly, I need more time to discuss this fully with your father at home.'

'It's already six o'clock. I'd like to know where I'm sleeping tonight. Please, Mum, may I stay here overnight?'

'Impatient as ever! Hang on, I think your father is coming into the house now. Talk to him, and if he lets you, you can stay there tonight. I'm passing my mobile to him.'

'Willow,' said Dad, 'it's so good to hear your voice. The house is very empty without you. I miss you terribly.'

'I miss you too, but I'm very happy here. We've several different activities and quite a few dogs. I couldn't wish for a better place.'

'Are you telling me you that you're not ready to come home yet?'

'I am. Mum agreed I could stay tonight, but I still need your permission.'

'I don't want to make a hasty decision.'

'Please, Dad, I so want to be here.'

'I don't know what to say ... er ... well ... erm ...' He hummed and hawed for a while. 'Alright then, if that's what you really want. You can stay there tonight, but you must call us first thing in the morning.'

'Thank you so much. I promise to call. Bye for now.'

I turned to Tania, smiling. She gave me a tight bear hug and then declared, 'I'm soooo happy, you're gonna stay in my room another night.'

The moment my head touched the pillow, I drifted off and enjoyed unbroken sleep. Immediately after waking up, I called my parents and told them how much I wanted to remain in the camp. They promised they'd let me know their decision in the afternoon.

I had lunch with Tania in Pumpkin Hall, and it was a pumpkin day! We had delicious pumpkin soup, followed by veggie burgers and roasted pumpkin pieces, and for dessert yummy pumpkin cakes.

On our way out, I saw Elena, the practical helper, walking hurriedly towards us with a broad smile on her face. 'Hello girls. I'm the bearer of good news! Willow, I had a long talk with both your parents. You'll be glad to know that you can remain here for the time being on condition you call them at least twice a day.'

'That's brilliant! Thank you so much!' I cried, smiling back and jumping up and down. 'You're a miracle worker. I can't believe it.'

'You'll get used to it pretty quickly,' Elena chuckled. 'Chris asked me to tell you that Edgar Houghton will see you tomorrow in Emerald halls after the morning ritual. I must dash, I've lots to do. I'll see you soon.'

Tania turned to me. 'That's really great! I couldn't wish

for a better room-mate.'

'Good to hear that. How about coming with me for a walk in the forest?' I asked.

'Nah, cheers. I'm not in the mood. I'm going back to our room. I'll see ya later.'

I ambled amongst trees for a while and then returned to Moonstone halls. Tania was lying on her bed with a faraway look in her eyes. I thought that she hadn't noticed me enter our room.

'Tania, you alright?' I asked, my heart beating faster.

She didn't reply.

'Can you hear me? Please talk to me.'

Tania's eyes were distant and unfocused. Leaning forward, I placed my head right in front of her face, hoping she'd say something. It appeared that she was looking, yet she didn't react. I touched her dreamy face very gently – she slightly moved her head, but the vacant expression in her eyes didn't change. She didn't say anything.

Not knowing what to do, I remained sat beside her. How long we stayed together, I couldn't tell. *Would a canine friend help?* I wondered. Having decided that that might be a good idea, I scooted out and looked for a hound in the vicinity of the halls. I couldn't find one, but then saw Liam walking with a red and white Husky.

'Hi there, I need a dog right now. Can I borrow yours?'

'Of course,' he replied, smiling. 'By the way, her name is Sky.'

'Thanks, Liam. Cheerio.' And then I said to the Husky, 'Come with me. You're needed pronto.'

The hound willingly lolloped along beside me as we rushed to Tania. It appeared that Sky knew what to do. Crouching on Tania's bed, she nudged her with her pinky-copper nose. Tania stirred – the dog moved closer and licked her face.

Slowly Tania lifted a hand and placed it on Sky's thick fur. The hound lay down and placed her head on Tania's shoulder. Gradually the far-away gaze faded and Tania noticed me.

We looked at each other – deep in Tania's eyes, I saw loneliness and a sea of sadness. Words were not needed; we understood each other without saying anything. We both spoke the silent language of unloved kids.

'Are you okay?' I asked. 'I was really worried about you.'

'Honestly, there was no need. I'm, like, alright most of the time, but when I'm very miserable, I go elsewhere and forget about everything. My trust restorer explained all that stuff.'

'Did anything happen?'

'No, not really. Sometimes, I get like this when I think about my parents.'

'Can I ask you about your family now?'

'I guess so ... first off ... I'm a twin.'

'Lucky you! I always wanted a brother or a sister. Having a twin must be so cool.'

'Nah, it wasn't. My parents had four girls and my dad was desperate for a son. He has said lots of times that it's difficult for a man to live in a house full of women.'

'What a stupid thing to say,' I protested.

'Abbey, my eldest sister, told me that they'd decided to try for a boy one last time. She said that they were thrilled when my mum became pregnant. Dad blabbed that he'd begged Lady Luck to give him a boy. When the doctor said that Mum was with twins, he declared that the kind lady had smiled twice after so many years of waiting, and instead of one son, she had given him two. Dad told the medics that there was no need to tell him the gender of the unborn twins 'cause he already knew.'

We sat silently for a while with the sea of sadness all around us. And then Tania took a deep breath and went on, 'Abbey said that Dad was over the moon when my brother was born, but disappointed when he found out that the second twin was a girl. He moaned that Lady Luck hadn't kept her promise.'

Tania was silent again. I looked at her – the sea of sadness was turning blustery.

'Perhaps, we could pretend ... that we're ... kind of ... sisters,' I suggested. 'What do you think?'

'That's a brilliant idea,' replied Tania, brightening up a little and smiling at me. 'You won't believe it, but you actually remind me of Abbey. She's about fifteen years older than you, so you and her look very different, but the way you accept me is the same.'

'Tell me more about Abbey.'

'Well, she's ace and she's got guts.'

'What d'you mean?'

'She stood up to my dad when he was mean to me. She always protected me.'

'Was he nasty to you even when you were little?'

'My dad couldn't stick me right from the start. He told everyone that I was a cry baby and that my twin brother, Noel, was a little angel, a really easy child.'

'But why?'

'I don't think he ever wanted me. He was always cold towards me. When he looked at my brother, his eyes lit up.'

'When my mum is angry, she says horrible things to me. She's never ever said that she loves me.'

'And your dad?' asked Tania.

'He's okay, but he can't control his temper when my mum drives him round the bend, and at times, he hits her. Afterwards, he apologises to me.'

'Your dad is a hundred times better than mine, believe you me. When my dad was angry with me, he called me an evil bitch.'

'That's really awful! Why was he so mad with you?'

'Well, I wasn't exactly an angel. I turned my anger on my twin; I dropped big toys on him and I scratched and bit him. I now feel bad about the way I bullied Noel; after all, it wasn't his fault they were nuts about him. In the end, my dad said that it wasn't safe for Noel to be left in the company of a devil child without an adult present.'

'That's so nasty!' I cried. 'How could he? What did you do when he was horrid?'

'I kinda turned to Abbey. When I was in the dumps, I pretended that she was my mum. On one occasion, my dad asked what had he done to deserve a hellish brat like me and why couldn't I be like my twin. Abbey then told him that my behaviour was his fault and that he should think about the way he treated me. Dad shouted back at her that I'd been born bad and that he was, like, a perfect parent to me.'

'I'm sorry about your dad. When my mum is furious, she says I'm a horrible mistake. What helped me was running and talking to my house. I named him George and he sort of became a good friend. You probably think I'm barking saying that.'

'Not at all. Other kids who come here have chats with their old houses. That's never happened to me, but then, I've lived in all sorts of different places.'

'So how did you find out about the Custodians' Sanctuary?'

'Billie brought me here,' replied Tania, stroking Sky. 'The first time I saw him was outside my school's gates. He approached me, wagging his tail. For around two weeks, I got a very special welcome after school. During the beginning of the third week, he was tugging at my sweatshirt trying to make me follow him. In the end, I did, and that's how I met Chris Light. I knew straight away I could trust him, so I agreed to come to the camp. It's the best thing that's ever happened to me.'

'Same here. Billie befriended me on Hampstead Heath and later he brought me here,' I said, glancing at my watch. 'I think we should be getting ready for supper now.'

We walked with Sky to the kennels and from there to Pumpkin Hall. After our return to Moonstone halls, I'd a long chat with both my parents, thanked them again for letting me remain in the camp, and told them how happy I was.

Late in the evening, Tania yawned. 'I'd like to go to

sleep now; talkin' about my parents has totally drained me.'

I got into my bed but couldn't stop thinking about Tania's family. Suddenly, a fuzzy image showed up in my head; it was a picture of two people painted in black and grey with a hint of murky white. The two figures were too dark for me to recognise them. The image left a taste of fear in my mouth and belly.

I don't know why the vaguely familiar memory showed up. No matter how hard I tried to push it away, every time I closed my eyes, it came back. At times, it re-emerged almost clearly and then faded away. I heard cross words, but couldn't understand their meaning. The two blurred grown-ups quarrelled; they shouted at each other. They spewed anger. Lots of anger. It was rage that tasted of cold food on smashed plates. Fury that radiated hurt and frustration.

I wanted to hide from that horrid recall; after cocooning myself in my duvet, I felt a little better. The quilt was like a soft shield between me and the cold anger. The hazy film snippet with the enraged voices briefly disappeared. Yet the second I closed my eyes, the ghostly picture show and fiery spat returned, challenging me to push them away.

I summoned an image of an air dragon in full flight to calm me down, but instead, Lava and Thunder lying motionless in the healing retreat appeared in my mind. Jumping out of bed, I sprinted to the door and then shot out of the halls. I ran away from the blurry memory. I ran away from the angry voices. I ran away from Lava and Thunder lying motionless in the healing retreat.

It was dark outside with only the moon shining faintly. I didn't care. My legs compelled me to move on. I had to charge forward, come what may.

After a while, I heard noise behind me. Fear stopped me dead in my tracks. Looking back, I saw Radar and two of his canine assistants.

I turned around and walked back to them, 'Sorry, Radar, I couldn't sleep.'

He looked at me with his green, thoughtful eyes and said calmly, 'There's nothing wrong with running; only here you mustn't go out on your own after dark. I know how much you love dogs, so right now, you have a chance to run with two.'

I thanked Radar and then turned to his assistants. 'Come on, hounds, let's get going.'

I sped along for a long time with the dogs bounding on either side of me. When I became exhausted, they accompanied me back to Moonstone halls. I got under my bed covers as quietly as I could, trying not to disturb Tania and immediately drifted off.

In the dead of the night, a loud scream jolted me out of my sleep.

CHAPTER TWELVE

Because Kids Need to Believe ...

I switched the lights on – Tania was sitting on the floor, her eyes and face contorted with fear. I shuddered when I noticed how scared she was. Having embraced her and guided her back to bed, I stayed by her side until she fell asleep.

In the morning, Tania appeared to be alright. She behaved as if she had no recollection of what had happened during the night. I don't know why, but I felt it might be best not to mention last night. I called my parents and told them that I was doing well. They were both in a rush, so we had only a brief chat.

After the morning ritual with its face-washing in the ceremonial water, I walked to my meet-up with Edgar Houghton, wondering what trust restorers do. I knocked on his door and he invited me to sit down in an armchair opposite him. His short brown hair matched the colour of his eyes. He was small in stature and not that old, perhaps in his late twenties. The grey jogging bottoms and the white t-shirt he was wearing sported a posh brand. In spite of his casual appearance, I was on edge and couldn't chill out.

'Hello, Willow, as you know, I'm a trust restorer and before we begin, is there anything you would like to ask me?'

'I do. Will we be talking about my parents?'

'Have you got any reservations about that?'

'To be honest, I can't see how talking about my mum is going to help me. It's not going to change her.'

'Talking about difficult experiences can be helpful.'

'The more I think or talk about my mum, the more miserable I become. What really helps me is to get away from the things she says and connect with dragons.'

'What does she tell you?'

'Well ... she ... says ... er ... that I'm a ...' I couldn't bring myself to finish the sentence. Gazing at the floor and chewing on my lip, I tried to work out why it was so difficult for me to tell him. After a massive pause, I mumbled, 'a horrible mistake.'

Now he knows that I'm rubbish and that even my own mother doesn't love me. I pictured a big macaque whispering in my ear in a funny way: *'Everyone can see that you're an unwanted mistake.'* It helped a little.

We sat in silence until Edgar said, 'I understand how hurtful these words are for you, so today you don't have to tell me about any other upsetting things your mother has told you. Do you feel ready to talk about her relationship with your father?'

'I guess that would be easier. My mum seems to do one thing extremely well and that's fighting with my dad. She says that she's with him because of me.'

'Do they argue in front of you?'

'They've a routine like clockwork. It starts with my mum spoiling for a fight; she says plenty while Dad says very little. He tries to be calm but Mum keeps on until he loses his cool. When that happens, nothing would stop them, not even an earthquake.'

'Your father doesn't say anything unkind to you?'

'Oh, no, never. He's alright, really. Though at times, he's in the dumps after my mum had a right go at him.'

'How does that make you feel?'

'I don't like it. He's tall and fit but Mum breaks him down bit by bit. I don't want to see him reduced to nothing.' The pressure in my head and chest became unbearable. 'Actually, it's not that easy to talk about my parents' fights.'

'Would you like to stop now? For some kids, the first

session can be quite difficult.'

'May I? I desperately need a good jog.'

'We can end now. Just to remind you that we'll be meeting twice a week. Thank you for coming to see me today.'

I was relieved when the session was over. All I could think about was moving my legs – I ran as fast as I could until the pressure in my head and chest ebbed away.

In the afternoon, Tania walked with me to Ruby halls. I was seriously impressed by the main room: the stained-glass windows depicted dragon horses as well as water and air dragons. Three walls were covered with paintings showing dragon horses with trees and shrubs in the background, while the fourth was hung with a large, colourful tapestry portraying forest animals on the ground with air dragons flying above them.

In the left-hand corner of the hall stood a large ceramic sculpture of a pack of Huskies running with four dragon horses. I particularly liked a sculpture displayed on a pedestal in the centre of the room, showing an air dragon made of metal crouching in a coloured glass cave.

Tania and I entered Fleur's room. It was out of this world – totally awesome. It had carvings of various kinds of dragons on undulating wooden walls.

Having introduced me to the activities organiser, Tania said goodbye and left. I wanted to ask heaps of questions, but then felt very shy and didn't say anything. When Fleur smiled at me, her cold grey eyes turned warm and welcoming – her friendly face melted my awkwardness away.

I liked her appearance: a slim, middle-aged woman with long, straight brown hair gathered in a ponytail. She wore a pink T-shirt and black trackie bottoms. *Is she into running? I* wondered. *If she is, then we've lots in common.*

'Have you had a chance to see our dragons?' she asked.

'Tania took me to the Dragon Horses' Pavilion. I loved it.'

'I can see you've a passion for all things dragon. They're magical creatures, often misunderstood by those who can't connect with the energy of good dragons.'

'The dragons in the pavilion were really special,' I said, 'But I can't stop worrying about Lava and Thunder.'

'It's a hard time for all of us, but we must remain positive and create a healing force.'

'I'll do that. I'm dead keen on dragons, completely captivated by them. What I can't understand is why people think they're bad.'

'Because dragons, just like kids or grown-ups, can go wrong. All of us wage a battle between the good and bad in our hearts. Not all dragons are trustworthy. On your very first day here, we were attacked by air dragons sent by the Nastorians.'

'Crumbs, I'd almost forgotten that. For a long time, long before I got here, dragons have helped me, so I've only seen their good side. Why do some dragons go bad?'

'Some of them do so because they were unloved, or they were treated harshly when they were young and don't know what friendship and kindness are. They protect themselves with aggressive behaviour, believing that attack is the best form of defence.'

'I don't get it. I hate to see anyone being treated badly or neglected.'

'How humans and dragons behave after unhappy experiences varies,' Fleur went on. 'Some, because of their own suffering, want to help others and become great healers. Now, shall we talk about the fun things dragons do in the camp?'

'Yeah, let's do that,' I replied enthusiastically. 'Dragons and fun are a great mix.'

'The celebrations of the Custodians' Festival begin with the dragon horses showing their skills; they form five groups, each with one rider from the Green, Blue, Brown and Red teams. This way, they create a moving colourful kaleidoscope.'

'Tania showed me the riders' outfits. They're mega-special. It must be ever so cool to be a dragon horse rider. I'm certain everyone would love to be one.'

'Most would, however, the privilege of riding also requires appropriate conduct; we expect them not to behave as though they're superior.'

'Do some of them think they're better just because they belong to one of the teams?'

'It's one of the traps they can fall into. Especially those who've had very unhappy childhoods; making themselves superior helps them to disown feelings of insecurity.'

'How do you become a rider?'

'First of all, you have to become a good Custodian and practise loving kindness towards humans, animals and dragons.'

'What about sporting abilities?'

'Experience riding ponies or horses is helpful as well as physical fitness. It's also important to develop good communication with the dragon horse, and have patience even when things don't go according to plan.'

'It's good to know that.'

'Now let me tell you about the air dragons; they'll fly to and from the four cardinal points and will perform some pretty amazing aerobatics. The festival will also include a costume parade by children and teenagers.'

'Wow, that sounds really awesome.'

'I'm glad you're passionate about dragons and the festival,' said Fleur, smiling. 'I enjoyed talking to you today. You can see me whenever you want.'

I walked out of Fleur's room feeling upbeat and strolled to Pumpkin Hall where I met Tania and Liam. While eating the veggie lasagne I'd chosen, my thoughts drifted to my meet-up with Edgar and the good feeling evaporated.

'I'm not sure I want to see a trust restorer,' I said, 'I felt funny after talking to Edgar.'

'Wait a minute,' said Tania, munching her nut cutlet. 'Give him a bit more time. After a while, it'll, like, work out.'

'Well,' said Liam, glancing up from the food piled on his plate 'I don't know why they're so obsessed with parents. I get really fed up when I talk about my dad.'

'How do you feel after seeing your trust restorer?' I asked Tania.

'She makes me feel better.'

'Do you think I could see her?'

'You gotta ask Chris.'

'I think I'll do that.'

Tania and I said goodbye to Liam and left Pumpkin Hall. On our way to our room, we came across Sky and Winter lounging in front of Moonstone halls and invited them in. It was great to have Winter sitting very close to me. Tania appeared chilled out when she was stroking Sky. Whenever she stopped, the hound pawed her arm, demanding more of the same.

'You know, it's cool to share a room with you,' I said. 'There's no need to pretend we're sisters, it feels real!'

'Same here. I told ya that you remind me of my eldest sister, and that Abbey always protected me when my dad was mean. She didn't beat around the bush; she told him he was a rubbish parent. In the end, he asked her to leave home. She didn't want to leave without me.'

'That was really good of her.' I felt happy that I had things in common with Abbey.

'She started to look for a place of her own but couldn't afford one, so she moved in with her boyfriend. There was no space for me in their tiny flat. After Abbey had left, I became frantic, I couldn't sit still for a second. Teachers noticed my behaviour and I was referred to a child psychologist.'

'Did they help you?'

'No way. My mum and dad convinced him that they were doing whatever they could and that I was impossible. He decided I was hyperactive and that my poor parents did their best, considering our large family.'

'What did he do for you?'

'Nothing,' replied Tania, 'in his report he wrote about sibling rivalry, but concluded that the main reason for my behaviour was ADHD. Do you know what that means? It stands for Attention Deficit and Hyperactivity Disorder. This way *I* was the problem and everyone seemed pleased because he'd stuck a label on me.'

'I think he's a useless child psychologist.'

'No lie! I totally agree with you. I deliberately did the opposite of what he'd asked me; I didn't answer his questions and argued with him about everything. That's when he also labelled me with Oppositional Defiant Disorder, or ODD in short. Eventually, he didn't want to work with me. My dad was triumphant: even a doctor couldn't stick me. He then wrote a letter praising that psychologist to the heavens. Something like, he was so lucky to get the best child therapist ever.'

The sea of sadness around us deepened. 'I think that psychologist is Machiavellian.'

'Come again?'

'Machiavellian. I found this word on the internet – it means a crafty, calculating person who uses clever lies and tricks to achieve his goals. In short, someone who has no scruples. Instead of helping you, that psychologist took your dad's side in the hope he would write good things about him.'

'Before secondary school everything at home was utterly horrible. My parents in the end decided they'd had enough and asked social services to find me a foster family, and that child psychologist supported their request. I'm beginning to like the word Machia ... how do you say it?'

'Machi-a-vell-ian. Were you placed with a foster family?'

'Yeah, but that didn't last for long. The first family did try really hard but I was very difficult and eventually, they gave up. I got two other foster families, but neither of these worked out either. By that time, I'd really lived up to my two labels, so they stuck on me like glue.'

'Did your parents keep in touch with you?'

'We met on a regular basis. The social worker convinced them to let me return home for one month's trial. It was so awful that before long, I was desperate to leave.'

'Was your father nasty to you?'

'Not directly. He did what the social worker had expected of him 'cause she kept an eye on us, but he sang my brother's praises all day long. He pushed my twin to support his football team and to watch his favourite films with him. I became tired of hearing how lucky he was to have such a wonderful son. But you know what? Sometimes, other kids can understand you better than grown-ups. Noel, my twin, was nice to me even though I'd bullied him when he was little. I think he kinda knew how unhappy I'd been at home.'

'How long did you stay at home?'

'Just the one month. I was picking up fights with my parents. They told social services that they couldn't cope, and that's when I was placed in a children's home.'

The sea of sadness threatened to engulf us. I looked at Tania's blank and unfocused gaze and knew that she was somewhere else. Sky once again turned out to be a great helper; she licked Tania's face until the Thousand Mile Stare disappeared. I then thanked the hounds and let them go out.

'Tania, when I'm unhappy, I connect with dragons and run with them. We need to believe in something bigger than ourselves; good dragons can help us. I know they can stand up to, and defeat, Machiavellian people.'

CHAPTER THIRTEEN

A Little Bird

With every passing day, I grew fonder of Tania – she was a great room-mate and I could tell her lots of things. Most of the time, she appeared alright, but then at times, she seemed to be elsewhere. She told me not to worry, but I really wanted to do something for her.

Before going to breakfast, I asked, 'Would you like to come with me for a run in the afternoon?'

'I'll think about that,' replied Tania. 'I ain't mad about running.'

'Well, I'd love you to come with me. I reckon I'll be needing a good jog after meeting Edgar.'

'I told ya that you can ask Chris to see my trust restorer – her name is Lavender. She's well cool.'

'I'll do that today.'

At the end of the morning ritual, I approached Chris, 'Can I talk to you?'

'Of course. Let's go to my chamber.'

'Actually, I just wanted to ask one question. Instead of Edgar, could I see Lavender? Tania told me that she's good'

'Did anything happen?'

'Nothing at all. It's just ... hard for me to talk to him about my family. Somehow, we always come back to my mum.'

'I wouldn't worry about that yet, it's still early days when taking into account that you've only seen him once. There's a good chance that after a few sessions, you'll get used to him.'

'Does it mean that I've to continue with him?'

'I'm afraid so. Many kids have difficulties in the early stages of seeing a trust restorer. Let me tell you that in the afternoon you'll see Louise Blake, our creativity guide. It might be a good idea to start thinking about your costume for the festival.'

Having said goodbye to Chris, I walked to Emerald halls. Sky sat proudly in front of the building, scanning the grounds in front of her. When she noticed me, she sprang to her feet and showered me with heaps of canine love.

'I'm happy to see you too,' I murmured into her ear. 'Maybe you could come with me to Edgar's room, having you there would make it easier.'

Sky bounded enthusiastically next to me. I knocked on Edgar's door and he invited me to enter.

'Can Sky join us?' I asked.

'She can, as long as she doesn't disturb us.'

I sat opposite Edgar. Sky positioned herself on the floor, leaning into my legs.

'How did you find our first meeting?' Edgar grinned – he smiled only with his lips though, his eyes were cold.

'Well, I was ... kind of ... feeling a bit down,' I faltered.

'It's not easy to talk about unhappy stuff, so it's only natural that you were upset when you told me about your mother saying unkind things to you.'

I looked at Edgar, trying to understand why I wanted to leave his room. 'It's just that ... I had all kinds of confusing thoughts afterwards ... even about my dad.'

'Can you tell me a bit more about that?'

'Dad is an English teacher. He has a lovely voice when he talks about books and poetry and when he explains things to me. It's only ...' I gazed at the floor and then stroked Sky's head.

'Take your time.'

We sat in silence for a long time, and then I went on, 'When he's angry ... he ... sort of ... becomes almost a different person ... that's when I'm afraid of him.'

'Are you afraid that he might hurt you?'

'Not me ... but my mum.' I looked fleetingly at Edgar – his eyes were indifferent. I shrank into myself with a lump in my throat.

'So your father can be good company, but at times he's very angry.'

I felt disloyal to my dad telling Edgar things about him. 'He's alright. He really is. I know that he cares about me. It's not his fault that my mum drives him mad.' I glanced up – Edgar appeared remote. 'He's a great teacher and he can be lots of fun. Actually, I don't want to talk about my parents.'

The silence returned. *Why is time passing so slowly?* I asked myself.

'Is there anything you'd like to tell me?'

'Don't think so. Right now, I just want to go for a run.'

'We can finish now. I'll see you next week.'

I thanked Edgar and walked out with Sky. The two of us ran together for a long time.

* * *

On my way to Ruby halls, I tried to decide whether to be a Georgian house or a unicorn. Just then, a twittering song snapped me out of my thoughts. Looking around, I spotted a small bird on a low branch not far away from me, singing its totally captivating tune.

I stood completely still with my eyes fixed on the bird, enjoying its contrasting colours: a red face, grey beak and black and white head. It had a golden-brown body and a white belly. The black wings with a wide yellow bar were striking.

I would have loved to remain there and admire the bird, but I knew that I had to see Louise. Reluctantly, I walked away, turning my head to catch one last glimpse while promising myself that I would identify the bird on the internet.

Louise greeted me with a big smile and friendly hazel

eyes. She was wearing a flowing patchwork dress – the main colours were mid-blue, navy, cream and white. Her brown hair was a work of art; a waterfall braid collected into a bun. I liked her immediately.

'Welcome, Willow. I'm a creativity guide. My name is Louise Blake.'

'Sorry for being late, but on my way here I saw a beautiful bird, and I just couldn't walk away from it.'

'Are you a birdwatcher?'

'Now that you've said it, I think I'm going to be one! It was really cool.'

Louise handed me a book about British birds. It didn't take me long to recognise the bird. 'That's a goldfinch,' she said. 'I love birds too. They definitely help your creative juices to flow. But now we have to think about your costume. Any ideas?'

'I'm going to be a goldfinch,' I said, spreading my arms sideways and moving them up and down. 'That's why I saw one today.'

'And that's final?'

'Totally, I don't have any doubts whatsoever.'

'Let's make a start then. Shall we begin with the bird's body, the head or the wings?'

'I'd like to start with the head, then the wings and the body will be last.'

Louise measured my head and produced coloured paper and a large card. She asked me to choose small feathers from boxes with all kinds of colourful plumage.

'I ... prefer not to use them,' I mumbled. 'Birds could've died ...'

'Allow me to reassure you that they're all synthetic.'

I was surprised how quickly – with Louise's help – I drew the different parts of the head, cut the coloured paper and the card and glued all the pieces together.

'Let the glue dry,' she said, 'and meanwhile we'll set about planning the wings.'

After designing the wings, I enjoyed gluing colourful

feathers to the bird's head. Having carefully studied a photo of a UK goldfinch, I did my best to create a convincing head and beak. I loved working with Louise and was disappointed that time had passed quickly.

'I tell you, little did I know that making a costume can be so much fun!' I said.

'Now that you know what to do, feel free to come here whenever you've a bit of time to spare. I'm always on hand to help.'

'I'll definitely do that. Thank you, and see you soon.'

While walking to Moonstone halls, I looked out for a goldfinch but couldn't find one. I spotted a robin though and observed it for a long time.

Tania was already in our room when I arrived. She was sitting on her bed, leaning over cream-coloured fabric.

'What are you doing?' I asked.

'Embroidering buttercups on my forest fairy costume.'

'Give me one minute to 'phone my dad.'

'Take your time,' she said.

Dad answered my call. 'I must tell you something really special,' I told him. 'I saw a goldfinch and a robin today and they didn't seem to be afraid of me. I could have watched them until the cows came home.'

'So now it's going to be birds, dogs and dragons. I'm glad that you love creatures of all sizes.'

'And, Dad, we're all preparing a costume. I'm going to be a goldfinch.' I twittered on and on about my outfit, the goldfinch, the robin and birds in general.

'You seem to be enjoying yourself,' Dad laughed. 'Even though I miss you, I think it might be good for you to stay there, but you still need your mother's permission. I just had an idea: would you like me to make a feeding table for birds?'

'Very much so,' I replied eagerly, 'but make sure it's out of reach of cats.'

'It'll be right in the middle of the garden and quite high up, so only cats with wings would reach it!'

'I'll say goodbye now. Promise to call very soon.'

Tania raised her head from her handiwork and smiled. 'I'm into birds. They really help me; when I look at them, I forget everythin' else. I told ya that I love trees, I discovered birds when I was checking out an oak tree.'

'That's great. Shall we go birdwatching together?'

'Sounds good to me. I'd deffo prefer that to running.'

I chatted with Tania until late. That night I slept well. I dreamed about a magical forest with lots of friendly, colourful birds. The wood was guarded by dogs and dragons. When I woke up in the morning, I thought that my dad was right: from now on it's going to be birds, dogs and dragons.

After the morning ritual, I hurried to Ruby halls; I couldn't wait to see Fleur again. There was something about her I really liked and connected with – though what it was, I couldn't tell.

As I was reaching Fleur's door, I was surprised to hear her speaking in a harsh and angry tone – something I hadn't heard since my arrival at the sanctuary. But when I knocked, Fleur hung up her mobile and welcomed me, all smiles. After sitting down, once again shyness sneaked in: I didn't know what to say.

'Do you like our camp?' she asked, grinning.

Fleur's warm welcome helped me to relax and talk freely. 'I love it. My dad said that I can stay throughout the summer holidays. Now I only need my mum to agree.'

'I'm glad you're settling in so well.'

'By the way, I saw a goldfinch yesterday and started making a goldfinch costume with Louise. This is such a wonderful place with birds, dogs and dragons. Just the thought that there are so many dragons here makes me feel on top of the world.'

'They're truly enchanting. If I get up early enough, I visit them in their pavilion and that makes such a wonderful start to my day.'

'Can I tell you something?'

'Go ahead.'

'I find the sessions with Edgar quite difficult. I don't like talking about my mum; it only muddles up my brain and creates lots of chaos. My head then feels like central London in the rush hour.'

'Talking about your family becomes easier with time.'

'I'd rather talk dragons with you; their magic works for me. I kind of feel ashamed of my mum pushing me away.'

'It would be good to share this with Edgar.'

'It's easier for me to talk to you.'

'I'm afraid that you'll have to continue with Edgar, but I'm happy to spend time with you. How about going to the Dragon Horses' Pavilion right now?'

'That'd be cool. Let me tell you, I wish I could sit an exam in Dragonology. Top marks guaranteed.'

'It looks that way,' Fleur laughed. 'You seem to know a lot about these awesome creatures.'

Having walked with Fleur to the pavilion, we located Fireball. While stroking his neck, deep calmness spread into my body and head. During the couple of hours we stayed there, I learned lots of new things about dragons. I especially loved Fleur's account of dragons' history.

'You can come and see me whenever you want,' Fleur reminded me. 'I enjoyed our dragon chat.'

'When I connect with dragons, they take me to a different world and I ... kind of ... feel great.'

'You seem to know what's good for you.'

'I do, kids need to believe in powerful creatures. When we connect with good dragons, grown-ups can't hurt us.'

Fleur smiled warmly. 'Shall we go together again to the dragons' pavilion? I think that'd suit you well.'

'It's an utterly brilliant idea. Let's do it.'

I said goodbye to Fleur and went for a run in the sanctuary's grounds. I couldn't stop thinking about Fleur, replaying our dragon chats over and over again.

CHAPTER FOURTEEN

Mirror of Doubt

I called my mum first thing in the morning, telling her how happy I was and asked again whether I could remain till the end of the summer holidays. To my huge relief, Mum seemed to be warming up to the idea – this gave me a massive buzz.

'Your father told me that you've discovered birds,' she said. 'Watching them is good for you; they can help you to be more patient.'

'They also help me to connect with nature. Please, Mum, can I stay?'

'You seem to be happy there. On the one hand, it's a good idea ... but on the other hand ... I'm still not sure ... after all ... I didn't see that place for myself.'

'I so want to stay here,' I begged. 'I'll be very upset if you make me go back home.'

'Alright then, you can remain ... but you'll have to call me at least twice a day. And call me immediately should anything untoward happen, no matter how small.'

'I will do it, I promise. Thank you for letting me stay.'

A lovely wave of calmness spread into my mind whenever I thought about remaining in the camp. I looked forward to seeing Fleur – thrilled at the prospect of another serious chat about all things dragon. After the morning ritual, I walked to Fleur's room.

'Good to see you,' she said, smiling. 'Do you still want to go to the pavilion?'

'Absolutely.'

'Well then, let's make a move,' said Fleur.

We walked out together. 'It's such an amazing place. I wish I could stay here forever.'

'There are many unhappy youngsters, so we couldn't possibly keep all of you in the camp. Kids spend their school summer holidays with us. Some also come here during the Christmas, Easter and half-term breaks. Very few visit over the weekend.'

'But what if something happens during the week?'

'We've a network of various helpers outside the camp. Humans, animals and old buildings such as your Georgian house.'

'I call my home George. The first time I heard him talking, I was very scared. Now I'm really happy we can chat. Actually, even before George talked to me, I had been telling him lots of things and it helped me an awful lot. But what do kids who live in a modern house do when they're down in the dumps?'

'There are all kinds of ways they can be helped. They may take up a hobby – sport, music and art can be very beneficial. Or they can turn to animals, especially dogs, for comfort and closeness. We've a network of hounds working for us.'

'I know. I met Billie on Hampstead Health in London.'

Fleur and I entered the pavilion. I breathed in the magic of dragons, wanting to keep that memory imprinted on my mind forever. 'Seeing all this, makes me worried that my mum might change her mind, and I'll have to go home before the end of the summer holidays.'

'Even if it comes to the worst-case scenario and you'll have to leave early, you'll keep in touch with other kids from the camp. And Billie looks ordinary enough for him to meet you on Hampstead Heath.'

'Will I be able to come here during the Christmas and Easter holidays?'

'That's not in my hands – Chris will decide. Don't worry

about it now, it's best to cross that bridge when you come to it.'

'You know, lots of amazing things have happened to me, and yet now and then they make me tired and restless.'

'New and exciting events can take their toll on us. You're still getting used to it all. Let's walk to Fireball – he knows how to make kids feel better.'

We located Fireball and I stroked his strong neck, connecting with his power and gentleness.

'There's no need for you to talk to me,' said Fleur quietly. 'Sometimes, it's good to be silent.'

I stood next to Fireball for some time, feeling upbeat. And then my thoughts drifted to Thunder and Lava. I closed my eyes and pictured them becoming strong again.

After leaving the pavilion, I asked Fleur, 'Can I go for a walk in the camp's forest? I'd like to be on my own for a little while.'

'Sure thing,' she replied and then suddenly became somewhat stern. 'But you need to be careful; not everything is as it seems in this place.'

I was taken aback when I noticed how serious her eyes were. I walked away with her strange words playing in my head.

Strolling aimlessly amongst trees, I remembered the goodwill Chris and Fleur had shown towards me. But then uninvited thoughts crept into my head: *Why are they so kind? How do I know that they truly want to help kids?* I walked for a long time, trying to shake off my doubts and confusion.

I sat on a fallen tree trunk and looked at a dog-rose shrub climbing up a tall oak tree. I liked the way its pale-pink flowers punctuated the dominant brown and green of the tree. The summer sun sneaked through the foliage, creating a pattern with the shadows formed by branches and leaves while the breeze made the interplay of light and shade dance on the forest's floor. I scanned tree branches looking for birds, especially for a goldfinch, but none showed up.

Hearing slow footsteps on crinkling leaves behind me, I turned my head and saw an old woman walking towards me. Unkempt wispy, white hair, deep wrinkles and a walking stick made me wonder how old she was. Her long, shabby, blue dress with frills on the front seemed to belong to bygone times.

She approached me. 'Do you mind if I sit here?'

Fleur's words, *"Not everything is as it seems in this place"* rang in my ears. I looked at her, not knowing what to say.

'I need to rest,' she went on wearily, 'I've walked for some time now.' She looked tired, leaning forward on her walking stick.

'Please, sit down,' I said. 'I'll be off in a minute.'

Having sat down, she introduced herself, 'My name is Phillipa Bennett.'

She appeared harmless, probably just a lonely old lady who wanted to talk to someone. 'I'm Willow Ashwood.'

'I assume you're one of the kids who stay here during the summer holidays. Do you like the camp?'

'I do,' I replied and then my doubts about talking to a stranger grew stronger. 'Actually, I should go now.'

'Have you had a chance to visit the Dragon Horses' Pavilion?'

'I have. They're awesome. My favourite is Fireball – we really took to each other.'

'I know what you mean. They're truly enchanting creatures. I love them too.'

If she likes dragons, she's probably okay, I thought. 'Did you work in the camp?'

'I did, until I discovered what's really going on. This camp isn't what it seems to be. It's run by people who control, manipulate and exploit kids.'

'I did have some doubts,' I mumbled.

'Don't you think this place is just too good to be true?'

Her words hit me hard. 'Are you telling me that the grown-ups only pretend to care about kids?'

'Sorry to be the bearer of bad news, but I'm duty bound to get you out of this so-called sanctuary.'

'What do you mean? Am I unsafe here?'

'You are! Look here, Willow, if you can't trust your own parents, you should not have faith in people you don't know very well. Be careful with what you tell them about yourself and your family. They'll use that knowledge against you.'

'I can't see Chris or Fleur do that.'

'Didn't Radar warn you that some highly trained Pretenders can camouflage their bad energies and mislead just about anyone? I think you should leave immediately. I know a secret way out.'

'I need time to think about that,' I muttered. 'I really must go now.'

Phillipa put a hand on my shoulder, 'I'm an old woman. I'll be eighty-four next month. I've devoted all my working life to children. Please trust me.'

'What you've said is so strange –'

'But sadly, it's true, life can be stranger than fiction. The dragons in this place are controlled by the adults who run the sanctuary. Their soft vapours may warm your heart, but a dragon's fierce fire may kill you.'

'But surely the dragons here are good,' I objected. 'They've risked their lives for us.'

'They fought to protect you because that's what they were ordered to do.' said Phillipa, grabbing my hand. 'Come with me before it's too late.'

I pulled my hand away from her and then heard the sound of charging hooves. I saw Volcano and Radar racing towards me. Phillipa sprang to her feet and sprinted to the camp's fence. I was astonished to see how fast she ran despite her advanced age.

Radar and Volcano stood by my side panting heavily. After steadying himself, Radar said, 'Phillipa is an impostor – she works for the Nastorians. They pay her handsomely for recruiting our kids. Did you have any unhelpful thoughts?'

'I had ... I had some doubts about ... Chris and Fleur.'

'She picked up on your uncertainty and tried to lure you out of here,' said Radar. 'Once you leave the camp, it can be very difficult to resist the power of the Nastorians. We're strong when we're united; that's when our collective energies protect us.'

'Sorry, Radar and Volcano. I really am.'

'It's quite likely that you'll have similar thoughts in the future,' said Radar. 'When you've any doubts, speak to Chris or Edgar.'

'Can't I talk to Fleur?' I asked.

'She's an activities organiser,' Radar replied firmly, 'not a trust restorer.'

'But I can tell her lots of things.'

'You have to do what Chris tells you,' Radar insisted. 'Right, let's make a move!'

'Jump onto my back,' said Volcano. I did as I was told and we set off to Emerald halls. *What a fab way to go back. It's totally amazing.*

I dismounted Volcano in front of the halls and said goodbye to him and Radar. I found Edgar typing away on his laptop. 'Have you come to see me?' he asked.

'Yes, hope you don't mind. May I tell you what happened today?'

'Fire away.'

'I met an old woman in the forest. She said her name is Phillipa Bennett and she did her best to get me out of here. It's really bothering me that I almost believed her. I was very lucky that Radar and Volcano came to my rescue.'

'What made you take her seriously?'

'I ... kind of ... wasn't sure whether Chris and Fleur ...'

'You can say whatever is on your mind.'

'Well then, I wondered why Chris and Fleur are so nice to me.'

'Trusting others can be a tall order for those who've been let down by their parents. Let me tell you that other kids in the camp have similar doubts from time to time.'

'I want to have faith in Custodians, but it's very difficult.'

'You need more time.'

'Believe me, it's so much easier to trust a house.'

'Chris told me that you turned to your Georgian home when you were unhappy.'

'I call him George. He's old and very run-down, but I really love him.'

Edgar laughed. 'You seem to have a heart that's big enough to hold dragons, dogs and old houses. In future, when uninvited doubts show up, connect with George and good dragons. They'll keep your heart warm and the candle of confidence burning.'

I said goodbye to Edgar, feeling somewhat better, but remained in the grip of dogged misgivings: *How could I doubt Chris and Fleur? Why did I entertain the idea that they could do something untoward?* Just then, my uncertainty morphed into a question: *Can I trust Edgar?*

CHAPTER FIFTEEN

Things that Refuse to Go away

On my way to Moonstone halls, I needed a monkey to help me with unhappy thoughts. I pictured a macaque jumping onto my shoulder and whispering in my ear in a clownish manner: *You should've gone with Phillipa Bennett. You don't deserve to be here, ungrateful little nothing.* This time, though, the monkey failed to help me.

Tania wasn't in our room – it was a massive relief to be on my own and think about my encounter with the Pretender. Feeling totally discombobulated, I flopped down into my bed. Just then, an unwelcome flashback gatecrashed my brain: I recalled the first time I'd overheard my mum saying angrily that I was a horrible mistake.

That uninvited memory now played in my head in slow motion with every dreadful detail; its clarity made me feel that it had taken place just the other day, rather than six years ago.

It had happened when I was in year three and aged seven. I was woken up in the middle of the night by my parents yelling at each other. Trying not to hear their enraged voices, I buried my head under my pillow. After what seemed to be an eternity, I fell asleep, but the angry voices woke me up again.

I was half-awake when I heard Mum shouting, *"If not for that horrible mistake, I'd have left you years ago. Both of you are the scourge of my life."*

"Eleanor," said Dad, *"Keep your voice down, Willow*

might hear you."

"As if I care! I wish she'd never been born. You stopped me from having an abortion. I regret I ever listened to you."

Dad's voice was no longer cross, just sad and tired. *"You were happy when you held her in your arms for the first time. You're saying this because you're angry with me."*

"I was pretending to be happy because women are expected to feel like that. I never wanted to have children."

"You're behaving like that irresponsible mother of yours. Why must you repeat what she did to you? How can you do this to Willow?"

That night, I lay in bed for hours, floating between dreamy wakefulness and light sleep. After drifting off, I dreamed about a family of macaque monkeys, two adults and their infant. My chief tormentor was a big macaque telling me repeatedly that I'd never been wanted. Its partner taunted me by reminding me that I was a horrible mistake. There was nothing I could do, so I let them have their fun. To be honest, I didn't mind the baby monkey, even though it snickered at me.

When I woke up in the morning, my head was shrouded in thick, dark fog; everything in my brain felt squashed and confused. And then the fight of that awful night whirred through my head like a short horror film. I didn't want to move a muscle, or do anything whatsoever.

Mum walked into my bedroom looking peaky. *"Hope you slept well,"* she said, feigning to be cheerful. *"Time to get up."*

I didn't say anything. All I wanted was to remain in bed and forget that I existed.

"Willow, you better make a move, or you'll be late for school."

I turned my back on her, curled up and gazed at the wall above my bed. Talking felt like a gargantuan effort.

"Get up!" Mum said irritably, pulling the covers off me. *"Do you hear?"*

I remained motionless.

"Now you listen to me," she shouted, shaking my shoulder. *"Get out of bed. Right now!"*

I looked at her with blank eyes. Mum flinched. *"Did you ... did you hear us last night?"*

I didn't have the energy to say anything. Closing my eyes, I curled up into a smaller ball.

"Alright then," Mum said wearily, *"you don't have to go to school today. I'll phone and tell them that you're unwell. I'll ask your grandmother to look after you. Don't you dare tell her that I quarrelled with your father last night."*

My grandma agreed to look after me. The moment she arrived, Mum grabbed hold of her handbag and left promptly.

I love my grandma – she's ace. I think that Dad inherited his interest in reading from her. Whenever I stayed with her, she took me to the local library and encouraged me to choose books. Unfortunately, that had not been happening very often; Mum doesn't get on with my grandma, so we see her once in a blue moon.

That day I didn't have the energy to talk to anyone, not even to my grandma. She looked at me and told me to remain in bed. It was true what Mum had said – I wasn't well.

"I'll be in the living room," she said. *"If you need anything, please call me."*

Throwing the eiderdown over my head, I tried to block out everything, but it didn't work. The war of words of that ghastly night unfolded in my head again, draining any dregs of energy I had. Mum's voice played loud, *"If not for that horrible mistake, I'd have left you years ago. Both of you are the scourge of my life."*

There was no hiding place from Mum's angry words; looming large and powerful, they controlled me. I dragged my uncooperative body into the kitchen and tried to eat the muesli Mum had prepared for me, but I wasn't hungry. Grandma appeared at the kitchen's door looking concerned. *"Would you like me to get you something?"*

"Thank you, but I can't eat right now. Perhaps later. I just want to sleep."

I returned to bed, hoping that sleep would give me a break from daunting memories, but muddled-up thoughts were swirling round in my mind. My head was buzzing and whirring and spinning with the energy of a demented computer. I couldn't switch off these churning thoughts for a long time.

Eventually, I fell asleep. The scornful macaques showed up again in a dream, poking fun at me once more, but even so, I didn't mind because I wasn't alone. And, as I said, I liked the little monkey.

Having woken up, Mum's mean words immediately returned. I was desperate to stop them, so I pictured the largest monkey from my dream sniggering at me in a funny way, *A horrible mistake. Your mother never wanted you.* And then, I imagined the little macaque looking at me in an impish way. The monkeys had helped; the harsh words became kind of flippant and silly. I heaved a sigh of relief and drifted off.

When I woke up, it was late afternoon. Mum had returned from work and my grandma was gone. I still didn't feel like getting up, so I lay in a daze for a long time.

In the end, I turned my head and whispered Mum's nasty words to the wall above my bed. From that day, the macaques and my house had shared the bad things that had been happening to me.

Over time, the mischievous little monkey became a steady companion. When I go to sleep, I imagine it curled up at the bottom of my bed and when I wake up, I picture it waiting for me to open my eyes. The small monkey is quite mischievous, but its playfully naughty ways help me to chill out.

That night is tattooed on my brain and on my heart. Every so often, the horrid flashback of the war of words plays in my head for no apparent reason. At other times, it appears when I'm home alone, or after I've watched something sad on television or the internet. Seeing a neglected animal or a sad child can bring back that unhappy recall.

But the most annoying thing is that it also happens when good things come to pass, or when someone is nice to me. It occurred after Sophie's mum had said, "*If you don't mind me asking, is everything alright? Sometimes you look very sad.*"

"*Everything is fine,*" I replied as casually as I could. "*Please don't talk with my mum about it. She'll start to worry and will ask a million questions.*"

Tania walking into our room snapped me out of my gloomy memories and brought me back to now. 'You okay?' she asked. 'You look out of sorts.'

I told her about Phillipa Bennett, the old woman with the surprising agility, and how I'd been rescued by Radar and Volcano.

'Believe you me, you were uber-lucky. She works as an actress whenever she can. Phillipa has lured a number of kids out of our camp. She often pretends to be proper ancient, but in reality she's in her forties, which is why her speed surprised you. Never leave the camp without talking to Radar first.'

'I've learned my lesson. Can I tell you something?'

'Go for it,' replied Tania.

'Now and then I have a flashback of my mum telling my dad that I'm a horrible mistake. After talking to Phillipa that memory has come back.'

'Well, pretty much everyone here has those kind of film snippets. My trust restorer explained why they crop up and what to do about them.'

'You've had them too?'

'Oh, yeah, in the past I had lots. They still show up from time to time.'

'Tell me about one of your bad memories.'

'I guess the worst one is when my parents told me that I was goin' to be placed in a children's home. You see, in my heart of hearts I was hoping that somehow, despite everything, they woudn't send me away.'

'How could they do that to you?'

The sea of sadness appeared in Tania's eyes. 'Well, I was looking for fights with them, and in the end, they decided they'd had enough.'

'Are you happy in the children's home?'

'You gotta be kidding! You hardly ever get a good night's kip in that place. Quite a few of the kids have nightmares and when they can't sleep, nobody else can either. Some of the staff are decent, but others couldn't care less. The social worker is looking for a new family for me, but with my history, I doubt anything will come of it.'

'Would you like to live with a foster family?'

'Dunno. Here I behave myself, but sometimes I can be a right pain. It's quite likely that my being fostered will be an exercise in futility. Lavender helps me to understand my behaviour.'

'I still have doubts about Edgar. He's sort of cold, and at times, the way he looks at me, I feel that he thinks that he's superior to me.'

'Well, to start with,' Tania laughed, 'it didn't go well with Lavender because I reckoned she'd be like that child psychologist I told ya about.'

'But she turned out to be okay?'

'Yep, she was very patient – she took heaps of rubbish from me, but didn't give up. I'm alright with her now despite havin' doubts every once in a while. Lavender encourages me to tell her how I feel about her and our meet-ups.'

'I'm happy with dragons and dogs, but I'm not so sure about the two-legged variety.'

'I think some people, like Lavender, are okay. I really struggled when I got here. I tell you, Lavender has been helpful.'

'Do you think it's worth your while seeing a trust restorer?'

'Deffo,' replied Tania, 'especially if you get a good one. But I think we'd better go to Pumpkin Hall now.'

After returning with Tania to our room, I watched a film on my laptop and afterwards, we chatted for quite some time.

'It's getting late and I'm dog-tired,' I said, yawning. 'Let's go to sleep now.'

Lying in bed, I kept thinking about my mum and Tania's family. It took me a long time to drift off. A nightmare about a witch sitting on my chest and suffocating me broke my sleep; I woke up cold and short of breath. When I nodded off again, I plunged into another nightmare; in a bleak dream-scape, devoid of any greenery, a demon chased me until I collapsed.

CHAPTER SIXTEEN

Strange Happenings

Despite my broken sleep, I woke up early. Whilst dragging my body out of bed, I thought that a visit to the Dragon Horses' Pavilion would make me feel better. I walked briskly, trying to shake off my weariness and before long reached the pavilion. The sight of powerful creatures and gentle, early morning sunrays streaming in through the windows were a welcome beginning to Sunday. Breathing in the energy of a new day, I sat down on a straw bale.

Some of the dragons were just waking up, stretching their legs and then milling around. Others stood by the windows, basking in the morning sun. Soon after my arrival, I noticed that a few trotted nervously around, raising their heads now and then and sniffing the air. Something didn't feel right, though what it was, I couldn't tell.

Fireball approached me. I stood close to him and stroked his neck and back. In spite of my disquiet, lazy thoughts, befitting Sunday morning, circulated in my head: *I'll spend a long time with the dragon horses. It'll be a slow day of not doing anything in particular.*

Suddenly, Fireball twitched sharply as a faint groaning was heard. I looked around but didn't see anything unusual. I heard the same noise again – only this time it was louder. A deep grunting followed, sounding like the breaking of a tree by a fierce storm. Some dragons stopped dead and listened intently while others rose on their hind legs.

The creaking and grumbling of distressed timber became stronger. I felt a surging wave of fear engulfing me and pinning me down. At that moment, the oak paneling above the main doors fell to the floor and blocked the exit. Alarm spread amongst the dragon horses with the young ones running around in a frenzy. The alpha dragons of the four teams told them to calm down.

When Fireball was passing by the pavilion's largest window, it shattered violently, showering him with shards of broken glass. He retreated swiftly, quivering. Even the big dragons looked scared.

Fireball regained his composure and took charge of the situation; in a commanding voice he ordered everyone to get out through the back doors. But as we approached the escape route, the doors slammed shut in front of us.

For a little while, the dragons stood in front of the rear exit, looking bewildered. Fireball approached the back doors and pushed them with the weight of his strong body, but they remained firmly shut. Turning around, he kicked them with his hind legs with increasingly frantic movements. Just then, the panelling above the doorway fell down and Fireball had to withdraw quickly.

All at once, wooden panels from the celling plummeted onto the dragons – making some break into a panic-stricken gallop. Fireball directed the smaller dragon horses to lie on the floor and the bigger ones to stand over them and shield them. Looking stunned, they followed his instructions. Fireball told me to join the small dragons – trembling, I crawled beneath one of the large creatures.

Shortly afterwards, a joist from the ceiling fell on Fireball – he writhed in pain, his legs almost caving in under the heavy weight. With an enormous belly-sinking jolt of horror, I realised that the attack was directed mainly at Fireball. Recalling Tania saying that a building can become a Nastorian, a scary thought invaded my head: *Is this what's happening right now?*

Fireball's will power and determination not to surrender to pain were as clear as day. I desperately tried to channel strength to him, but my thoughts kept returning to Radar.

Tania had told me that on Sunday mornings, he trains dogs, wolves and other forest animals in security matters. I prayed that his ever-rotating ears were picking up the sound of breaking wood.

The building continued to shower Fireball with pieces of timber, causing him to shudder in agony. And then I heard Volcano commanding the dragons to listen to him.

'Despite all our precautions,' he said in a sombre voice. 'Nastorian forces have taken over the pavilion. The only way we can defend Fireball and ourselves is by feeling loving kindness to each other.'

Volcano continued to talk to the dragons, urging them to connect with uplifting experiences. His voice became softer, almost hypnotic, when he directed channelling of kind thoughts to everyone in the sanctuary. I joined in. The combined energies of all present seemed to slow the shedding of timbers until the assault had stopped altogether.

It was a huge relief to see Radar and his assistants storming in through the shattered window. Radar appeared shocked when he saw the wooden debris.

After a little while, Chris Light, Ophelia Leech and other grown-ups entered the building through the broken window. Chris stared at the destruction in the pavilion, shaking his head in disbelief and then told Ophelia to attend to Fireball.

Whilst the body healer was examining Fireball's injuries, the dragon collapsed to the floor. My brain went numb when I saw Ophelia's agitated face. Fireball's scales were broken in several places and blood was running down his body. Ophelia knelt next to him and then asked me to bring clean water. I located a tap and dashed quickly back with a freshly filled bucket. She then cleaned and dressed the dragon's wounds.

'We must get him to the healing retreat immediately,' cried Ophelia. 'There's no time to waste. He's too big for us to carry; he'll have to walk. But first I must give him an elixir to make him stronger.'

She took a potion from her remedy kit. I stood as close as I could to the injured dragon and channelled loving kindness to him. When I looked at Radar and his assistants, I knew that they joined me in sending healing energy to Fireball.

'You must take your medicine!' Chris said firmly.

Fireball made futile attempts to lift his head. My heart sank. The other dragons moved closer and enveloped him in soft vapours. Eventually, he managed to raise his head and slowly opened his eyes. Chris supported his head while Ophelia opened the dragon's mouth and poured the potion down his throat, imploring him to swallow.

I could see how difficult it was for him to retain the first mouthful. My heart sank lower. Ophelia and Chris persisted until he took four measures of the elixir. Fireball then looked a little more alert, and Ophelia and Chris somewhat less distressed. I breathed a huge sigh of relief.

Chris asked the other adults to remove the wooden wreckage from the doorways. Radar and his trainees joined in the clearing task, carrying in their mouths whatever they could until all the debris was removed.

'Let's help him to his feet,' said Ophelia.

Many hands helped Fireball to rise from the floor. I could feel my throat closing and tears welling up when I noticed his trembling legs and the deep pain in his eyes.

He tried to reposition his body by tentatively stepping forward – every tiny movement caused his large body to writhe in anguish. The dragon horses around him produced a large cloud of good vibes that enveloped him. Fireball again slowly placed one hoof in front of the other.

After a few small steps he had to rest – it took Fireball a long time to reach the healing retreat, but eventually he got there. A gigantic wave of relief swept throughout my body when he crossed the threshold of the building.

Ophelia then led him to the Dragons' Hall of Recovery where he lay down on straw. The body healer placed calcite crystals around him. Fireball closed his eyes – I hoped that he had drifted into a deep, invigorating sleep.

'I'd like everyone to leave now,' Ophelia requested in no uncertain terms. 'I'll keep you updated about his progress.'

* * *

The morning ritual was delayed until early afternoon. Standing in a circle, Chris told the kids who got up late about the pavilion attacking Fireball. Looking around, I couldn't help but notice dread swirling around.

'You must remain strong,' Chris told us calmly. 'The Nastorians successfully lured the Dragon Horses' Pavilion to join them. We mustn't allow fear to triumph.'

'How did they do it?' asked Ollie in a trembling voice.

'All buildings have a life force and a will of their own,' replied Chris. 'Young structures are easier to manipulate than older ones. We'll review all security and will find out how the Nastorians managed to gain access to the pavilion. Radar will take care of all necessary improvements.'

'What about the pavilion?' asked Tania. 'It's now a disgustin' Nastorian. Surely the dragons ain't gonna live there.'

'It will need a comprehensive restoration,' said Chris, 'as well as a deprogramming and then reintegrating into our community.'

'But where will the dragons spend the night?' asked Ollie, looking very worried.

'They'll sleep in the open air,' answered Chris. 'When it rains, we'll bring them into one of the halls.'

'I'll have a dragon horse in my room,' called Liam.

Kayla also declared her interest. 'I'd love to look after a little one.'

'Thank you for your offers,' said Chris. 'But right now, I urge you to face adversity with courage. The Nastorians injured fireball's body but they didn't break his spirit. Follow his example. I now ask you all to continue with your plans for today.'

Tania invited me to watch birds in the forest, but wanting to be on my own, I declined joining her and walked to Moonstone halls. After entering my room, uninvited film snippets of the assault by the pavilion forced their way into my head.

When the horrible flashback became unbearable, to make myself feel better, I looked at pictures of Georgian buildings on my laptop. Having read a ton of books and searched the net about this architectural style, I like to think that I know loads. I also love learning new words about the different parts of old buildings.

Lying on my bed, I connected with George, my house, trying to picture him in his prime when he was a well maintained town-house. Despite my best efforts, images of George looking neglected and unloved dominated.

In the end, I settled on picturing my home in its current state. To begin with, I visualised George's staircase: a continuous dark handrail, twisting and winding up from the ground floor all the way to the top, supported by beautiful wooden spindles that had seen better days. Over time, some had been replaced with plain timber poles.

The balustrade on the lower two floors had been strengthened with ugly steel straps. The unsightly repairs led me to imagine how my house would look after a total revamp. I decided that the first thing I would do, would be to restore the staircase to its original Georgian splendour.

I was enjoying planning George's renovation when a picture of Fireball's injuries showed up in my mind. It was quickly followed by images of Lava lying motionless on the forest's floor, and Thunder being hit by Nastorian fire. Closing my eyes, I tried to channel loving energy to the three dragons, but mingled snippets of injured dragons and damaged buildings sabotaged my efforts.

I got up and went for a run, hoping that a four-legged running mate might join me, but no dog turned up. On my way back to my room, I bumped into Chris. It was good to see him – his calmness was very welcome.

'How are you feeling?' he asked with a concerned look in his eyes. 'It's a difficult time for all of us, even more so for you having witnessed the attack. If you need additional sessions with Edgar, I can arrange that.'

'I'm still not sure that I can tell him everything. He's kind of ... a bit ... offish.'

'You've only seen him twice. I think you need more time.'

'I'll do what you tell me, but sometimes you know straight away how you feel about people. I don't think it's going to get any easier.'

'Have one more session with him, and if after that you'd still want to see someone else, come and talk to me. Now, let me share with you some good news. I've come from the healing retreat, Lava and Thunder are making a steady recovery.'

'And Fireball?'

'It's still early days. He's young and strong and that's why he's likely to pull through. We must keep him in our thoughts and our hearts.'

'I'll do my best. Thank you for letting me know about the dragons. I'll see you soon.'

Late into the night, whenever I closed my eyes, movie shows of the onslaught on Fireball played in my head. I kept my eyes open for a long time, trying to avoid the uninvited pictures while struggling to figure out how the pavilion had turned into a Nastorian.

When sleep freed me from intruding images, I was woken up by a terrifying nightmare of losing Fireball. I knew that I'd have to keep my eyes open to prevent dreadful recalls and night terrors from haunting me. Lying quietly, I urged reluctant, slowly-moving time to hurry up. I waited for ages for dawn to break and release me from the tyranny of intrusive memories.

CHAPTER SEVENTEEN

The Battle Within

Having got fed up with lying in bed and warding off dreadful film clips of the attack by the dragons' pavilion, I got up at the first light of dawn. Hoping not to disturb Tania, I quietly dressed up and slipped out of our room.

I walked out of Moonstone halls and sprinted into an early morning run. After a while, broken sleep and tiredness took their toll – I stopped jogging and strolled aimlessly in the forest. Playing images of Fireball regaining his strength helped me to feel a little better.

The morning was bright and pleasantly warm. Inhaling the scent of wild jasmine, I urged it to dispel the lethargy of sleepless nights and the heebie-jeebies in the pit of my belly. Looking at other early-risers, I realised that they, too, were fearful. Even the good weather couldn't banish the pervading dread.

The welcome snippets of Fireball looking healthy quickly faded and my mind started playing up: I was afraid of an imminent Nastorian attack; I was afraid of trees falling on me; I was afraid of Moonstone halls turning into enemy assailants.

Just then, uninvited images of Fireball's injuries invaded my head. I tried my hardest to send the injured dragon healing energy. But despite all my good intentions, crushing doubts had taken over my entire brain: *Can the*

Custodians protect us from the Nastorians? Are we safe here?

Unexpectedly, I heard a voice. 'Morning, Willow.'

Looking around, I saw Fleur standing beneath an old oak tree. For a moment, I wasn't sure whether she was an image I'd conjured up or a real person. I decided to find out what was really going on. 'What are you doing here so early?' I asked.

'Whenever I can, I go for walks at the crack of dawn,' Fleur replied, smiling broadly. 'I like this time when everything is peaceful and the world is slowly waking up. What got you out of bed?'

'I couldn't sleep and got totally bored with lying in bed.'

'Were you thinking about Fireball?'

'I just can't get my head around the pavilion attacking him. He's so friendly and helpful – he doesn't deserve what happened to him.'

'You need more time to come to terms with that dreadful event. Yesterday, in the battle between kindness and cruelty, the Nastorians won. I'm afraid that there's a constant conflict between good and bad everywhere, even in our hearts.'

'There were many good dragons in the pavilion, and yet, they couldn't stop the destructive energy. Are the Nastorians more powerful than the Custodians?'

'Sometimes malicious forces can have the upper hand. I'm sorry, I can't talk to you any more,' said Fleur in a somewhat sharp voice. 'I've got to go now and help with the planning of the restoration of the pavilion.' And then, she walked away.

I was baffled by her sudden departure, but had too many things on my mind without dwelling on this. I returned to Moonstone halls. Tania was in bed with her eyes half open. 'Where have you been?' she asked.

'I couldn't sleep, so I went for a run.'

'I feel ya. I can't stop thinking about yesterday.'

'Let's have breakfast and after that, would you like to

visit Fireball with me?'

'I'd love to,' replied Tania.

We made our way to Pumpkin Hall and ate breakfast unusually quietly. Coriander made delicious pancakes with scrummy toppings of fresh berries and crushed nuts. She also prepared a fruit salad made of apples, peaches and mangos. I always loved her food, but on that morning, I didn't enjoy what I ate.

Having eaten breakfast, Tania and I walked to the morning ritual. The circle was cast, but anxious-looking kids whispered to each other while shuffling on their feet. Chris raised his hand and asked everyone to listen to him.

'The pavilion's attack has unnerved us all,' he said gravely. 'Yesterday, the Nastorians triumphed. It's quite likely that they'd masqueraded as Custodians and that's how they managed to gain access to the pavilion. They inflicted severe injuries on Fireball, one of the most courageous dragons we've ever had. After the ritual, we'll go together to Emerald halls where we'll discuss yesterday's events.'

Kids appeared subdued during the ceremony. Even the special water on my face seemed to have lost some of its uplifting energy. I looked at Ollie and recoiled when I saw how unhappy he was. *He lost both of his parents and now he's faced with the possibility of losing Fireball. Why has he had to suffer so much?* I asked myself, wanting badly to do something for him.

After the ceremony, I approached Ollie. 'You look a bit shook up. You can come and see me anytime you want, you know.'

'Thank you,' he murmured.

We all walked to Emerald halls and sat in a circle on the floor. Chris gave everyone a crystal and then he spoke to us, 'Fireball's condition is serious. Lava and Thunder are slowly getting better, but they still need your healing energy. Focus with all your heart on our dragons making a full recovery. Don't allow doubts to distract you.'

Despite my best efforts to stay with images of the injured

dragons regaining their strength, one thought continued to badger me: *How did the Nastorians, or the Pretenders, succeed in converting the pavilion right under the noses of so many Custodians?*

'We'll stop now sending healing thoughts to the injured dragons,' said Chris gently. 'I'd like to tell you why our nemeses targeted Fireball. The Nastorians know full well that they'd never break his integrity and that he would never join them, and that's why they attacked him. Fireball showed his mettle when he protected the smaller dragons and Willow during the assault. We must have confidence in what we believe in, even when faced with adversity.'

'How did they manage to enter the pavilion? Why didn't our dragons notice their nasty vibes?' I blurted out before I could stop myself.

'The answers to your questions are still unknown,' replied Chris. 'The only thing I can say is that there are Pretenders amongst us, impostors of the highest echelon. They are fraudsters who have masked their malice so well that even the dragon horses have been misled.'

My dread and unease increased; I felt alarm pulsating in my body and all around me. I recalled Radar telling me that he'd rather face a Nastorian than a Pretender. At that moment, I realised how frightening and daunting a hidden enemy can be.

'Are they still here?' asked Tania.

'I'm afraid so,' said Chris. 'I'd like you all to be vigilant and report anything unusual to Radar immediately. We'll do our best to unmask them.'

'It's really scary,' muttered one of the small children, sitting close to me.

'You may feel that we should have prevented the attack and that we can't protect you. Don't allow fear and doubts to take over. I ask you to use this difficult time to find the courage we need to drive away our adversaries.'

'How can we do that when we don't even know who they are?' demanded Liam.

'We'll expose them,' said Chris. 'Right now, connect with the strength that helped you to survive dark moments when you were let down by your parents, by the very people who were supposed to care for you. I beg you to continue to believe in loving kindness. We need your good energy to help our injured dragons. When misgivings and despair threaten to dampen down any good energy you have, think about the brave dragons that were prepared to lay down their lives for others.'

'We gotta fight for Fireball, Thunder and Lava,' called a teenage boy.

'I understand how you feel, but fighting is not our way,' said Chris. 'We'll help the dragons with goodwill and compassion. I'd like you all to visit the dragons in the healing retreat every day. Two volunteers will stay there for an hour and then, they'll be replaced by two other kids throughout the day. Your presence will help the dragons to mobilise their own healing powers. Before I end this meeting, let me tell you that you can have additional sessions with your trust restorer, or if you prefer, you can see me.'

After the gathering, I walked to Emerald halls for my meeting with Edgar. He smiled when I entered his room, and I decided to give him another chance.

'The attack on Fireball has affected everyone in the camp. How are you feeling?' he asked.

'Last night, I couldn't sleep and now I see Nastorians everywhere. And worse yet, I'm now overwhelmed by uncertainty and fear. Normally, I've lots of doubts about myself, but since the assault, I'm not sure about anything.' I gazed at the floor when tension gripped my shoulders.

'Does it feel as if someone pulled a rug from under your feet?'

'Totally.' Looking up, I noticed that his eyes were cold.

'What had happened in the pavilion was completely unexpected. We're all still in a state of shock. More time is needed to come to terms with such an appalling incident.'

'Why did it happen to Fireball? I just don't get it. Why didn't Radar detect the Pretenders?' I felt unbearable pressure in my chest – sitting back in my chair, I tried to calm down and force my lungs to take in air.

'Are you alright?' asked Edgar. A lump in my throat prevented me from saying anything.

At that moment, I knew for sure that I couldn't tell him how I really felt. There was something about him that made me feel uncomfortable. I needed to talk to Fleur about dragons – just then, an image of the injured Fireball showed up in my unruly brain. My chest threatened me with an explosion.

'I'm sorry,' I mumbled after a massive silence. 'I must go for a run. May I?'

'We can finish now. Take it easy today.'

I scooted out of Emerald halls and took off, picturing Lightning, my imaginary green air dragon flying above me. But then, an uninvited image of Thunder flying lopsided with an injured wing appeared next to him. I gave up on running and walked to the sanctuary's forest, looking out for birds.

Having located a robin, I watched it closely; I loved the changing hues of its orange-red breast when it hopped between branches. After the robin flew away, I decided to see Fleur, thinking that talking about dragons would make me feel better.

I walked to Ruby halls where Billie danced rings around me. As always, there was no holding back; I received lots of enthusiastic canine love. I said goodbye to the bouncing hound and then knocked on Fleur's door.

'Hello, Willow,' Fleur greeted me warmly. 'Did you come to see me because of Fireball?'

'Yes, I can't stop thinking about what has happened to him.'

'I'm happy to see you but, as I told you, Edgar is the best person to help you.'

'I tried! I talked to him this morning. I don't know

what's wrong with me, but I felt worse afterwards.'

'Perhaps, Fireball made you feel unhappy and not Edgar. What do you think?'

'Could be. I keep asking myself why the kindest and most caring dragon got so badly hurt.'

'The Nastorians know that they'd never succeed in manipulating a true Custodian like Fireball into joining their ranks, and for this reason they want to destroy him.'

'Chris said something similar at our meet-up today. I'm really struggling with the thought that Fireball was punished for being good.'

'Until there's some kind of a resolution, it might be difficult to let go.'

'Do other kids feel like this?'

'They do,' replied Fleur, 'even adults may become preoccupied with shocking things. How are you feeling right now?'

'A little bit better after watching a robin and getting lots of doggie love from Billie.'

'Connecting with a bird, an animal or a dragon can be helpful.'

'Yesterday morning, I went to the Dragon Horses' Pavilion to do just that, and that's when all hell broke loose. Now, dreadful pictures of the pavilion attacking Fireball haunt me.'

'How about running with a dog?' asked Fleur.

'Even that might be difficult. I now see Nastorians everywhere.'

'Can you think about any happy experiences with your family?'

'I can, but then the bad things come back. I hear my mum say horrible things, and I see her cold eyes.'

'Does she say unkind things in front of people who aren't family?'

'Never! We play happy families when we aren't at home.'

'It doesn't sound as if your mother would like to join us

anytime soon.'

'What do you mean?' I muttered, shuddering.

'Well, you told me that she's caring in front of other people, but at home, she says horrible things to you. How does she really feel about you?'

'I'm not sure – it's all so confusing. I want to believe that she cares about me, but at times, I think she hates me.'

'Perhaps, because of your own unhappiness, it's so difficult for you to stomach images of injured dragons.'

'You've hit the nail on the head. It doesn't take much to upset me. I hurt when I see a homeless dog or cat; I hurt when I see a sad kid; I even hurt when I see my home in a state of disrepair. I don't want to be that sensitive. There are times when I think, it'd be easier to be a Nastorian or a Pretender; at least I wouldn't be so miserable.'

'I'm afraid I have to agree with you,' said Fleur. 'From what I know about the Pretenders, in the beginning they have misgivings about causing upset. With continued practice, they become completely blind to the suffering of others, and eventually they enjoy inflicting pain and humiliation.'

'How can they? I don't get it.'

'Power is addictive. The Nastorians love being in control and do whatever they want, even if it means hurting others.'

'That's awful!' I cried.

'For them, it's gratifying. They particularly enjoy gradually breaking down kids or grown-ups; stripping away any good feelings they have about themselves until there's nothing left. For instance, a Pretender is very helpful until someone trusts them, and then, they drive the knife in. They use underhand tactics with a smile on their face, feigning to be caring. It's very confusing and it creates a lot of self-doubt – when that happens, they become decent again. In the end, their prey becomes dependent on them.'

'I don't believe it!'

'Let me give you another example; a teacher who is

also a Pretender may encourage a talented pupil to study hard for a scholarship. But eventually, that teacher does not support their pupil's application on the grounds that the kid wasn't ready. The Pretender might say that he didn't want their *protégé* to go through the heartache of failure. Feeling defeated, the pupil remembers the initial validation and craves more approval from their teacher. The mixture of praise and fault-finding can be toxic.'

'I don't like the sound of that. I think I'll go now. Thank you for talking to me.'

I walked out of Ruby halls with Fleur's words *"It doesn't sound as if your mother would like to join us anytime soon"* playing in my head like a broken record. Every step intensified the disquiet and fear caused by nightmarish questions: *Does it mean that my mum is a Pretender? If she's an impostor, am I one too? Do I deserve to be in the sanctuary?*

CHAPTER EIGHTEEN

The Calcite Healing Retreat

The prospect of my mum being a Pretender was trying; it drained my energy whenever I thought about it and snuffed out the little self-respect I'd only just begun to have. At night, my sleep was broken by nightmares. While during the day, I was bedevilled by film clips of Mum pushing me away at home, yet playing happy families in front of other people.

Eventually, I decided not to think about Mum altogether and instead focus on the injured dragons. True to his word, Chris had arranged for Tania and me to watch over them. Having entered the retreat, I was surprised to see Radar in the reception area. He approached us with a serious expression in his eyes.

'Please listen carefully,' he said. 'I've noticed unusual frequencies in the retreat. We must all be very vigilant; should you observe any change in the energy in the halls of recovery, let me know right away.'

A chill travelled down my spine. 'I'll do anything for our dragons,' I whispered.

'Vile, disgustin' Nastorians,' said Tania. 'I hate 'em. How can they go after injured dragons?'

'I will check all visitors before they proceed to the halls of recovery,' Radar told us. 'I ask you again to be on the lookout for anything out of the ordinary, no matter how trivial it might appear.'

Tania and I walked into the Dragons' Hall of Recovery – the calm atmosphere embraced me like a gentle, warm wave.

One of the walls had a stunning tiled mosaic, depicting a red air dragon in full flight on a sky-blue background. I stopped in my tracks when I saw large, honey, blue and green crystals. I stood there chained by their beauty while inhaling their energy and letting it spread into my mind and body.

The dragons' hall had a large open area and a number of individual dens. We found Fireball in a den with Ophelia sitting by his side, giving him his remedies. She smiled and invited us to join her.

'I'll have to check on Lava and Thunder,' said Ophelia. 'Can you look after Fireball for me? Your company will do him a world of good.'

'We're gonna do our very best,' said Tania.

Tania and I crouched on either side of Fireball and channelled healing energy to him. I tried my hardest to link with his fighting spirit, willing him to be the strong dragon he'd once been. While focusing on Fireball's injured back, I felt a surge of heat and vitality in my hands, which I then placed on the dragon's dressed wounds. I heard Tania whisper, 'Get better, Fireball.'

Our efforts were abruptly interrupted by visitors. I saw Coriander Meadows enter with two men I hadn't seen before. 'I've brought two renowned body healers from one of our temporary sites to help Fireball,' she announced.

The air suddenly turned cooler. I decided to act immediately. 'I'll be back in one minute,' I muttered.

I shot to reception looking for Radar, but I couldn't find him anywhere. Having located Ophelia in the apothecary, I asked her where he might be. She told me that he'd to go out because of an emergency.

'Coriander came to visit Fireball with two body healers,' I blurted out. 'The temperature suddenly dropped when they entered his den.'

Without saying a word, Ophelia ran out of the apothecary with me following closely behind. I immediately noticed that Fireball was unhappy.

Ophelia was angry when she spoke to Coriander. 'Who are these so-called body healers? You should have checked with me in advance to find out whether you could bring them to see Fireball.'

'I'm sorry,' said Coriander, taken aback. 'I thought it was the best thing to do.'

'Let me introduce myself,' said one of the men smoothly, smiling broadly – one of those grins that only involve moving your mouth, his eyes remained cold. 'My name –'

'Don't bother,' snapped Ophelia. 'You're to leave immediately.' I had never heard her talk in such a commanding, icy tone.

'Please,' said the other man, 'just give us one minute of your time.'

'You're going right now,' Ophelia reiterated sharply. 'Do you hear me? Right. Now!'

The men left Fireball's den, walked briskly through the reception area and out of the building. Tania, Ophelia and I followed them and were surprised to see two dragon horses waiting outside. The two men jumped on their backs and galloped off. At that moment, I noticed Radar and his canine assistants charging at full speed towards us.

Radar, panting heavily, almost bumped into Ophelia – breaking his run at the last moment. 'I was called to a false emergency,' he gasped. 'The Pretenders knew that the two impostors wouldn't get past me, so they created a distraction.'

'I'm so sorry. I really am,' apologised Coriander, looking crestfallen. 'I wanted the dragons to get better quickly and that's why I didn't check security with you. Now, I understand that they used the identities of two renowned body healers ... I fell into their trap ... Sorry again, I should've known better.'

'We'll put this incident behind us,' said Radar. 'The Pretenders outplayed us today. They mustn't succeed again. Let's focus now on keeping our dragons safe.' He then turned to Tania and me. 'Your hour with Fireball is up.

You might want to stay here and connect with the calming frequencies of different calcites – ask one of the assistants to tell you about their unique qualities.'

Tania and I left Radar in the reception area and walked with Ophelia back to the Dragons' Hall of Recovery.

'Jade will finish her shift soon,' said Ophelia. 'When she's free, ask her to tell you about the calcites. She loves sharing her knowledge of crystals with others. I now have to go back to the apothecary.'

We found Jade with Fireball. She was holding a beautiful grey crystal in one hand while the other was on his chest. Her eyes were closed and I knew she was channelling healing energy into his heart; she hadn't noticed us enter the den. Tania and I stood quietly, hoping not to disturb her.

A few moments later, two loud teenage boys entered. Jade raised her head and smiled. 'I'm glad you've come to stay with Fireball.'

'We'll watch over him for an hour,' said one of the boys. He'd short dark hair, sallow complexion and was wearing ripped jeans and a white shirt.

'Is there anything we need to know?' asked the other one. I liked his unruly mousey locks and the black T-shirt with a large wolf's head printed on its front.

'Fireball is stable,' replied Jade, 'but his condition is still serious. Send him lots of healing thoughts. Should you notice any change in him, let Ophelia know immediately.'

'Is there any chance you might show us the calcites?' I asked Jade.

'I'd love to,' she replied, her face breaking into a smile. 'Let's go to the Crystals' Room. While we're there, we could also channel loving kindness to the dragons.'

'They're really something,' Tania gushed. 'I mean, as good as they come. I really love Fireball, Lava and Thunder.'

While Tania was talking, I recalled her telling me that Coriander had been working in the sanctuary for many years, and yet she'd brought two charlatans to see Fireball.

Is she one of them? These niggling thoughts persisted, freaking me out.

'Did Coriander make a mistake?' I dared to ask. 'Or is she a Pretender?'

'Dunno,' replied Tania. 'If she's a con artist, then she's a pretty good one. I always liked her, but then, I guess I'm biased 'cause of her cooking. I think with my stomach.'

'I was very surprised by what happened today,' said Jade. 'She's the last person I'd have suspected. Now, Tania and Willow, Radar's asked us to create healing energy. Let's talk about crystals and not impostors.'

We entered the Crystals' Room. I didn't know where to look – never before had I seen so many beautiful crystals arranged in a way that their colours and vibes made me feel chilled out to my core. I totally immersed myself in the soothing atmosphere around me, noticing Tania doing the same.

'The positioning of crystals,' said Jade, 'creates a grid of a powerful healing force.'

I didn't want to talk; I didn't want to do anything; I just wanted to enjoy the enchanting display and peaceful atmosphere. After a while, I sighed, 'They're out of this world. Totally amazing.'

'I'm soooo in tune with them,' Tania declared. 'All I can think about right now are crystals and nothing else.'

Jade was upbeat, completely in her element. 'The calcite minerals generate solid yet gentle vibes that can be used to help fragile dragons, animals or humans. When our charges are strong enough, we let them connect with other, more potent crystals, chosen for their individual needs.'

'Is it always best to start with calcites?' I asked.

'Most of the time,' said Jade. 'Occasionally, Ophelia decides on something different.'

'How do you know which ones to use?' asked Tania.

'I learn a great deal from Ophelia. She is very good at arranging grids for different ailments or injuries.'

'Why were different calcites placed in the Dragons' Hall

of Recovery?' I asked.

'The honey-coloured one cleanses toxins and brings the body into alignment for optimal well-being. The green helps to stimulate the immune system and prevent infections because it absorbs negative energy. The blue mineral is used for strengthening immunity and for pain relief. After the shock of an injury, it's instrumental in creating inner peace and healing.'

'When d'you use a pink calcite?' asked Tania.

'Pink is good for the development of compassion for others. I don't think Fireball, Thunder or Lava need this particular mineral,' Jade laughed. 'They're already the kindest and most caring dragons you could wish for.'

'I love the brown one,' I said, inhaling its frequencies and enjoying a feeling of calm in every atom of my body.

'Brown acts as a stabiliser when you're faced with conflicting priorities,' Jade went on. 'It also boosts wisdom.'

'And the other calcites?' asked Tania.

'Black enhances grounding and stability. Grey brings about serenity and detachment from problems. Red energises you and gets rid of bad thoughts. It also helps kids who have had unhappy experiences. Orange promotes happiness and safety.'

'Can I hold one?' I asked.

Jade walked to the back of the room where wicker baskets with different crystals stood proudly on top of chests of drawers. She chose a few pieces and handed them to Tania and me. We were both given three minerals coloured red, orange and grey.

'Use them to make yourselves stronger, and then you'll be in a better place to help others. And now, while you're holding the crystals, let's concentrate on sending lots of healing energy and loving thoughts to the injured dragons.'

For a while, the three of us stood in silence. I pictured Lava, Thunder and Fireball looking healthy and taking part in the morning ritual.

'You can stop now,' Jade told us. 'However, before

you go, I'd like to show you the celestite collection.' She opened a large ornate wooden box with brittle pale blue, almost grey, coloured clusters. They worked their magic on me: happy memories of fooling around with Sophie and her Chihuahua showed up in my head.

'Celestite removes sadness, stress and low mood,' said Jade. 'It brings peace and harmony. It also encourages creativity. This delicate mineral is really good for us.'

'When I look at them,' said Tania. 'I see clearly that Fireball's heart is totally kind.'

'Sadly, the Nastorians see his kindness as a threat to their way of doing things,' said Jade. 'In recent years, they've managed to recruit only a few of our dragons.'

'I find it hard to believe that any dragons would have joined them,' I remarked.

'Many noble dragons were offered precious gemstones and power, but chose to remain honourable. Fearing them, the Nastorians have been striving to annihilate them and wreck their good reputation.'

'It ain't fair,' protested Tania.

'In Europe, the Nastorians have been successful in creating a huge rift between dragons and humans. In the Orient, the dragon is considered to be spiritual and good. For centuries, in Chinese folklore and art, dragons have been symbols of power, strength and good fortune, and till the present day they command much respect. Modern popular Japanese culture ascribes them magical healing powers.'

'I believe people in Europe will reconcile with dragons,' I stated. 'All they have to do is to meet our dragons. I'll tell them how much they've helped me.'

'Kids like you will show the way,' said Jade.

'Wow, you're a cool crystal teacher and a great dragon enthusiast,' said Tania, smiling. 'I wish you worked in my school.'

'Your school is not ready for me.'

'That's a real pity,' sighed Tania.

Tania and I thanked Jade for her time, said goodbye and set off to Emerald halls.

'I'm gonna tell my trust restorer about Coriander visiting Fireball with two impostors,' said Tania. 'She's good at explaining things – I feel better after seeing her.'

'Talking to Fleur about dragons helps me.'

'Yeah, she's, like, a dragonologist through and through.'

'Right now,' I uttered, 'I could do with someone telling me that Fireball will be alright. I've this gut-wrenching fear that something awful is going to happen to him.

CHAPTER NINETEEN

The Power of Words

In the morning, looking at the three calcite pieces crowning my bedside cabinet, I felt ready to face the day. Breathing in their gentle and uplifting energy, I stretched and jumped out of bed.

While making our way to Pumpkin Hall, Tania and I talked about Fireball. During breakfast, I observed Coriander and noticed how tense she was. Her customary warm smile was nowhere to be seen; she was tetchy and ill at ease.

After the morning cleansing ceremony, Tania and I went to Ruby halls where we worked with Louise Blake on our costumes. Tania appeared chilled out when she was embroidering buttercups on her forest fairy dress. I was surprised to find out how quickly, with the creativity guide's help, I progressed with the wings of my goldfinch costume. I also started planning the bird's body.

Time to visit the injured dragons arrived quickly – Tania and I hurried to the healing retreat. In the reception we were met by Radar's most trusted assistants: Winter and Sky. After the attack on Fireball, Radar appointed the two Huskies to share guard duties; the hounds took turns in patrolling the building. Despite knowing us well, the dogs sniffed Tania and me thoroughly before allowing us to go to the halls of recovery.

We found Jade standing by Lava's side. The dragon horse appeared now healthier and fitter with a focused expression on her face.

'Hello, Tania and Willow, good to see you both,' Jade greeted us cheerily. 'Look at Lava: she's so much better.'

'This is great news,' I said. 'How are Thunder and Fireball?'

'Thunder has been making steady progress, but Fireball still needs lots of healing energy.'

'That's exactly what we're gonna do,' said Tania. 'We'll give Fireball tons of love.'

I smiled at Jade. 'Before we go to Fireball, may I ask if I could help in the Crystals' Room?'

'Would you be interested in cleansing crystals?'

'Totally,' I replied eagerly.

'In that case,' said Jade, 'come to the Crystals' Room after your hour with Fireball.'

We waved bye to Jade and moved to Fireball's den. Tania and I sat down on either side of the dragon horse and focused on sending him loving kindness.

After a while, Fireball raised his head and seemed a little perkier. He welcomed us by sending gentle pastel-coloured vapours in our direction. When our hour was up, I said goodbye to Fireball and Tania and walked to the Crystals' Room.

Jade asked me to do the best job ever; I had a great time holding and cleansing beautiful crystals and loved every moment of it. I left the retreat feeling both energised and calm and walked to Ruby halls, hoping to have another chat with Fleur.

Having knocked on Fleur's door, I entered her room – she didn't smile when she saw me. *Had I done something wrong? Why is she so cold?* I wondered. An army of grasshoppers invaded my belly, giving me the heebie-jeebies.

'Can I talk to you?' I mumbled.

'Now, look here, Willow,' Fleur snapped irritably, 'I'm tired of you clinging onto me. As you know, I'm an activities organiser and not a trust restorer.'

Her words knocked me sideways. 'I'm sorry,' I muttered, 'I thought you didn't mind me coming to see you.'

'But I do! I've enough on my plate without you badgering me.'

'Oh ... okay ... would you like me to leave now?'

'It might be best,' she said flatly, without looking at me. 'As I've told you already, I'm very busy.'

Fleur got up, walked to the door and opened it. I scooted out, brushing against her in my hurry to get out. I left Ruby halls in a stunned daze, feeling baffled. *Why did she talk to me like that?*

I ambled back in the direction of the healing retreat. On my way, I pictured a large macaque jumping playfully onto my shoulder and whispering in a jolly manner: *Nobody likes you, not even the grown-ups working here.* The chirpy monkey helped me a little.

Radar and Winter were in the reception of the healing retreat. I greeted them and stroked the hound's head. Winter licked my hand and then sniffed it intensely for a long time. Afterwards, he turned his attention to my right arm. I expected Radar's assistants to check every visitor, but why was the Husky so diligent with me? Had he identified an unusual energy or scent?

Radar got closer to me with his nose twitching and he, too, sniffed carefully. 'The frequencies on your right side are highly unusual,' he commented. 'I can recall something somewhat similar, but not quite the same.'

Now I was completely confused. 'I don't know what to say. I haven't gone anywhere special or done anything extraordinary. Do you suspect anything?'

'I'm not sure yet, but both Winter and I have picked up an unfamiliar energy that requires further investigation. What did you do today?'

'I cleansed crystals in the Crystals' Room and afterwards I went to see Fleur.'

'Continue with your usual activities,' Radar instructed me, 'and report to me anything out of the ordinary.'

I said goodbye to Radar and Winter and walked out of the retreat with miserable thoughts circulating in my head: *All of a sudden Fleur doesn't want to know me. And somehow, there's some weird energy on me.* Having decided to talk with Jade, I hurried to the Crystals' Room. Jade was there, arranging amethysts.

'Hello, Willow,' she welcomed me, smiling. 'You've done a great cleansing job. You look out of sorts. Has something happened?'

'Sorry for taking up your time ... er ... Can we talk briefly?'

'Sure thing, go ahead.'

'Well ... Fleur had told me that I could visit her whenever I wanted ... but today ... she said that I ... badger her.'

'It's out of character,' remarked Jade, looking surprised.

'I like her and, above all, I started to trust her. I don't understand what's brought on this new attitude towards me.'

Before Jade could say anything, Sky bounded in with her tail wagging. While I was stroking her head, the Husky moved slightly back and sniffed my hand and then my right arm. I guessed she was analysing the smells her superbly clever nose had detected.

'Winter and Radar have already identified something unfamiliar on me,' I said, 'and now it seems that Sky has done the same.' Sky looked at me, turned around and left.

'Let's leave the scent and energy trailing to the hounds and come back to Fleur. What you've told me is quite curious, she's normally true to her word and reliable. Perhaps you could talk to her – she probably has a plausible explanation.'

'I'll think about that. May I stay here and look at the crystals?'

'Of course, I'd recommend holding a celestite cluster, a blue lace agate and a creamy calcite. They will make you feel better. I'm afraid I've to go now. I'll see you soon.'

I stayed for some time connecting with the crystals

Jade had suggested while trying to figure out Fleur's new attitude towards me. In the end, I settled on talking with her in the hope of clarifying things.

I walked back to Ruby halls, not knowing what to expect. Fleur was now all smiles. 'Good to see you, Willow,' she said warmly.

I didn't know what to make of this see-saw of greetings. 'May I ask you something?'

'Go on.'

'Why were you so unwelcoming when I came to see you earlier?' I blurted out. 'I don't understand –'

'You're over-sensitive. I was very busy. Sometimes I need to be left alone so that I could get on with my work.'

'It was, like, the way my mum behaves; she can be quite unpredictable.'

'That's for you to deal with,' said Fleur sharply. 'I'm not interested in your relationship with your mother. As I've said, I'm an activities organiser, not a trust restorer.'

'But you were so friendly to begin with! It kind of feels, like, you've misled me.'

'Whatever,' she spat, 'just don't you tell me that I'm dishonest. I take exception to that.'

'I ... I didn't mean to upset you.'

'You can be really irritating at times. I'm not surprised that your mother rejects you when she's angry – that's when she shows her true feelings. I can only assume that you're even more annoying with her than with me.'

'Do you think she pushes me away because I'm a nuisance?'

'Quite likely. You've managed to nark me with your clinginess and unrealistic expectations. Let go, Willow! Give me a break.'

'Sorry for bothering you,' I mumbled. 'I'll go now.'

I left the halls, feeling scared and disorientated. I walked slowly, carrying horrible thoughts: *Fleur has worked out that I'm a pain in the neck. Now it's only a question of time before Chris, Ophelia and Jade will also find out. Fleur is nobody's fool; she was the first to discover that I'm a clinging pest.*

I returned to Ruby halls and knocked on Fleur's door. She invited me in, looking surprised.

'I just wanted to apologise for the things I've said. You're an activities organiser and I shouldn't have bothered you with my mum.'

'That's okay, Willow. I'm glad you've understood what I've been saying and I hope this won't affect our friendship. Despite all your shortcomings, I'm very fond of you. However, there are a number of weaknesses you've to work on.'

'Deep down, I know that I'm a waste of space, especially when I'm in the company of my friend Sophie. Everyone likes her because she's bubbly and fun.'

'How is her mother with you?' asked Fleur.

'She's good to me, though I often feel that I don't deserve it.'

'Well, you've made progress today. Coming to terms with the fact that you've got to change is the first step forward. Right now, let me focus on my work.'

Having said goodbye to Fleur, I left Ruby halls and ambled nowhere in particular. I no longer had to pretend that I wasn't a flawed nobody. After a long time, I meandered back to Moonstone halls.

I opened the front door – a child charging towards me at high speed startled me, snapping me out of my thoughts. Stepping back, I recognised Ollie's face when he hurtled past me. I got the impression that he didn't notice me. Wanting to keep him safe, I hurried after him. I knew full well that running would help him – it always worked for me – so I kept a good distance between us, letting him run freely.

Ollie sped for some time. When we reached the forest, he gradually slowed down, ground to a halt and sank to the forest's floor. With shoulders hunched forward, he looked aimlessly around with blank eyes. I shuffled my feet heavily so that he would hear me approaching him. He turned his head in my direction.

'Heya, Ollie, mind if I sit next to you?'

'If you want to,' he half-whispered, shrugging his shoulders indifferently.

'I'm also into running. I love it.'

Ollie didn't say anything. His eyes were unfocused and remote. We sat in silence for a long time. Then looking at the ground, he faltered, 'Why ... why did they leave me? I ... I thought that they cared about me.'

He said that his parents died in a car crash, so why does he think that they wanted to leave him? I didn't know what to say. 'Sorry about your mum and dad,' I mumbled.

His eyes remained glued to the ground, 'I'm so angry with them. Why ... why did they do that ... they still have each other ... I'm all alone.'

'Your aunt is alright with you?'

'She's okay ... but she works all the time and hasn't that much time for me ... My mum said that she'd always love me ... Why did she leave me?'

'She didn't want to leave you,' I murmured, 'It was an accident.'

'Do you think she loved me? Then, I ... I wanna die ... I wanna be with them again ... You know, we're a family.'

'You don't want ...' I couldn't bring myself to finish the sentence – a voice in my head was yelling, *You're too young, far too young, to talk about dying.*

'My aunt said that my mum and dad are now angels in heaven ... How do I get there? Are there stairs to heaven?'

Once again, I didn't know what to say. 'I ... I ... don't think –'

'Fireball will die.'

Fear engulfing me like wildfire. 'Why do you say that?'

'He will, sure as anything ... I'm telling you ... good people and dragons die ... Sometimes ... I'm afraid that my aunt will die.'

We both turned our heads when we heard movement

behind us. I heaved a sigh of relief when I saw Billie, the dog, bounding towards us. He slowed down and walked calmly to Ollie and then plastered his face with licks. He positioned himself next to Ollie, almost sitting on his lap. Ollie put his arms around the hound and buried his head in his neck. He didn't make a sound, but I knew from his quivering shoulders that he was crying.

It felt so wrong. So horribly wrong. *Why should he suffer so much?* Once again, I experienced a strong urge to do something for him – to make him feel a little better. When Ollie's shoulders stopped moving, I asked, 'What do you enjoy doing?'

'I love watching films, especially cartoons.'

'So how about coming with me to my room and watching as many cartoons as you want on my laptop?'

'I'd like that,' he replied, looking a bit brighter, and then he turned to Billie. 'Let's make a move, Mr Dog. We're gonna watch cartoons.'

We walked back to Moonstone halls and I let Ollie gorge himself on all kinds of animated shows. Doing something small for him made me feel better. Ollie seemed to trust me – if only I could do the same and have a little bit of faith in myself.

* * *

During some days, I thought that I deserved to be rejected by Fleur, but then, at other times, I was angry with her for pushing me away. All the while, a persistent thought bedevilled me: *Am I good enough to remain in the camp?*

Eventually, I decided to leave.

CHAPTER TWENTY

A New Friend

Even though I had decided to leave the sanctuary, I couldn't bring myself to do so. I knew that I'd miss Tania, the dragons and the dogs terribly. In the end, I settled on delaying my departure and on seeing Lavender, hoping that she would make it easier for me.

After the morning ritual, i approached chris – looking at his calm eyes, i felt somewhat better.

'Is everything alright?' he asked in his amiable and caring voice. 'Shall we go to my chamber and talk?'

'Er ... I just wanted to ask whether I could see Lavender? I know it's all my fault ... only ... it's difficult for me to tell Edgar how I feel ...'

'Are you sure about that?'

'I am, I just don't feel comfortable with him.'

'In that case, I'll ask Lavender to work with you. When would you like to see her?'

'Today, if at all possible.'

'I've a meeting with her at two o'clock this afternoon. I'll ask her to see you instead of me.'

'Thank you. I really appreciate this. I'll be on my way now.'

* * *

Lavender stood up when I entered her room, walked briskly towards me with a big smile on her face as if she'd known me all my life and shook my hand. 'It's good to meet you, Willow.'

She looked about thirty, of middling height with neat features and jet-black, shiny, straight hair cut at chin level. Her blue eyes matched the colour of the long dress she was wearing. Unease stopped me from smiling back. *Why is she so friendly? She doesn't even know me.*

'Tania told me that you work with her,' I muttered.

'I do,' Lavender said in a soft voice. 'Can you tell me a little bit about yourself?'

'well ... I'm ...' I wanted to tell her lots of things, but something held me back. I pushed back into my armchair and didn't say anything.

We sat in silence for a while until Lavender said, 'May I ask you a question?'

'Go on,' I replied, shrugging my shoulders.

'I know that you had a few sessions with Edgar. Why didn't you want to continue with him?' She was leaning slightly towards me as if she was trying not to miss anything.

'Er ... I'm not sure myself. It was ... kind of ... hard for me talk to him.'

'Try to think about it. If you tell me what didn't work for you with Edgar, I'd do things differently.'

'He was asking questions about my mum, and I prefer not to think about what she says.'

'Would you rather avoid talking about your mother?'

'I can't see the point, it just upsets me.' I replied, feeling exasperated: *Why can't they get it that it's best to steer clear of what makes you unhappy.*

'Was there anything else that Edgar said you that you didn't like?'

'It's not only what he said ... It's also ... sort of ... his cold attitude.'

'Do I appear distant?'

'No, not at all.' *What's wrong with me?* I wondered. *I didn't like Edgar because he was offish, and now I've doubts about Lavender because she is very friendly.*

'Have you any ideas why it's difficult for you to talk to me?'

'Perhaps ... because, like, I don't usually talk about

myself.'

'Even when something upsets you?'

'When I'm upset, I go for a run ... and ... at home ... at times, I was telling stuff to my house.' *Now Lavender will think that I'm barking.* I had a strong urge to get up and scoot out of her room as fast as I could.

'There's nothing wrong with speaking to your house. You're not the only kid in this place who does that. What would you like to talk about today?'

'Dragons,' I answered, relaxing a little. At that moment, I twigged why I was so edgy. Fleur was mega-friendly in the beginning. *Will Lavender change her mind about me once she gets to know me?*

'What do you like about them?'

'They're strong and ...' *This is way too similar to what had happened with Fleur,* I thought. 'Actually, I'm not in the mood for talking about dragons right now.'

Lavender asked me loads of questions and I gave her very short answers. Perhaps, after all, seeing a trust restorer wasn't for me. Sometimes, she did more talking than me.

It was a relief when the meet-up was over. I left Emerald halls and wandered aimlessly in the camp's grounds. When I reached the sanctuary's forest, I decided to look for a goldfinch, knowing that a colourful bird would help me to forget everything.

Wandering amongst trees, I noticed a slim woman ambling along with a basket of wild mushrooms. She wore a loose, white T-shirt and black leggings. Her long, curly brown hair was gathered in a ponytail. Hoping that she hadn't noticed me, I tried to creep away quietly but she'd seen me.

'Hi there,' she called, 'can I talk to you?'

I hesitated, remembering that Radar told me not to talk to strangers. Eventually, I replied, 'Sorry, not now. I must go.'

She smiled warmly. 'I'll be quick. I used to come here for many years, so I thought it'd be good to talk to someone from the camp. By the way, I'm Destini Badley.'

'You ... you stayed here?'

'I had been coming here for around ten years. This place is still very special to me and that's why I bought an old cottage nearby.'

'You bought a cottage? Wow, that is so cool,' I remarked, feeling impressed.

'Let me tell you that some people who have had an unhappy childhood can be very successful. I don't like to think about the past, so I throw myself into my work. When I'm focusing on the task in hand, I forget about everything else.'

I liked Destini – I didn't have a job to escape to, but, like her, I have to do something when I'm down in the dumps. 'I know what you mean. I'm okay when I run.'

Destini moved closer to me. 'I love running, too. I go for a jog every day.'

'Do you have a dog? They make wonderful running mates.'

'Sort of ... I've a really amazing pet. She's totally unusual; something between a dog and a big cat. She has the shape and loyalty of a hound together with the suppleness of a panther. Believe me, she's a perfect mix. You couldn't wish for a better pet. I hope it's alright for me to ask about your family. Do you live with your parents?'

'I do,' I said, feeling the customary pressure in my chest, 'but my mum ...' Half way through the sentence, I thought it might be best not talk about my family.

'My dad had died from cancer and my mum became very depressed after his death,' said Destini casually with no expression in her eyes.

'Sorry to hear that.'

'In the end, I was placed with a foster family,' Destini went on. 'You know, for many years, I was ashamed of going into foster care, but with the help I got in the sanctuary, I understood why my mum couldn't cope and I'm okay about it now.'

Clashing thoughts crowded my head: *She looks alright – she stayed here, so there's no harm in chatting to her.* Other thoughts urged me to be careful: *You don't know her. Walk away now.*

'When I didn't do what my foster parents told me, they were really mean. I spent half of my childhood dreaming about having a real home.'

'And you've one now. That's really something! I'm mad about old buildings. I live in a Georgian house.'

'Georgian buildings are very special. I love that architectural style. Actually, you didn't tell me your name.'

'Sorry, I'm Willow Ashwood.'

'Would you like to see my home? It's a quaint seventeenth-century cottage with a thatched roof. I'm sure you'll love it.'

'I need permission to do that.'

'I'm literally fifteen minutes' walk from here. If you come for a brief visit now, nobody would even notice.'

I was paralysed by my wavering and indecision. 'I'm not –'

'Come on! You worry too much. You look the sporty type, so if we scram now, we could be there in no time.'

'I don't think I –'

'Don't sweat it. Let's get cracking.'

'Well, I'm not sure ... You know what, I will come with you.'

We moved swiftly to the fence surrounding the camp. Destini dislodged a small section and we walked through it, she then carefully replaced the loose panel. I was now outside the sanctuary.

We reached Destini's home and I really liked the half-timbered cottage. Like George, it had a long history and reminded me of a bygone era.

Looking at the picturesque building, I recalled the special terms I had read about thatched roof cottages in my books on architecture and on the internet. I loved the sturdy black wooden posts at each corner of the front *façade* and the timbers framing doors and windows. The cottage also had horizontal beams just below the thatched roof and at first-floor level. The infill panels were whitewashed render.

Destini spent a few long moments undoing three high-security locks. When we entered the cottage, I was flabbergasted to see a strange creature pacing around the living room. I stood there, gaping at the extraordinary animal. It had the suppleness and movements of a big cat in a giant dog's body, the size of a St Bernard. Destini had told me about her pet, but seeing it moving in front of me was breathtaking.

The broad head had well-developed cheekbones with plentiful fur around the head and neck. The amber eyes were very large and the ears droopy. The body had a short, dense, copper coat with slightly bushier hair on the thighs. The wagging thick, short-haired tail appeared to be strong and flexible.

'Her name is Charity,' Destini said proudly. 'Isn't she beautiful? Please, make yourself at home.'

I sat on a settee and the peculiar beast positioned herself close to me, behaving as if we were old friends.

'What do you think of my pet?'

'She's out of this world. Totally amazing.'

Destini served up Danish pastries and orange juice. I tucked into the fresh pastries, thinking: *Perhaps, after all, it wasn't such a bad idea to come here. The half-timbered cottage is cool and Charity is mega-special.* 'It must be great to have a place of your own,' I said, 'and a really unique pet.'

'When I was growing up, I never had anything and that motivated me to do well. My mum lives in a small rented flat and she didn't accomplish much in her life. I'm fixed on doing things differently. I hope that you'll be successful, too.'

'I'd like to be a vet and look after animals. Wow, I feel completely chilled out with Charity almost sitting on my feet.'

'You seem to be having a good time with my pet,' remarked Destini.

'I love her soft coat,' I purred while stroking Charity, 'it's soooo smooth.'

'Shall I 'phone Elena and ask whether you could stay with me this evening?'

'I'm not allowed to walk in the forest on my own after dark.'

'Oh, don't worry about that, Charity and I will accompany you back. Charity can be as gentle as a lamb or as fierce as a lioness. She's very protective of me and my friends. I'll go next door and make that call.'

Destini had returned and said that I'd permission to stay for a meal. I suggested we go for a run with Charity before eating. It seemed that the creature had understood what I'd said because she was on her feet in a split second, looking at us expectantly.

It didn't take long to leave and after a few minutes we reached open land. I admired Charity; she was a picture of suppleness and agility – beauty in motion.

After we had returned to the cottage, Charity spread herself on the floor of the living room; her stretched muscles appeared to be semi-fluid. I sat next to her and stroked her.

Destini let me decide on the cuisine and I chose an Indian. We cooked rice, a vegetable curry, and my favourite chickpea dish. The enjoyable mix of eating scrummy food and a giant creature with a velvety coat pushing against my legs made me feel happy. I looked at Destini, feeling grateful for her invite.

'Thank you for everything – it was really good. You're so lucky to have this amazing animal.' Charity rubbed her head against my leg. 'But I think I should go now.'

'Well, Willow, if you want, you can be my guest for a few days. We can do lots of interesting things together.'

I was astonished at the speed with which she spewed new ideas. 'I don't think my mum and dad would let me,' I mumbled.

'If you decide to stay with me, I'll talk to your parents and will come to an agreement with them. I think your mother's first name is Eleanor, isn't it?'

'Yes, Dr Eleanor Ashwood. Do you know her?'

'Not very well, but I believe we've met a number of times. Does she work as a clinical lead in a hospital?'

'She does. Wow, it's so weird you know my mum!'

'I work as a senior manager in another hospital; I've met her at conferences and on training days. Now, Willow, would you stay with me if Elena and your parents agree? I've two weeks off work, so I'll have plenty of time for you.'

I looked at Destini's friendly eyes while stroking Charity's sleek coat. 'I'd like to accept your invite. I'm not sure I'm right for the sanctuary.'

Destini left the room again. She returned with a broad smile on her face. 'Your parents and Elena are happy for you to stay with me.'

CHAPTER TWENTY-ONE

The Elite Alliance

Despite the age gap, Destini and I seemed to have lots in common. We talked about old houses, dragons, dogs, pets, birds and trees. Before going to sleep, we watched a film together. The following morning, we went for a jog with Charity.

My new friend was an excellent and willing cook who liked to please her guests. She asked me what I wanted for lunch and prepared a vegetarian spaghetti and an apple and plum crumble.

Having eaten a large portion of the first delicious course, I tucked into the yummy dessert, enjoying every mouthful.

'You seem to like the crumble. The fruit is from my garden.'

'It's really good,' I said appreciatively, taking a second helping.

'I'm glad you like my cooking. Willow, I'm getting very fond of you and that's why I want you to do well, above all, I want you to be happy.'

'What do you mean?'

'Let me clarify, when you're in touch with your feelings, anyone can hurt you. I can teach you how to push your feelings down, so that you won't be upset by your own unhappiness or that of others.'

I was totally surprised by she'd said. 'But I *do* feel and I *want* to care. When I'm miserable, I want to help others. I don't even like the sight of a neglected old house.'

'You'll learn how to walk away from a troubled human,

dragon, or any other creature. And you'll also find out how to take no notice of tumbledown buildings in desperate need of renovation. After letting go of your sensitivity, you'll leave the Nobodies' Club for Kids with Sad Eyes.'

'Does it mean that I won't be able to visit the Custodians' Sanctuary?'

'You won't be needing the camp. I'll introduce you to exceptionally loyal friends. We're sort of a large family and we do everything to help each other, and I mean it, literally, anything. You'll always be able to count on one us. These friends have transformed my life. That's how I got the job I'm doing now.'

I recalled Fleur telling me that my mum wasn't ready to join the Custodians anytime soon. Scary questions circulated in my head: *Did Destini talk about the Pretenders? Could it be that my mum one of them?*

For a while I couldn't say anything. 'You told me that you'd met my mum and yesterday she allowed me to stay here. Does she know the same mega-loyal people?'

'We'll talk about this another time. Firstly, I'd like to explain a few things.'

Blood thumped around my body in panic. 'No, I'd like to know now, right now. Otherwise, I'll worry myself to death. Who are these people?'

'I think you need more time.'

'I can't wait,' I insisted, 'I must have an answer now.'

'Er ... you're very impatient –'

'Always have been,' I blurted. 'Please, tell me.'

'Alright then,' Destini agreed reluctantly. 'Some of our members hold top positions and this way we help each other to progress.'

I felt dizzy, as if I was whacked on the head by a cricket bat. *What's the connection between my mum and Destini?* 'Are you ... is my mum ... a Pretender?'

'I told you, I need more time to prepare you.'

'I must know,' I begged. 'Please, tell me.'

'In that case, the answer is yes. We are, and we'd like

you to join us. Don't you want to be close to your mum? By the way, we call ourselves the Elite Alliance, which is much nicer than Pretenders.'

Scathing thoughts had taken over: *Why won't you face up to reality? All your life your mum has been playing the best mother ever in front of other people, while telling you at home that you're a horrible mistake.*

I took a deep breath, fearing a complete meltdown. 'Did the Alliance help my mum?'

'The Elite Alliance helped her secure a senior management position after she had been qualified for about eighteen months.'

'How did they do it?'

'They discouraged better qualified applicants with more experience from going through the selection process.'

Slumping back, I wanted to curl up and disappear. Nagging thoughts showed up with a vengeance. I buried my head in my hands, trying in vain to stop the onslaught of dreadful questions: *If my mum is a Pretender, does it mean that I'm one, too? If I'm a Pretender, would I be able to connect with good dragons? Will I survive without them?*

Destini put her arm around my shoulders. 'I'll look after you,' she said gently. 'You can trust me. At times, in order to get where you want to be, it may be necessary to pretend and receive help from powerful people.'

'But it doesn't feel right.'

'Many things aren't what they should be. When you're offered a gift, accept it gratefully. This is your big chance to get close to your mum, have loyal friends and a great future.'

'It's the complete opposite to what Chris says –'

'Chris is an idealist,' Destini cut in dismissively. 'In real life, it can be much harder to progress without contacts. Think about your mother – she had to live with the knowledge that her own mother didn't want her. The Alliance smoothed things for her after she had got into trouble at school, and she was given another chance to sit her exams. They also helped her to get a place on a clinical psychology course. You wouldn't want your mother to be a failure, would you? I'm sure that you love her.'

'I do ... and I want her ... to love me ...'

'Now, it's your golden opportunity to get what you want. Don't let this fantastic moment pass you by. Will you join us?'

'Don't ask me ... right now ... I'm totally confused.'

'Look here, Willow, I want the best for you. Why so unappreciative?'

'I can't make up my mind,' I said after a long pause, feeling very weary and disorientated. 'I want to be close to my mum, but I don't think I could be unfeeling. I'm far too sensitive for that. Deep down I know that I'm worthless, I've tons of doubts about myself, but I do know that I won't be able to ignore anyone in distress.'

'With practice, you'll learn gradually to be less sensitive.'

'The one thing I'm certain of is that I can't do it. And right now, I can't even think straight. I must go for a run to clear my head.'

'Charity and I will come with you.'

'I'd like to be on my own.'

'Well, this option is not available. The three of us are going out together, or you're staying in, and that's that.'

'Please, I need a bit of time alone.'

'You'll have to get past my pet,' Destini said harshly. Charity jumped off the settee, stood in front of me and bared her long fangs.

'Alright then, let's go together.'

Destini kept close to me – her proximity stopped me from losing myself in running. I enjoyed the movement of my legs but my head remained heavy and confused. After our return, Destini told me that she'd give me more time to consider her offer.

I thought in a loop about the advantages of becoming a member of the Elite Alliance: Would my mum treat me differently? Would things at home be easier? Yet at the same time, I had lots of doubts about overcoming my sensitivity. By the end of the day though, I knew that I couldn't join.

'Well, Willow,' Destini said, smiling warmly, 'did you think about the benefits of becoming one of us?'

'I did ... but I can't ... cut it. I'm far too easily affected by the suffering of others.'

'That's an unfortunate weakness!' Destini said angrily. 'An indulgence you can't afford.'

'I'm telling you, there's nothing I can do about it. I can't hack it.'

'I'm beginning to lose patience with you,' snapped Destini. 'You'll remain with me until you see the error of your ways.'

Destini told me, in no uncertain terms, that I would have to remain indoors, and I did so for over a week. Staying in the cottage was unbearable. These were the longest days I'd ever experienced. I was desperate to get out and run, but all I could do was pace – like a caged animal – in circles in the living room. Charity behaved as if she were my shadow during the day and a prison guard at night.

Having confiscated my mobile, Destini was in complete control of any contact I had with the outside world. I was only allowed to call my parents with her sitting next to me. Destini embroidered a tapestry of clever lies every time she spoke to my dad. She insisted that I back her up, so I had to recount trumped-up stories. Destini and my mum got on well; I overheard them chatting and laughing.

After eight dreary days of Destini doing her best to convert me to her way of life, she said that she had to go out. Just before leaving, she warned me: 'Charity will look after you, but don't you even think about going anywhere. My pet can be very unpleasant if her charges try to leave.'

When Destini was opening the front door, a loud noise startled me. I was stunned to see two large dogs burst in. It took a few moments before I recognised Winter and Sky.

Charity sprung to her feet and growled at the intruders. She crouched down and then pounced on Winter, biting him while striking Sky with her powerful tail. The Huskies yelped in pain but didn't retreat.

Sky and Winter turned on her at the same time. Charity, using her superior speed and elasticity, jumped out of the way and the hounds collided. With another high leap, she landed on top of a sideboard.

Destini's pet was larger than a Siberian Husky and strikingly more supple than any hound. My heart sank when I realised that she was using her elasticity and agility as effective combat weapons. The fierce look in her large eyes told me that she'd fight to the bitter end. She surveyed the battleground and swooped down with her dagger-like claws spread out in front of her.

'Winter, Sky, watch out!' I shouted. 'She'll scratch you.'

Charity pounced on Sky. I watched with gut-wrenching alarm, but Sky swerved at the last moment, saving her head and eyes from injury. She hadn't moved far enough though, and Charity had scratched leg back. I flinched when I heard Sky howl in pain.

Winter ran to Charity and hurled his strong body at her, causing her to lose her balance. The Huskies then turned on Charity. Winter sank his teeth into her back and she yelled in anguish. Destini grabbed a poker from the fireplace and ran towards the fighting animals.

'Sky! Winter!' I cried. 'Destini is attacking you.'

Winter turned ninety degrees, jumped on Destini and pushed her to the floor with his front paws. Charity noticed the Husky attacking Destini and sprang on Winter – her sharp claws missed his eyes, but they cut into the side of his head. Enraged with pain, the hound bit the paw that had struck him. Charity's yowl pierced my ears and my heart.

'Winter, don't bite her again,' I shouted. 'She's badly injured. Let's get out of here. Winter, Sky, we're leaving right now! Do you hear me? Right now!'

Sky was lying on top of Destini, growling into her horror-stricken, pearly white face. At that moment, I knew without a shadow of a doubt that I couldn't ignore Destini's plight. I dragged Sky off her, holding the hound back by her collar. 'Thank you,' she whispered. 'I'll remember this.'

'I helped you and Charity because I hate seeing anyone suffer. I hope Charity will recover quickly. I'm leaving now.'

With a Husky on either side of me, we set off on our way back to the Custodians' camp. All I could think about was getting the dogs to the Calcite Healing Retreat.

We walked at a fast pace and promptly reached the gates of the camp. Sky and Winter barked the security code four-and-a-half times. We had waited for a while. When the gates opened, I was surprised to see Chris.

'Willow, it's good to have you back,' he said. 'I've been very worried about you. We need to talk right away. I'd like you to come with me to my chamber.'

'I'm sorry I left,' I mumbled, my eyes fixed firmly on the ground and my face burning.

'I'm not angry with you,' Chris said calmly. 'I just want to understand why you went to Destini's cottage.'

I felt a big wave of relief sweep into my head. 'I'll tell you, but first could we take the Huskies to the healing retreat? I'm afraid that they're injured.'

'I'll walk with you there.'

Radar was in the reception of the retreat. 'Willow, I'm glad to see you safe and sound!'

'Thank you,' I murmured, my face hotter than ever.

Radar moved closer to me with his nose twitching. I looked at him while he sniffed my hair intensely for a long time. 'Willow, I'm picking up some unusual vibes on you.'

'I'm not surprised,' I mumbled, 'after staying in Destini's cottage. It had a really weird energy.'

'Right now,' said Chris, 'we must look after the hounds.'

I walked with Chris and the Huskies to the halls of recovery. We found Ophelia attending to Fireball.

'Hello,' I muttered, feeling massively guilty that the dogs needed help because of me. 'Sky and Winter were attacked by Destini Badley's pet, a strange hybrid between a dog and a big cat.'

'It's not the first time she injured one of our animals. I'll take the hounds now to the Canine Hall of Recovery,' said Ophelia while leading the Huskies out of Fireball's den. I breathed a sigh of relief, knowing full well that Sky and Winter would receive excellent care under the watchful eye of the body healer.

I said goodbye to Ophelia and left the retreat with Chris, thinking, *Can I tell him everything? What will he think of me if he finds out that my mum is a Pretender?*

CHAPTER TWENTY-TWO

The Face behind the Mask

Chris and I walked from the Calcite Healing Retreat to the Amber Chamber in silence. After reaching his room, Chris's calmness and the gentle energy of the lit amber lamp on his desk, relaxed me a little.

'Why did you leave the camp so suddenly?' he asked amiably.

'It was ... kind of ... the result of how I was feeling ... after talking to Fleur.'

'Clearly that conversation upset you. Can you tell me what happened? Please start from the beginning.'

'Well, Fleur had told me that I could see her whenever I wanted, but more recently she said that I'm a nuisance. I was angry with her, though later I realised that she had found out that I'm a waste of space. Deep down, I know that anyway. She, like, confirmed it.'

'Did she upset you?'

'Totally, what she'd said completely derailed me. I was scared – don't ask me what of. At that time, I could hardly think straight.'

'Now that some time has passed, have you any idea what you were you afraid of?'

'I haven't got a clue; all I know is that I felt disorientated.'

'Did Fleur's words remind you of anything?'

'Come to think of it now, it was a bit like my mum telling me that I'm a horrible mistake. I heard her say that lots of times, and every time those words get to me.' I did my best to fight back tears and to appear chilled.

'Willow,' said Chris in his gentle and concerned voice, 'I can see that you're upset about the things your mother has told you. It's alright for you to have your feelings.'

'What's the point?' I blurted out before I could put the brakes on. 'That's when chaos takes over. I recall my dad hitting my mum. I ruined her life; she's with him because of me. At times, I think she's right; perhaps I should never have been born.' I buried my head in my hands, trying to regain my composure.

'Take your time,' said Chris.

'They're only words. Why can't I get over this? Worse things can happen. You know, little Ollie lost both of his parents in a car crash.'

'Did Fleur make you feel the same way your mother does when she says unkind things to you?'

'Maybe ... all I know is that I didn't expect her to change so quickly. Afterwards, I'd lots of crushing doubts just about everything. I didn't know what to do with myself. The same lousy stuff was going round and round in my head. Eventually, I thought about leaving the camp. I bumped into Destini in the forest and she invited me to her cottage.'

'Am I correct in saying that you'd left because of Fleur?'

'Possibly, I had disappointed Fleur and I didn't want to let other people down. In the end, I thought it might be best to leave before someone else found out that I'm worthless. I was certain that whatever I'd do, I'd never be good enough.'

'In this place, we all accept you as you are. The kids who come to our camp have similar self-doubts. I'd like you to remember that there's nothing wrong with you – the problem is your mother's inability to love you.'

'When I'm here and you say this, I believe you. But the doubts return pretty quickly. If I can't run and connect with dragons, then I hate myself.'

'It'd be good to share this with Lavender. I'd like to talk now about something different; how was your stay in

Destini's cottage?'

'During the first day, I had a whale of a time. Destini was very friendly and cooked really yummy veggie food, but later she hard-pressed me to join something called the Elite Alliance. This would've meant that I'd have had to ignore my own unhappiness and that of others. It's something I can't hack.'

'So, you don't think you can shut your feelings down?'

'Well, at times I wish I could, because then I wouldn't be so upset by my mum's words. You've said that she doesn't know how to love me, but I still want what she can't do. Why am I so stupid?'

'It's the most natural thing in the world to want your mother's love. That's what every child wants and needs. I would like to come back now to what Destini had told you. Do you think you might miss out on other things if you disown your feelings?'

'Sure thing. I might not be able to love dragons, dogs and other animals.'

'What about good friends? I know that you and Tania get on well.'

'But she might change.'

'Like Fleur did? Is that what you're afraid of?'

'I haven't got an inkling. At times, I'm very confused.'

'I'd like you to discuss this with Lavender, she'll help you to make sense of it all. How is it going with her?'

'I saw her only once. She seems alright.'

'Even if it might be hard in the early stages, please give her a chance. Also, can I ask you that in the future, you come and talk to me before you take drastic action?'

'I'll do that,' I promised. I'd have loved Chris to be my trust restorer, I knew I could tell him lots of things.

I thanked Chris, said goodbye to him and left. He didn't tell me off despite my leaving the camp. *Will Tania and the other kids be as forgiving?* I asked myself.

Having reached the entrance of Moonstone halls, I took a deep breath, opened the front door and sneaked quietly to the girls' wing. When I entered my room, Tania raised her head from her laptop, gave me a big grin, jumped off her bed and squeezed me so hard I feared she might break my ribs. 'Welcome back,' she said happily. 'It's really great to have you back. All of us were worried about you.'

My face was on fire. 'So everyone knows that I ... I cleared off with ... Destini?'

'We do, I mean, the whole camp was looking for you. Radar got the dogs to track down your scent and they traced it to Destini's cottage. But to get in, they had to wait until she opened the front door.'

'I feel awful about causing Radar problems, like he didn't have enough already trying to identify the Pretenders amongst us.'

'Honestly, no need to feel so bad about it. I scarpered too. Lavender helped me to understand why I did it.'

'I think I know why – it was because of Fleur; she kind of confirmed that I'm rubbish. I reckoned I didn't deserve to be here.'

'You're deffo not rubbish, sure as anything. I told ya that you remind me of my sister Abbey, she's ace.'

'You aren't disappointed in me?'

'Nah, not one bit. Believe you me, I ain't behaved too well in the camp in the past.'

Like Chris, Tania accepted me with all my stupid mistakes. We chatted until late and then went to sleep. I drifted off immediately, but nocturnal intruders invaded my dreams. I had a bizarre nightmare; everyone I knew turned into aggressive demons. They had captured me and I helped them to trap kids, animals and dragons.

In the morning, I didn't want to get out of bed and face the day. In the end, I sat up, but thinking about Destini made me flop back. All I wanted was to curl up and do nothing. When Tania returned from the bathroom, I pulled the bed covers over my head.

'Outta bed, you lazybones! What's the matter with you? You look half-dead.'

'I'm tired. I don't want to do anything whatsoever.'

'Tell Lavender about that. C'mon, chop-chop, we gotta leave now!'

I forced myself to get up, got ready and walked with Tania to Pumpkin Hall. We located Liam and sat next to him.

'I'm gonna be honest,' said Liam, smiling at me. 'I worried about you, I'm sure glad you're back.'

'You probably heard,' I gabbled, all flustered, 'that I went off with Destini.'

'They never stop, those rotten Pretenders.'

I liked him for not blaming me. 'I'll see Louise tomorrow after the morning ritual. How about a chat after that, at around eleven?'

'Sure. Let's meet in the front garden of Emerald halls. I'm off now. See ya later.'

As Liam was leaving, I saw Ollie walking towards us. 'Can I sit here?' he asked, pointing at the place Liam had just vacated.

'Sure thing,' I said, making a big effort to sound cheerful.

Ollie fixed his unhappy eyes on me, 'Why did you go away? I thought you'd never come back.'

All at once, I realised that my leaving the camp scared him. *How could I do it? Why didn't I think of Ollie?* 'I'm sorry. I really am. That was so stupid of me.'

'You know ... in my dreams you were killed in a car crash ... I saw you next to my parents ... I was waiting for the police to come and tell us that you ... were dead.'

A voice in my head was screaming at me, *Now look what you have done? You made friends with a child who went through so much and you've frightened him.* I steadied myself and said, 'How can I make it up to you?'

'How about watching cartoons on your laptop?' he asked, looking hopeful.

'You can hang out in my room and do just that. You know what? You're welcome to my laptop anytime, and that's until we all go back home. Is it a fair deal?'

'Yeah, I like that. Thank you.'

Kayla joined us. I liked her keen interest in Ollie – she sounded jolly and funny when she was talking to him. I recalled her wanting to take care of a little dragon after the attack by the pavilion.

'Hi, Kayla,' I said, smiling. 'How are you?'

'Alright,' she replied flatly with a hard look in her eyes. She then turned to Ollie. 'I'll be waiting for you in my room in the afternoon. You get to decide what we do.' She said goodbye to Ollie and Tania and walked away, blanking me.

Caring girls like Kayla don't like me, I thought. *I'm sure Ollie told her how my vanishing act alarmed him. Perhaps, I should tell her that it's alright for her to dislike me, because I, too, don't like myself much.*

Tania, Ollie and I made our way to the morning ceremony. After the face washing, Alfie and his charges performed a new dance routine, moving rhythmically in their unified fashion. Usually, I was captivated by their synchronised steps and jumps, but during that morning, my mind was elsewhere.

By the end of the canine show though, there was a massive surprise; we saw Fireball walking slowly towards us with Ophelia by his side. When they reached the circle, we all gathered around them.

'Fireball insisted on coming to the ritual. I still don't know how to stop a determined dragon. I couldn't do anything,' Ophelia laughed, 'as you can see, he's bigger than me.'

It was great to see Fireball looking stronger. I put my arms around his neck and connected with the kindness he radiated towards everyone. Fireball was visibly delighted when kids hugged him. I held Ollie's hand and walked with him to Fireball. The dragon horse lowered his head and Ollie rubbed his nose.

At the close of the ritual, Chris announced, 'I think it's now time for Fireball to return to the healing retreat.

I'm going there myself, so if anyone would like to talk to me this morning, you know where to find me. I've some important news to tell you this afternoon. I'm asking everyone to come to the Celestite Chamber in Emerald halls immediately after lunch.'

Having watched a blue tit and a robin for a while, Tania and I walked to the retreat where we were greeted by Chris and Radar.

'Can we check on the Huskies?' I asked.

'Of course,' answered Chris. 'I'm sure they'd love to see you. But before you go, let me tell you that Fleur has left the sanctuary.'

'Wow,' Tania gasped in disbelief, 'she's slipped off just like that, without any warning?'

Why am I sorry to hear that she is gone? I asked myself, but out loud I said, 'Why did she leave?'

'You'll find out very soon,' replied Chris. 'Willow, in view of what you went through with Fleur and Destini, I'd like you to see Lavender on a daily basis. Right now, visiting the hounds will do you a world of good.'

'After seeing the Huskies,' said Radar, 'I'd like to talk to you.'

Tania and I went to the Canine Hall of Recovery where Sky and Winter performed their customary welcoming dance around us. They definitely didn't blame me for their injuries. Chris was right, I felt better after stroking two prancing hounds.

We went back to the reception area. 'Can we talk now?' I asked Radar.

'We can,' he replied. 'Chin up, Willow. You may not believe it, but your stay in Destini's place was of great help to me.'

'I don't get it,' I said, not sure what to make of it all.

'Well,' Radar explained, 'when you got back yesterday, I detected some unusual energy on you. The vibes that you had picked up in Destini's cottage had some resemblance to those in the pavilion after the attack. I noticed them on you without much difficulty because they weren't as heavily masked as those in the pavilion. I can say with confidence that this similarity is enough to connect Destini with Fleur.'

'It appears that Fleur and Destini worked together,' said Chris, 'and from that Radar and I have deduced that Fleur is a Master Pretender of the Supreme Order. Very few Pretenders ever reach this advanced level, which is why she has managed to mislead us for such a long time. Destini, however, is considerably less advanced than Fleur. The worst part of it all is that Fleur was responsible for the attack by the pavilion; she had regular access to the building and that's how she had converted it into a Nastorian.'

'Woah,' I uttered, 'that's incredible. I still can't get my head around Fleur being a Pretender. In the beginning, she was ever so kind.'

'I'm telling ya,' cried Tania. 'I also thought that she was fab.'

'Appearances can be misleading,' said Chris, 'especially when it comes to Master Pretenders of the Supreme Order. Willow, I wanted to tell about Fleur as soon as possible so that you don't beat yourself up about going to Destini's cottage. However, I ask both of you not to disclose this to anyone else, I'll inform all the kids about these new developments after lunch.'

I was completely confused about Fleur. I was glad that her cover was blown and that Fireball was safe, yet at the same time, I missed her. I kept asking myself: *Why do I want to see her, even now that I know that she's a Master Pretender of the Supreme Order?*

CHAPTER TWENTY-THREE

The Riddle

While having lunch with Tania in Pumpkin Hall, I overheard animated voices – picking up fragments of chatter, I realised that the talk was all about Fleur. Rumours had spread like wildfire that she'd scarpered and there were all kinds of guesses as to why she'd taken off. After lunch, it seemed that everybody was keen on getting to the meet-up with Chris quickly. I walked briskly with Tania and other kids to Emerald halls.

The gathering took place in a large room I'd never visited before. I loved the beautiful bluish-grey minerals placed on every available space. The bright summer sky and sunshine dropped in through the windows, enhancing the delicate hues of the translucent crystals and joining them in the creation of cool and gentle vibes. We all sat on cushions on the floor in a circle.

'What you see in here are celestite crystals,' said Tania. 'Everyone loves them – they kinda make you feel better even after horrible things had happened.'

'They're really special,' I agreed, inhaling deeply and trying to chill out. 'Add a dragon to the mix and you could manage just about anything.'

Chris asked everyone to stop chatting and settle down. The room fell silent with kids looking at him expectantly. Then he began, 'The important news I'd like to share with you concerns Fleur Embers. You've probably heard by now that she suddenly left without warning. I'm saddened to have to tell you that Fleur misled us.'

'What?!' Liam called out. 'Does it mean that she's a Pretender?'

'The answer to your question is unfortunately positive. Yes, Fleur is an impostor. I know that some of you were quite fond of her, and I must acknowledge that she was a good activities organiser.'

Gasps of disbelief erupted. I already knew that Fleur was a con artist, but hearing this again made me feel worse. Against what I knew was right, deep down, I still hoped that everything had been a terrible mistake and that Fleur would remain in the sanctuary.

'How come she had been working here for over a year?' demanded Liam angrily.

'Fleur had been able to deceive us for a long time,' answered Chris, 'because she is a Master Pretender of the Supreme Order. She'd learned the most advanced techniques of the craft of pretence and trickery, and that's how she masked her destructive energy with the vibes of a Custodian. What upsets me most is that Fleur was responsible for the attack by the Dragon Horses' Pavilion.'

I heard shocked voices all around me. 'Radar wasn't able to detect her evil energy?' asked Kayla, looking discombobulated.

'He did,' replied Chris, 'about a year ago, Radar told me that at times, Fleur's vibes intrigued him and that he couldn't link them to any other familiar frequencies. I didn't do anything about it because she appeared to be doing good work with both kids and dragons. I thought that she was a Custodian with unique vibes, but still one of us. Fleur had successfully duped me.'

'In that case,' said Liam loudly, trying to be heard above the din in the room. 'It's safer not to trust anyone. I'm telling you, absolutely nobody! That's the only way we can protect ourselves.'

'I think,' said Kayla, looking at Liam and then at Chris, 'that Liam has a point. Better safe than sorry.'

'That's right,' agreed Ollie, 'Fleur nearly killed Fireball.'

'Our work here is to help you to trust again,' Chris went on. 'I'd like to remind you that most grown-ups and kids are kind. I know that there are also Nastorians and Pretenders, but as Custodians we believe in the good in humans, dragons and animals. Nastorians see their own malice in others, which is why they suspect everyone. They can't understand kindness without a hidden agenda.'

'How did you find out that Fleur is a Pretender?' asked a teenage boy.

'Well,' said Chris, 'after the attack by the pavilion, Radar detected heavily masked hostile frequencies in the pavilion. Following Fleur's sudden departure, he thoroughly investigated the energy in her room and some of the vibes had resemblance to the energy Radar had identified in the pavilion. Radar also traced similarly heavily disguised frequencies in the healing retreat after the visit of the two fake body healers –'

'And that's why,' interrupted Kayla, 'we gotta be very careful.'

'Too riiiight, I couldn't agree more,' Liam declared vehemently. 'Otherwise, how can we protect ourselves? If you would've done something straight away after Radar had told you about Fleur's unusual vibes, the attack by the pavilion could've been prevented. Our trust can be our downfall.'

'At that time, I didn't think that uncommon vibes alone

were sufficient for me to act. I like to see the good in people and not assume the worst immediately. Also, if someone lets me down, I still give them another chance if they choose to change.'

'That's not how I see it,' said Liam. 'Every time my father reduced my mum to tears, he afterwards promised he wouldn't do it again. But, guess what? He continued to bully her again, and again, and again.'

'Perhaps your father can't change without help,' said Chris. 'The challenge is to remain a Custodian and have faith in others even when our fingers get burnt. The cost of distrust may have a greater price tag attached to it. That's when kids and grown-ups either avoid forming close friendships, or they hurt others. Humiliating and damaging those around them gives them a sense of superiority and power that often comes out of wariness and fear. I'd like you all to talk to your trust restorers about Fleur – sometimes, we learn more from unhappy events than from good ones.'

Liam remained unconvinced. 'I don't get it. What d'you mean?'

'When things go well, we don't always stop to think why they went so smoothly. We're more likely to ask questions and learn from our experience when something untoward occurs. Adverse events can get the best out of humans and dragons. Look at Fireball, even when he was attacked, he chose to protect the smaller dragons and –'

'But he nearly lost his life,' protested Ollie.

'Thankfully,' said Chris, 'he survived and helping others made him feel better about himself. Let me give you other examples. Many great works of art and literature were created because of suffering. You can also use misfortune to raise awareness and campaign for a change. Some adults who had unhappy childhoods can be very driven and become hugely successful. It's not what had happened to you that matters, but how you dealt with it.'

'Only at times, when it all feels too much,' remarked Kayla, 'you just don't know what to do.'

'Even during dark moments,' said Chris, 'see the light at the end of the tunnel. Whatever comes to pass, have faith in others.'

'I'll have faith in Fireball,' said Liam, 'even if he makes mistakes because he has proved himself. I know he deserves it.'

'It may take a while to work through Fleur's betrayal,' said Chris, 'It's time now to end our meeting. Let me remind you all that you can have additional sessions with your trust restorer, or see me.'

I walked out with the other kids, feeling better. Thinking about Chris's kindness, I wondered whether he was also touched by neglected buildings. Tania then accompanied me to Lavender's room. Despite Tania telling me that Lavender helped her, I still had niggling doubts about trust restorers. I said goodbye to Tania and knocked on Lavender's door.

'It's good to see you,' she welcomed me warmly. 'How have you been?'

'Alright,' I mumbled.

'What would you like to talk about today?'

'I don't have the slightest idea.' I just sat there chewing on my lip. I turned my attention to my right hand and picked at a piece of skin that had become loose around my index finder.

Lavender didn't rush me – after a long silence, she went on, 'Now, would it help you to be more relaxed with me, if you knew that I didn't have a happy childhood myself?'

Curiosity got the better of me – I perked up and looked

at Lavender. 'Your parents didn't want you?'

'I think they wanted me, but both were very busy with the family business. I'd lots of au pairs because I always made sure that they didn't stay very long. I came to the sanctuary at the age of twelve.'

So, you're one of us, I thought. 'Did your stay here help you?' I asked.

'It did. I also found out what I wanted to do. During my time here I helped my room-mate, and that's when I decided to be a trust restorer. Looking after kids makes me feel better. What works for you?'

'I love running and picturing dragons and I love dogs.'

'Then you're in the right place,' Lavender laughed. 'Can I ask about the meeting with Chris? How did it go?'

'It was good. You probably know that Fleur turned out to be a Pretender. He told us about that and also talked about trust.'

'How do you feel about Fleur now that her true colours have been exposed?'

I wanted to tell Lavender how I really felt. I wanted to tell her that Fleur had been a permanent and unwelcome resident in my head. I wanted to tell her that I still liked Fleur. 'It's all sort of very confusing. I feel ashamed ...'

Lavender waited for me to continue but I remained silent. After a while she said gently, 'I hear all kinds of things from the kids I work with. We all can think or do things we aren't proud of. You can tell me whatever is on your mind.'

'Do you really want to know? It's ... it's ... so crazy.'

'Let me be the judge of what's crazy. Sometimes when we talk about what bothers us, we can create clarity and feel better.'

'Well then, I know that Fleur is a con artist, but somehow

... she's still important to me.' I was hugely relieved to spit it out.

'First of all, I'm glad you've shared this with me,' Lavender reassured me with a smile on her face and in her voice. 'Am I correct in saying that you've mixed feelings about her?'

'You can definitely say that. I think I'm going nuts.'

'Have you felt like this before?' she asked softly.

'Perhaps a bit ... but not exactly the same.'

'Tell me about the last time you had similar feelings.'

'I'm not sure about my mum. At times, she drives me round the bend.'

'Can we talk about your mother?'

I was torn between an urge to keep my feelings about my mum in a locked box in my head, and desperately wanting to understand the grip Fleur had on me. 'Well, how about talking about her briefly?'

'We can do that, but do let me know when you'd like to stop. How do you feel about your mother and Fleur?'

I glued my eyes to the floor. 'Most of the time I love my mum, but there are times when I'm angry with her or even hate her. I'm cross with Fleur for injuring Fireball and deceiving us, but I still like her. You must think I'm barking.' I raised my eyes to look at Lavender – she didn't appear to be shocked.

'I don't think that at all. Tell me about your relationship with Fleur.'

'In the beginning it was great, but recently she changed unexpectedly. By the end of it all, I was totally confused because she said that I'm a nuisance, but somehow, she was still fond of me.'

'And with your mother?'

'I hate it when she tells me that I'm a horrible mistake,

but then, perhaps ... it's alright for her to say that ...' The familiar pressure in my chest returned with a vengeance – I could hardly breathe. 'Actually, I don't want to talk about my mum. It makes me feel awful. Can I go now?'

'You can. Thank you for letting me know that you wanted to stop. I look forward to seeing you tomorrow.'

After my return to Moonstone halls, Tania asked, 'How did it go with Lavender?'

'She was very patient with me, but I still couldn't tell her everything.'

'Oh, don't worry about that. To begin with, I was, like, really unfriendly towards her. I didn't want her to feel sorry for me. I wanted her to feel sorry for herself for 'aving to work with me.'

'What did you do?'

'During the first meet-up, I said nothing at all. During the second one, I ignored what she said and talked about something completely different. She took lots of rubbish from me, but she didn't give up.'

'She's alright then?'

'She deffo is. I can tell ya, she does care.'

'I'll try to remember that. The way I'm feeling right now, I think I could do with a good run. I'll see you later in Pumpkin Hall.'

I spotted Winter milling in front of the halls and invited him to join me – the two of us ran for a long time. But jogging didn't give me a break from Fleur; despite my best efforts, I couldn't stop thinking about her.

Feeling defeated, I hugged Winter good-bye and walked to Pumpkin Hall. Lavender wasn't appalled by what I'd said about Fleur, so I decided to tell Tania, too.

I met Tania at the entrance of Pumpkin Hall. I chose a table in a quiet corner by the rear garden. The moment we sat down, I asked, 'Can I tell you something?'

'Fire away.'

'I feel very confused about Fleur.' I blurted out. 'Despite everything, I still miss her.'

Tania looked baffled. 'Why? You know that she's a Master Pretender.'

'That's what bugs me. I feel very guilty and frustrated with myself.'

'Did you tell Lavender?'

'I did. It seems that my mum and Fleur might have something in common. Don't ask me what.'

I had chosen a veggie burger, made with a flat mushroom and vegan cheese. I loved Coriander's cooking, but right then my appetite had disappeared. All I could manage was one bite. 'Can l tell you how I really feel?'

'Go for it.'

'I want to see Fleur again.'

Tania was horrified. 'For the love of dragons, don't say that! She nearly killed Fireball!'

CHAPTER TWENTY-FOUR

The Squatter in my Head

Despite shocking Tania by telling her that I wanted to see Fleur, I couldn't stop thinking about that top-notch con artist – telling myself off didn't work. I tried to make light of my hang-up about Fleur by picturing a playful macaque saying in a clownish voice: *You like Fleur because you're a cheat yourself, a fake Custodian.* But the mischievous monkey failed to improve the situation – I couldn't see anything funny in my fixation on a Pretender.

After the morning ritual, I went to Ruby halls and, with Louise's help, I glued black and yellow feathers to the wings of my goldfinch costume. Having completed the wings, I created a wireframe of the bird's body and tail. I then I stitched material to the frame. I thanked Louise and left Ruby halls.

I walked to the front garden of Emerald halls for my meet-up with Liam. I had the impression that he accepted me even though I behaved like a total muppet.

Liam was sitting on a bench, looking at his mobile. When I got closer, he raised his head and smiled. I parked myself next to him. 'Hiya, Liam, what's up?'

'If you really wanna know, then I'll tell ya,' he sighed. 'I'm still getting my head around Fleur being a flipping Pretender.'

'How do you feel about her?'

'Well, I'll be honest with you, I liked her because she appeared to be strong – I can't imagine Fleur being bullied by anyone. My dad treats my mum like a doormat and completely controls what she does and every penny she spends, but she never stands up to him. She always says that she'll leave him, but she's never even tried!'

'Perhaps, she's afraid of him.'

'She could've left him if she gave it her best shot. I feel angry with her for being so weak, and now I feel cross with Fleur for hoodwinking us.'

'Now that you've told me how you feel about Fleur, I'll be honest with you, too. What bugs me is that Fleur has become even more important since she has made off.'

'Well, Fleur kinda feels unreal, like a nightmare. Unfortunately, she'd been way too convincing, so I assume we need more time to get used to the idea that she's an accomplished liar. Can I ask you a something?'

It was good to hear that I wasn't the only one trapped by Fleur's state-of-the-art trickery. 'Go ahead.'

'D'you feel that something bad is going to happen any moment? I feel like this most of the time, I just can't relax.'

'That sounds familiar. Though my problem right now is that I think that I don't deserve to be here.'

'I totally disagree with you,' said Liam firmly, looking me in the eye. 'I want you to remain and so does Tania. How about having supper together?'

'That would be great. I usually go to Pumpkin Hall with Tania. Would you like to join us?'

'I'd love to. Perhaps, between the three of us, we'll talk about something other than Fleur.'

We chatted for a while and then I said good-bye to Liam and went for a walk. Before I'd gone very far, I heard a noise and was surprised to see Radar running towards me.

Looking at his serious face gave me the willies. 'Radar,' I cried, 'has anything happened?'

'I don't want you to be out on your own, not even during the day. But you can go for walks with a hound.'

'Why this new rule?'

'I'm fearing another attack by the Nastorians. They

pinned their hopes on Fleur and Destini, but now that these Pretenders have failed them, there might very soon be another battle. The Custodians' headquarters in the Himalayas have sent a squadron of air dragons – I'm expecting their arrival this afternoon. I hope their presence will be a sufficient deterrent. Come with me to the kennels and I'll get a dog to go with you – they've superb hearing and can pick up sounds from a long distance.'

'I don't want to be any trouble. I don't have to go for a walk.'

'You'll actually help our Border Collies. They love herding anything that moves, including kids!'

'I like the thought of being watched over by a dog,' I remarked.

'In that case, feel free to take them with you as often as you want.'

I left with six dogs – looking at them bounding around me made me feel safe. While walking, I thought about Fleur, the permanent resident in my head. *Has she become so powerful because she's changed from a friend to a foe? Will Lavender help me drive her out from my faulty brain?* At that moment, all I wanted was to serve an eviction notice on her.

After returning the dogs to their kennels and having lunch with Tania, I made my way to Lavender's room for our daily meet-up. Lavender greeted me with her friendly smile. 'How are you today?' she asked.

'Right now, I'm okay. I went for a walk with the Border Collies. Dogs have what it takes to make you feel better.'

'I'm glad to hear that. Are you happy here?'

'I love it. It's the first time ever that I don't feel like a weirdo. I don't know why, but it's easier for me to chat with the kids in the camp.'

'Could it be because you've stuff in common?'

'Perhaps, in this place I feel less ashamed of my mum not wanting me. Here I go – I told you that I don't want to talk about my mum and now I'm doing just that.' *Do I know what I want? Or am I just confusing Lavender and myself?* I wondered.

'We can stay with your mum or talk about something different. What would you like to do?'

'Actually, may I tell you something that keeps playing on my mind?'

'Sure thing. That's one of the reasons why you come to see me.'

'Well ... it's about ... Fleur,' I faltered, 'I told you already that I still like her. What I didn't say is that I ... I want to see her.'

Lavender didn't appear surprised or appalled by what I'd said. *Would anything shock her?*

'It can happen to anyone,' said Lavender in her warm voice, 'that they might want to have contact with someone they know full well they shouldn't.'

'Why do I think about her all of the time? No matter how hard I try, she still controls me. She wasn't even nice to me towards the end. Why can't I let go?'

'Fleur touched something deep in your mind and your heart. She activated feelings you've been pushing down for a long time. It's probably easier for you to be in touch with these more recent feelings linked to Fleur rather than to your mum. Can we talk about your mother?'

'I don't know ... I'm afraid of being in the dumps and then hating myself.'

'Please, tell me, what do you *like* about yourself?'

'What's there to like? I'm a mistake ... My mum stays with my dad because of me. At times, he loses his cool and hits her.' I took a deep breath, trying to push back tears. 'That's not fair that she's to suffer because of me.'

'Who told you that?' asked Lavender, looking dismayed.

'That's what my mum says when she's angry with me or my dad.'

'Can we talk about your parents?'

'Not sure,' I mumbled, looking at my feet. 'Alright then, just for a little while.'

'When your mum says these unkind words, what do you do?'

'I go for a run with imaginary dragons. Sometimes, I picture funny monkeys.'

'Do you think that running helps you to avoid the hurt these words cause you?' asked Lavender in her soft voice.

'Perhaps,' I said after a massive pause. The familiar pressure in my head and chest becoming steadily unbearable. 'It's not only what she says ... I'm also scared of her anger. When she loses her rag, she's very mean.' Gazing at the floor, I feared that my chest would implode like a building collapsing in on itself.

'What does your father do when your mum is angry?'

'To start with, he tries to remain calm, but when she drones on and on, eventually he loses his cool. But mind you, my mum never stops once she's started a fight.'

My head was banging from the inside and confusion started taking over; uninvited film clips of Mum yelling at Dad played in my mind. At that moment, I knew without a shadow of a doubt that I had to run and get away from it all. 'Sorry,' I muttered, 'but I've to go now.'

'It's probably enough for one session. You've done very well – in the long run, it'll help you. Take it easy today. I'll see you tomorrow.'

I sprang up to my feet and bolted out of Lavender's room like a spooked cat. Once outside, I was glad to see Sky, sitting tall whilst scanning the grounds in front of her. Crouching down, I stroked her beautiful head and then put my arms around her. I shuddered when waves of fear and despair threatened to drown me. The pressure in my chest nearly stopped me from breathing. 'Run, Sky, run,' I cried, sprinting forward.

Sky joined me. Moving my legs in a warp speed, I tried not to think, knowing only too well that revisiting my talk with Lavender would be like jumping onto a sinking boat. We ran together for a long time until I became tired and had to slow down. Sky was panting heavily by my side.

I walked with Sky to Moonstone halls. Wanting to be on my own, I was relieved to see that Tania was out. I collapsed on to my bed, Sky snuggled up close to me.

As I was closing my eyes, I promised myself that I wouldn't allow anyone to whip up scary feelings again. This pledge relaxed me and I drifted into the land of nod.

I woke up feeling refreshed and very, very hot. Sky was lying next to me with her head on my shoulder. I stroked the Husky's thick fur – she opened her piercing blue eyes and looked at me.

'Thank you for your company,' I murmured into her ear, 'but I must move away from you because you're as hot as an electric blanket. Actually, if you want, you're free to go now.'

The Husky licked my face and jumped off my bed. I opened the door and she left. A little while later Tania walked in and the two of us went to Pumpkin Hall. Liam was already there, beckoning to us to join him. Tania and Liam seemed to like each other and I was hoping that the three of us would become good friends.

'I'm going home for the weekend,' said Liam, looking out of sorts, 'will be back on Monday.'

'Why?' asked Tania. 'Did anything happen?'

'We've been invited to an uncle's sixtieth birthday party and my father insists on me showing my face. Unfortunately, I've to go. Tania, would you like to meet me and Willow after lunch tomorrow?'

'Count me out,' replied Tania. 'There's a number of things I gotta do. I also have to work on my costume.'

'Shall we take the Border Collies for a walk?' I asked Liam.

'Let's do that,' he said. 'I love them running around me.'

* * *

The following day, I walked with Liam to the kennels and we invited the Border Collies to join us. While we were chatting, the dogs ran in circles around us, diligently discharging the duties of trusted guides. No one could ever accuse a Border Collie of not having a work ethic of the highest standard!

'I dread going home tomorrow,' said Liam, sighing. 'I hate it when my father bullies my mum – he criticises her for just about everything and anything.'

'My mum would've started World War Three! She could enter the Guinness Book of Records for waging the longest fight any couple ever had.'

'I tell you, my mum wouldn't dare; my dad puts her down an awful lot and she doesn't say anything. The truth is that I'm afraid of him too.' A faraway look appeared in Liam's eyes and then he zoned in again. 'I hate myself for being such a coward.'

'Come on. There's no need to be so hard on yourself.'

'I don't want to be a spineless wimp. At other times though, I worry I'll end up like him.'

The dogs barked and herded us towards the centre of the sanctuary. Radar's warning about a possible attack sprang to mind, giving me a massive dose of the heebie-jeebies. I wondered whether the dogs picked up a sound inaudible to humans. Before we got very far, I heard the beat of flapping wings. Looking up, I saw a large squadron of air dragons.

'Are those ours?' I cried. 'They could be Nastorians. Let's hurry back.'

'Those are Nastorians!' shouted Liam. 'We must leg it. Right Now!'

CHAPTER TWENTY-FIVE

Lavender

Liam, the dogs and I ran at lightning speed to Emerald halls. My worst fears materialised; a hostile air dragon squadron was drawing closer to the centre of the camp. I was terrified of them setting fire to the wooden buildings in the sanctuary; shuddering at the thought of injured dragons and other animals becoming trapped inside the healing retreat.

I came to an abrupt halt when I saw happy kids and grown-ups standing in front of Emerald halls – some smiling while others talking excitedly. Tania, looking thrilled, sprinted towards me. 'Willow!' she cried. 'Check it out! Our dragons have arrived. Aren't they amazing? What a parade!'

'I'm sorry,' said Liam. 'I was convinced they were Nastorians.'

'No worries at all. Believe me, so was I.'

The air dragons flew north, east, south and west. Having completed five rounds of flying to the four cardinal points, they performed astounding loops, cartwheels and other aerial manoeuvres.

It was an awesome demo of power and spectacular unison. The aerial display was firing up my insides and my brain. I knew that this *tour de force* would be imprinted on my mind forever and would come to my rescue during lousy moments. 'Aren't they out of this world?' I declared. 'Totally awesome.'

Liam looked overjoyed. 'This is it,' he raved, his eyes

glued to the dragons. 'The best parade in the history of the universe. They're as precise as a military air show. I could stand here and watch them till the cows came home.'

After finishing the breathtaking aerobatics, four air dragons landed on the ground, while eight remained guarding the skies above and beyond the camp. Everyone gathered around them, basking in their strength and defence know-how. Standing in close proximity and linking with their powerful energies, I was completely in tune with them. A lovely wave of *joie de vivre* engulfed me.

'The dragons will take turns in providing aerial cover,' Chris announced. 'I think we're safe for the time being. It's unlikely that the Nastorians would attack us with our air dragons exhibiting their might. Let me remind you that the Custodians' Festival will take place on the third Sunday of August. So, those of you who've not yet decided on your costumes, do hurry up. Now, I'd like you all to continue with your scheduled activities.'

Chris approached me. 'Can we talk briefly?'

'Sure thing,' I replied.

After entering his room, I connected with the warm energy of the amber stones of the lamp on his desk. 'How are you finding your meet-ups with Lavender?' asked Chris, looking at me attentively.

'She's alright and very friendly. It's only our conversations always return to my mum, and ... it's not easy for me to talk about her.'

'What do you find difficult?'

'It's ... like ... I have a box in my head where I keep stuff about my mum, if you see what I mean. Talking about her opens that box, and then there is chaos and confusion.'

'Are you afraid of these feelings?' he asked in his calm and caring voice.

'Not sure. I just don't want them to take over.'

'Talking about your mother could help you to empty that box.'

'Actually, it's so much easier to run and forget about

everything.'

'Would you like always to run away from yourself?' I didn't say anything for a few drawn-out minutes and then Chris went on, 'Why won't you give Lavender a chance? She has an excellent track record of helping kids.'

'Tania says she's good and she doesn't put any pressure on me. It's my fault, really. Only at times, I find it all too much.'

'A lot of kids, and even grown-ups, find facing their past daunting. However, with time it becomes easier. Let me tell you that for some, telling their story helps them from the outset.'

'I'm definitely not one of them,' I said without any hesitation whatsoever. 'But if you want me to stick with the meet-ups, then I will.'

'I'd like you to continue with Lavender. Thank you for talking to me. You're free to go now.'

Having left Emerald halls, I saw Winter and Sky lying on the grass in the front garden – I invited them to join me for a run. When I got tired, I ambled aimlessly with the Huskies by my side, trying not think about my conversation with Chris.

I hugged the Huskies goodbye and walked to the creativity room where I continued working on my goldfinch costume. I glued golden-brown feathers to the bird's body, white feathers to the belly and black ones to the tail. Stepping back, I enjoyed looking at my completed handiwork and then put my costume on.

'Well, Willow,' Louise said, 'you look really well. I think we can say your costume is finished now.'

'I'm almost sorry to hear this. I loved working on it.'

Louise chuckled. 'You're very welcome to help others with their costumes.'

'With pleasure, but not right now. In twenty minutes I've a session with Lavender. I'll see you soon.'

I left the creativity hall and called my dad, telling him that I had completed my goldfinch costume and that everything was fine. On my way to Lavender's room, I reminded myself that she could help me to find out why Fleur had so much power over me. But knowing that this was in some way linked to my mum gave me the heebie-jeebies.

Lavender greeted me with her customary smile, both warm and caring. 'Are you feeling more relaxed about seeing me?' she asked.

I smiled back. 'I think so, it's good that you let me have choices.'

'In that case, what would you like to talk about today?'

'Well, I want to find out why I'm so hung up on Fleur, even if it means talking about my mum.'

'We can do that, but do let me know when you'd like to stop.'

'I will.'

'Well then, you told me that Fleur was very friendly in the beginning and shared your strong interest in dragons. That's why it was only natural that she became important to you. So, to start with, she offered you a steady friendship.'

'But now I know that she's a Master Pretender of the Supreme Order, why can't I let go? That's what bugs me.'

'When Fleur suddenly changed her attitude towards you, she caused a lot of hurt and confusion. Despite the unkind things she had said to you, part of you still wants her to like you. Can I go on?'

'Will it help?' I asked.

'Quite likely. If not immediately, then in the long run.'

'Let's continue then.'

'Letting go of someone with whom you'd a special relationship may take a while. Understanding your reaction is the first step forward. In a way, Fleur took your mother's place because she'd been friendly and then pushed you away. Your relationship with your mother has been characterised by her being caring in front of other people, or when she's in a good mood, and rejecting you when she's angry. It's as if you've transferred your feelings from your mother to Fleur.'

Despite her telling me, during a previous meet-up, that something connected my mum and Fleur, I looked at Lavender in disbelief. What she'd just said was totally and utterly weird! It freaked me out. Without me even knowing, Fleur somehow became a mother substitute. 'I had no intention ... of doing that ...' I faltered. 'I don't get it.'

'This can happen without us being aware of it. It often comes to pass when there's still unresolved emotional stuff.'

'Wow, you're telling me that Fleur ... kind of ... replaced my mum. That's really strange. I can't get my head around it.'

'It'll sink in gradually. Otherwise, why do you think she has such a hold over you?'

'I've no idea,' I mumbled. 'It sounds really strange. But then, is there anything I can *do* about it?'

'As I said earlier, understanding yourself is fundamental because it creates clarity. The next step is for you to be more accepting and appreciative of yourself. If you do that, approval from people like Fleur would be a bit less important. Please, tell me what you do well and list your good qualities.'

'I don't think I've any ...'

'Let me help you. I know you love animals – what does it say about you?'

I shrugged my shoulders. 'Not much, most kids like animals. What's the big deal?'

'Perhaps, not all. Let me ask another question. Would you let Tania down?'

'Never,' I said vehemently, 'she's suffered enough. Her own parents didn't want her.'

'It seems to me that you're a good friend.'

'Actually, I'd like to ask you something. Do you think that I'm ... that I'm ... a ... you know what ... and that's why I like Fleur?'

'Do you mean a Pretender?' said Lavender calmly. 'No,

not at all. Your heart is in the right place. Didn't you just tell me that you care about Tania?'

I heaved a huge sigh of relief. Lavender didn't think the worst of me. *Can I tell her that my mum is a Pretender? Will she be as forgiving and understanding when she finds out?* I told Lavender that I wanted to end the session, said goodbye and left her room.

Talking to Lavender about my fixation on Fleur made me feel like a roller coaster. A niggling thought grated on me: *Is there another reason as to why I'm hung up on Fleur other than her replacing my mum?*

When I returned to my room, Tania was already there. She was totally focused on her laptop – that usually meant that she was playing a computer game and got lost in cyberspace. She briefly raised her head. 'Give me just a couple of minutes, will ya? Right now, I'm crushing it.'

'Take your time,' I said. My phone buzzed with a text – I opened it and was stunned to see a message from Fleur. I almost trembled with excitement; electricity was charging throughout my body. Fleur asked for my email address so she could write to me.

I knew I shouldn't respond, but my brain had shut down, relinquishing complete control to my hand, which hurriedly typed my email address. After sending the message, I waited impatiently for a reply, checking my emails non-stop.

'Are you expecting something?' asked Tania. 'You seem to be obsessed with that 'phone of yours.'

I didn't want to tell Tania that Fleur had contacted me, so I excused myself and went for a walk. Having bumped into Winter, I invited him to join me.

Moving briskly with the Husky in tow, I tried to think about dragons, the Custodians' Festival and Coriander's yummy food, but my thoughts kept drifting back to Fleur. At that moment, she had complete control over my unruly brain. At last, the email from her arrived:

Hi Willow

I'm writing because I'd like to clarify why I was unkind to you.

I knew that I'd be leaving the sanctuary and not wanting to hurt your feelings, I thought it was best to end our friendship.

With the benefit of hindsight, I should've done it differently. If I upset you, then I'd like to offer my sincere apologies. I hope you understand and forgive me.

After my departure, I've realised that you're very important to me. I keep thinking about you and our dragon chats. We seem to have lots in common, and that's why I miss you so badly.

It'd be great to see you. If you decide to give me another chance, I'd do my best for you.

I'm waiting for your reply.

Fleur

I read the email a thousand times until every word was engraved on my brain. *So, Fleur cares about me! She didn't mean it when she told me that I was a nuisance.* Just then another thought sneaked in: *She's a Master Pretender of the Supreme Order – you can't trust her.* Yet I read the email yet again and decided to meet her. *Perhaps this would help me break my fixation on her,* I reasoned with myself and then I replied:

Hi Fleur

Let's meet up. Can you suggest a time and a place?

I sent the email right away so that I couldn't change my mind and plopped down on the ground. *Did I do the right thing?* My thoughts were interrupted by the sound of footsteps – glancing up, I was surprised to see Liam walking towards me.

'I was looking for you everywhere,' he said. 'How are you doing? Tania told me that you hardly talked to her today. She's worried about you.'

I did my best to appear chilled out. 'Oh, everything is cool, I just needed a bit of time for myself. That's all.'

'Shall I leave you alone then?'

'Actually, I'm okay now. Let's go for a walk.'

I kept thinking about meeting Fleur. It seemed that Liam noticed that I was totally zoned out because he told me there were a number of things he had to do. After saying goodbye to him, I checked my mobile, feeling relieved when I saw an email from Fleur.

Hi Willow

It was good to hear from you and thank you for your prompt reply. You've made the right decision – I'm confident that you won't regret it.

I'll meet you at midnight, just outside the back gardens of Pumpkin Hall. Once I'm there, I'll text you.

Under no circumstances, let anyone know of our meeting.

All you need to bring with you is a change of clothing. I trust you. Please don't let me down.

Can't wait to see you.

Your friend

Fleur

The certainty of meeting Fleur made me feel dizzy and utterly confused. My need to see her was shrouded with fear and doubts: *Will it mean that I won't be friends with Tania and Liam? Will it spell the end of my visits to the sanctuary?*

During supper in Pumpkin Hall, I could hardly talk, let alone eat the food on my plate. But you can always rely on a teenage boy to polish off an extra meal – Liam gratefully accepted my veggie burger. It wasn't far from the truth when I told my friends that I was out of sorts, and that I'd be returning to Moonstone halls.

Having followed Fleur's instructions to the letter, I got under my bed covers without changing my clothes. When Tania entered our room, I pretended that I was asleep. She spent a little while on her laptop and afterwards turned in. I lay silently with my mobile in my hand under the blanket, waiting impatiently for the minutes to hurry up. The text message, I both badly wanted and dreaded, appeared:

I'm waiting for you.
Please be careful.

While getting out of my bed as quietly as I could, I tried to steady myself. Carrying my trainers and a small bag of clothing in one hand, I tiptoed out of the room and gently closed the door behind me. I put my trainers on and slunk out of Moonstone halls, checking that no one was following me.

I reached Pumpkin Hall with my heart thumping loudly against my ribcage. I looked around and continued to the rear gardens. Fleur was waiting for me. My blood ran cold when I noticed that she wasn't alone.

CHAPTER TWENTY-SIX

New Vistas

Fleur walked briskly towards me with a broad smile on her face. 'Willow, should the need arise, Charity will protect –'

Before she could finish her sentence, I heard a noise. Trembling, I looked around and saw Chris Light, Radar and a number of Border Collies circling us.

'You've set me up!' Fleur snapped, giving me a look that could kill. 'I'd have expected better from you.' Charity bared her long fangs.

'No, Willow did not,' said Chris in a steely voice. 'Her friends were concerned about her, so they talked to me. I decided to observe her and followed her to your meeting place. I'd like you to go right now. I don't want any animal to be hurt.'

Fleur shot another Vulcan Death Glare in my direction. 'You'll hear from me,' she said in a voice frosty enough to extinguish flames. 'I'll not forget this in a hurry.'

To my huge relief, she walked away with Charity.

My face was on fire – I didn't have the courage to look at Chris. 'I'm sorry,' I whispered. 'I really am. I've let you down yet again. Do you still want me to stay here?'

'Yes, I do,' he replied calmly. 'I'm not cross with you. Right now, go back to your room. I'd like you to talk with Lavender about tonight's events. She'll help you to let go of Fleur.'

Chris, Radar and the hounds accompanied me to the entrance of Moonstone halls where I said goodbye to them.

I tiptoed into my bedroom, but Tania heard me.

'Glad you're back. You alright?' she asked.

'I might as well tell you,' I mumbled, feeling grateful that Tania couldn't see my very red face in the dark. 'I went nuts and agreed to meet Fleur. Did you tell Chris about me behaving like a demented idiot?'

'I did 'cause I worried about you. To be honest, after what you've told me about Fleur, I suspected something like that. I'm very happy you didn't scarper with her.'

'Let's go to sleep now. I'm knackered.'

'Don't beat yourself up, I've done heaps of stupid things,' said Tania, yawning. 'Night night.'

In the morning, self-doubts flooded me like a burst dam: *Why did I agree to meet Fleur? Is it because we've lots in common, not only dragons, but also other stuff? Am I a Pretender?* Despite Chris telling me that he wanted me to remain in the sanctuary, I thought I should leave.

After breakfast and the morning ritual, I walked to Emerald halls, dreading facing Lavender and explaining my brain's breakdown. She greeted me in her customary friendly manner. At that moment, I wanted to be anywhere else but not with Lavender – she was way too nice and too accepting of me.

'I'll make it easier for you,' she said in her friendly and caring voice. 'Chris has already told me that last night you went to meet Fleur. Can we talk about that?'

'We can ... only ... I'm not sure myself why I did it,' I muttered with my face burning and my eyes fixed on my trainers.

'That's alright, we can work it out together. I assume that she contacted you, or was the other way around?'

'She sent me a text message ... and I ... I ... replied.'

'How did you feel when you've received her message?'

I didn't say anything for quite some time – the seconds were ticking away incredibly slowly. Lavender waited patiently. 'That's the difficult bit,' I admitted eventually, with my brain going into self-hatred mode. 'I'm really ashamed ...'

'You can tell me whatever is on your mind,' said Lavender gently. 'I'm asking because I want to help.'

'I was actually ... excited ... I know that I'm a complete muppet ... Do you still want to see me?'

'Very much so, I don't walk away from kids when they go through a difficult time.'

'Even when they behave like brainless imbeciles?' I briefly glanced at her.

'That's not how I see it. I'll continue seeing you even after you've made mistakes.'

I looked at Lavender in surprise. Did she really mean it? Her eyes were sincere. 'So, for you, it was only a mistake?'

'Absolutely – when I was your age, I did all kinds of daft things. Let me tell you about one of them. I was desperate for my very busy parents to notice me, so I convinced one of my friends to let me stay overnight. I didn't tell my parents though, and in the end, they contacted the police.'

'Wow, you had guts,' I said appreciatively, warming to Lavender and feeling that I could tell her everything. 'I wouldn't have dared. The most important rule my mum drilled into my head was that I must behave in front of people who aren't family.'

'And at home?'

I laughed. 'Well, it's the complete opposite, practically anything goes. When she's angry, she says nasty things to my dad and me. I hate it when she is super nice to me in front of other people because I know that it's a charade. Come to think of it, my mum is a brilliant actress. What a wasted talent! She's good enough to win an Oscar! And that's why ... that's why ... I think … that ... she … could be ... a Pretender.'

'Are you ready to talk about your mother today? If not, it can wait.'

'Actually, I'd like to talk about her. Ever since Destini told me that my mum is a Pretender ... I've been having crazy thoughts about her and myself ... I'm still trying to get my head around all that stuff.'

'Firstly, Willow, let me tell you that your mother was lured out of our camp by the Pretenders, or the Elite Alliance, as they like to call themselves, when she was sixteen. She joined them because they promised her unquestionable loyalty and a great future.'

'I find this difficult to come to terms with,' I mumbled, 'and quite confusing.'

'Allow me to clarify. Your mum, despite behavioural problems, did well in school and showed an interest in studying either medicine or psychology. After joining the Pretenders, they encouraged her to choose psychology and promised her a career in this discipline. Progression in medicine is highly structured. A medic can progress only after working for a specified number of years in their chosen speciality. In comparison, psychologists with very little experience can be shot through the ranks.'

'Destini told me that the Elite Alliance helped my mum to become a senior manager after being qualified for only eighteen months. Is it true?'

'I'm afraid so. They'd do just about anything for each other. If there are any problems or complaints at work, they always protect and exonerate one of their members. Mutual allegiance is an absolute priority; it comes before everything else.'

'Do you think my mum assumed that I'm here and that's why she let me remain?'

'It's a distinct possibility.'

'Destini also said that she wants me to join them ...'

'It looks that way,' said Lavender gently. 'The Alliance expects its members to recruit newbies all the time, they particularly like young people.'

I slumped back in my chair. Just then, my brain started throbbing inside my head. 'I think I need time to work it all out ... Actually, may I ask you something?'

'Please, do.'

'Why is my mum pushing me away?'

'Before I answer your question, let me tell you a little bit about disruption in attachment early in life. Your mother never knew her father. Her mother, your maternal grandmother, suffered from something called post-natal depression and because of this, she didn't bond with her daughter. Eventually when your mother was two years old, she was placed with a foster family. Secure bonding provides a child with a solid emotional foundation for the rest of their lives. In the absence of good attachment, there's an undercurrent of frustration, anxiety and anger. When your mother is in the grip of strong emotions, she rejects you, the way she was rejected by her own mother.'

'That's so unfair, it's not my fault that her mother couldn't look after her.' I said, trying to ignore the thumping inside my head.

'Perhaps, another way for you to view this is that your mother doesn't know how to love you. I hope this would slightly ease the hurt you've been carrying all your life.'

The pounding inside my head increased as if my brain was trying to escape from my head and hide somewhere. 'It's all ... very confusing ... I don't really get it. Why does she push me away? Why does she fight over everything and anything?'

'Your mother as a child learned to get attention by being difficult and doggedly oppositional. She was placed in a children's home after a number of foster families couldn't cope with her. Throughout her life, her relationship with others was embroiled in strife. It's quite possible that for her, conflict means closeness.'

'Now I'm ... completely baffled.' The constant hammering inside my head threatened a complete brain malfunction.

'Your mother pushed down her feelings of hurt and disowned her emotions. That's what the Elite Alliance teaches them. Sadly, when she does that, she doesn't acknowledge that what she needs, above all, is to be loved.'

'But then, whenever Dad tries to be nice to her, she

always spoils for a fight.'

'As I said earlier, that's her way of being close to him. Deep down, she craves love, but at the same time, she's afraid of closeness and possible rejection.'

'I don't know what to make of this ... When I'm unhappy, I want to look after homeless animals and run-down buildings.'

'I assume that your Georgian home is one of them,' Lavender chuckled.

'Absolutely, it has been neglected for far too long.'

'What I'd like you to take from our session today is that your mother, because of her own unhappy childhood, doesn't know how to love you. Willow, you're a special kid, only your mother can't appreciate you.'

'I don't feel very special at all, not even one little bit. Quite often I feel like a weirdo and that's what some kids at school call me. At times, when I'm down in the dumps, I hate myself.'

'When that happens, think about the saying, "What does not kill you, makes you stronger." I've slightly changed it to: What does not break you, makes you stronger.'

'Are you telling me that I can be strong because my mum pushes me away?' I liked that idea – it felt like a speck of light in a very dark room.

'Did your mother break you? Are you hurting anyone because you're unhappy?'

'No ... not really, on the contrary ...'

'When you feel low, you want to look after animals or buildings. You transformed your unhappiness into a force for the good.'

'Do you really think that I'm strong?'

'I do,' Lavender said softly, looking me in the eye, 'and this'll help you to do well in life without any help from the Elite Alliance. Also, I'd like you to remember that you're kind. Willow, you're one of us – you're a Custodian.'

I left Lavender's room with lots of mixed feelings and a very painful head. I liked the idea of being strong, but I struggled with the thought that I'm special and that I'm a Custodian. I had an urge to sprint and run away from it all, but then decided to think about what Lavender had said. After a while, I walked to Ruby halls. It was good to see Tania in the creativity room. She was working on her forest spirit dress.

'Glad you came,' she said. 'How is it going with Lavender?'

'She was alright with me, even though I'd gone to meet Fleur. I'm beginning to like her.'

'I love talking to her. I'm very fond of her because she's the complete opposite to my dad. He doesn't give two hoots about me.'

'It was good today, but I still find it difficult to accept the nice things she tells me.'

'You'll get used to that, bit by bit,' Tania reassured me.

I checked yet again my costume and tried it on. 'What do you think?' I asked Tania.

'Looks great. You're doing ultra-well. I still gotta embroider tons of flowers.'

Louise approached us. 'Tania,' she said, 'I'd like you to try on your dress so that I could see if any alterations are needed.'

Tania put her outfit on and the creativity guide checked it thoroughly. 'Are you happy with it being so loose?' asked Louise.

'I do. it kinda looks more fairy-like this way.'

'Can I help you with the wings? I'm now a bit of an expert after making mine.'

Tania accepted my offer, chose an intricate weave of a transparent material, and we worked together on the sprite's wings. Before leaving Tania folded the dress and placed it in a bag. 'I'll continue working on it in my room again,' she told Louise. 'Otherwise, it ain't gonna be done before the festival.'

Tania and I thanked Louise and walked out of Ruby halls. I gasped in delight when I saw Billie running towards us with his tail wagging. I murmured in his ear, 'It's great to see you.'

'As loving as ever,' Tania said to the hound. 'Even though you didn't have time for a wash, I'm gonna cuddle you.'

Billie walked with us to Moonstones halls. He stayed with us for a couple of hours and then walked to the door. Tania and I gave him another hug and let him go.

* * *

The Custodians' headquarters had decided that the air dragon squadron would remain in the sanctuary until the end of the school holidays.

The air dragons patrolled the skies on a regular basis. If I wanted to see them, all I had to do was to look up and enjoy the sight of at least one quartet flying above the camp.

Every morning, the squadron flew to and from the four cardinal points and created different formations. That view never failed to thrill me and always made me feel upbeat and happy.

During some days, I had to run and escape from what was happening in my discombobulated head; I'd scoot then to the kennels and invite a dog to join me. My legs drove me on and on until I felt calmer. On other days though, I was okay.

I called my mum, hoping that she wasn't in one of her endless meetings. She answered the phone with a voice that was unusually gentle, 'Willow, it's so good to hear you. I miss you so much – I can't wait to see you.'

Did she mean it? I asked myself. *Or did she say that because she was in a room with other work colleagues?* I played mum's affectionate words in my head many times, savouring the warmth in her voice. *Would returning home be a new beginning?*

CHAPTER TWENTY-SEVEN

The Custodians' Festival

With the additional air dragons patrolling the skies above and beyond the sanctuary, we all enjoyed a peaceful week, doing what we liked best. I wrote poetry, and with Louise's help, drew and painted all kinds of dragons. I also started making mosaics. Alfie took us for long walks outside the camp with the Border Collies. The hounds herded the stragglers, keeping us as one group.

At long last the time for the festivities arrived! After the morning ceremony, everyone got ready for the sanctuary's most important event. I overheard loud and excited voices as well as less noisy, lively chattering.

Tania and I walked to the sanctuary's amphitheatre carrying our costumes that had been carefully packed in large bags. Standing by the entrance, I admired the breathtaking natural formation of the amphitheatre – it nestled between grass-covered low hills with gently sloping land leading to a circular field that was used as an arena.

Although clearly loved and looked after by the sanctuary's gardeners, the tops of the slopes gave the impression of a riot of wild flowers. Swathes of jumbled buttercups, cornflowers, daisies, harebells, dandelions, rugged robins, yellow and red poppies were punctuated by four entrances and paths that led to the arena.

Some flowers had migrated down from the top, sprucing up the dominant green with the occasional small splashes of white, blue, yellow or red. The unhurried inclines were used as seating areas.

'It's called the Valley of Brave Hearts,' said Tania. 'Legend has it that some proper gutsy humans and dragons who survived persecution hid in this place.'

We positioned ourselves at the bottom of the seating area from where we had a good view of the arena. I ran my fingers along the grass, enjoying its suppleness and coolness.

The dragon horses and their riders were waiting just outside the arena. When the riders mounted their horses, a wave of thrilled voices swept over the seating areas. Looking at the colourful outfits of the riders, I felt a big buzz of excitement.

The four groups of five mounted dragon horses positioned themselves at the cardinal points of the arena. The Greens in the north, the Blues in the east, the Browns in the south and the Reds in the west.

Chris, wearing a scarlet habit with a yellow sash, stood in front of a microphone on a small stage. 'Good afternoon, kids, grown-ups, dragons and animals,' he announced. 'The day we've all been waiting and getting ready for, the most special event in the Custodians' calendar, has finally arrived! The dragon horses and their riders will start our celebrations – their astounding team work will be followed by air dragons displaying amazing aerobatic skills. So, the festival is commencing right now! Musicians, let us have a rhythm befitting this phenomenal occasion, and everyone else give a big hand to the dragon horses and their riders as they enter the arena.'

A group of kids drummed out a powerful beat with a rat-a-tat-tat. The dragon horses trotted to the centre of the arena where they formed a circle and breathed fire above their heads that merged into a flaming ring rising upwards, like an incandescent crown. I was completely still, looking in breathless wonder.

The dragon horses turned around as one and cantered back to the outer edge of the arena. Then all twenty reared on their hind legs at the same time and shot fire from their great open mouths, creating a circle of fire punctuated by regular intervals. I was spell-bound by their precisely co-ordinated movements.

Having executed another superb U-turn, all the dragon horses trotted to the centre of the round field again. A dragon horse from the Green Team stepped forward and walked to the Blues. The drummers stopped briefly and when they re-started the same beat, a dragon horse from the Blue Team joined the one from the Green Team and together they cantered to the Browns. After another short pause, a dragon horse from the Brown Team joined the first two, and the three of them trotted to the Reds where they were joined by a dragon horse from the Red Team.

The four dragons cantered to the outer lane along the edge of the arena. This was repeated until five groups were formed. The drumming tempo gradually accelerated until all the dragon horses were galloping along the outer lane.

The riders' cloaks flowed behind them, creating multi-coloured waves. A rush of energy shot into every muscle of my body – I sprang to my feet and clapped for all I was worth. A chorus of appreciation erupted across the sitting areas. I wasn't the only one standing! Some of the kids were jumping up and down.

'Aren't they stupendous!' I cried. 'How can they be so precise?'

'They've had tons of practice,' said Tania, smiling happily.

The five squads galloped ten laps and left the arena to thundering applause and yelps of joy.

'Wow! Wasn't that incredible,' Chris exclaimed. 'I've seen them perform on many occasions, but every single time, without fail, I'm overwhelmed by their co-ordination and timing. Show how much you have enjoyed their performance and give those fabulous dragon horses and their riders another big hand.'

The amphitheatre exploded with clapping and shouts

of approval. My brain was totally clear and comfortable, snugly fitting inside my head and taking in every detail.

'Now our air dragons will perform an equally gripping show,' Chris declared in a high-spirited voice. 'They will fly north, east, south and west. Flying in the four directions symbolises the spread of loving kindness and compassion. They'll also delight you with amazing aerobatic manoeuvres and formations. Everyone put your hands together and clap as loud as you can, so that the air dragons can hear you!'

The drummers introduced a fast rhythm that culminated in three loud staccato strikes. A green air dragon came from the north, a blue flew in from the east, a brown materialised from the south and a red flew in from the west. The air dragons turned around and flew to and from the four cardinal directions three times. Then, when they were over the arena, the air dragons raised their heads upwards and shot huge fireballs.

A tingle travelled down my back; it was an awesome display of power and precision. I was totally enthralled by the formidable air dragons. I looked at Tania: her big eyes sparkled with gusto. I sensed that just like me, she was totally in the now – the past had ceased to exist. And, what's more, it didn't matter.

Afterwards, they performed three tight pirouettes and then flew towards the circular field. As they approached it, all dived down at the same time. The drummers produced a loud strike and they once more rose up to the sky, twice looping the loop. Then all of them flew away from the centre of the arena accompanied by deafening cheers.

'Wasn't that a spectacular show of supreme mastery of timing and strength?' Chris enthused. 'Just in case what they've accomplished thus far wasn't brilliant enough, they'll now thrill you with stunning formations. They will begin with a diamond shape.'

The drummers produced a crescendo beat that culminated in three powerful strikes. The green dragon was the head of the diamond while behind him, to his left, flew the red dragon and on his rear right, the blue one. The brown dragon completed the diamond. The dragons flew away and returned in a new configuration.

'This is gargantuan, totally scintillating,' I cried. 'I'm loving every second.'

'You and your big words,' Tania grinned.

'I'm afraid that's what happens when your dad is an English teacher.'

'What you're looking at right now is called Finger-four formation,' Chris announced. 'As you can see, this resembles the tips of four fingers without the thumb. Military squadron also create this form.'

The dragons flew to the east and returned with six additional dragons in a V formation. Glancing around, I saw kids clapping their hands, stamping their feet, shouting, cheering and laughing. I tell you, the place was rocking.

Chris went on, 'The awesome V pattern you are looking at now is based on migratory birds. Some scientists say that by synchronising their flapping, birds and can improve the efficiency of their flight.'

'Where did these extra dragons come from?' I cried. 'What a view! Are they from the reinforcement sent by the Custodians' headquarters?'

'Nah, they aren't,' said Tania. 'The Nastorians would love to attack us durin' our festival, so they're patrolling the skies beyond the camp. They're young dragons in trainin' and it's their mega big day to show what they can do.'

After the dragon squadron flew to the west, Chris announced, 'I hope you all enjoyed the dazzling aerial display as much as I did. The air show has now come to an end. We will have a break for an hour during which you can get refreshments from the stalls by the entrances to the amphitheatre. Today, you're going to have some of Coriander's most delicious goodies – so without further ado, go and treat your taste buds.'

'After sitting down all this time. I now need to move my legs,' I said.

'Likewise,' laughed Tania. 'Let's get cracking.'

I ran up the hill with Tania closely behind me. There were all kinds of food and drink stalls, as well as little souvenirs made by kids working with the creativity guide. I chose a scrumptious chilli-flavoured popcorn, while Tania opted for pumpkin ice-cream. 'You can always trust Coriander to sneak pumpkin into everything!' she chuckled.

The hour passed very quickly and we resumed our seating spot on the grass.

'And now,' Chris announced, 'it's time for the fun part of this phenomenal day. After the breathtaking display of formidable power, Alfie Doggard and his Border Collies will entertain you with a light-footed spectacle. The dogs, just like their larger friends before them, possess the same spellbinding timing and co-ordination. Let our dog whisperer and his charges hear how much you want to see them.'

The drummers introduced a progressive rhythm and we all joined them clapping along. When the tempo had accelerated to a powerful crescendo, Alfie, with six black and white Border Collies, walked to the centre of the arena. The musicians reduced the volume of their drumming and the dogs positioned themselves in a straight line at regular intervals. Alfie stood in front of the hounds and walked towards them – all six Border Collies moved back in unison in small, crisp steps with their eyes fixed on their trainer.

Alfie skipped to the left and the line of hounds moved in springy steps in the same direction. They repeated the same move to the right and did the whole routine three times. Afterwards, the dog whisperer knelt down and stretched his arms sideways – two dogs simultaneously jumped, one over his left arm and the other over his right arm. The remaining four dogs repeated the same move.

The drummers now played a new flowing rhythm. Alfie moved his hands clockwise and the hounds turned in the direction dictated by him. When he moved his hands anticlockwise, the dogs followed faithfully. The dog whisperer introduced different variations and the Border Collies executed all of his commands, with their eyes glued to his hands.

The canine show ended with a conga line; a dog stood on its hind legs behind Alfie and placed its forepaws on his back. One by one, all the remaining dogs took the same position with each placing its forepaws on the back of the one in front. With little steps they moved to the rhythmic beat provided by the drummers.

'Thank you, Alfie, and your dancing troupe for a wonderful performance,' said Chris. 'We've seen incredible feats by dragons and dogs, so now it's time for us to enjoy your creative inventiveness. Please put your costumes on. The parade will begin in half an hour. The three best costumes will win a weekend in the sanctuary during term-time.'

Having taken the goldfinch costume out of my bag, I stepped into the bird's frame and fastened it securely to my neck, arms and legs. I then attached the wings to my arms and put on the bird's head.

'How do I look?' I asked Tania.

'Seriously?' she laughed. 'If you start twittering, you'll pass as the real thing.'

Tania put on her cream chiffon dress and placed a daisy garland on her long, loose hair. Her matchstick arms and legs went well with the flowing garment, creating an ephemeral presence – it seemed as if she might float away at any moment. Her gossamer wings sparkled when she moved.

Looking around, I was really impressed by the various costumes. There were many kids dressed as animals, ranging from a mouse to an alpaca. Three small children presented themselves as garden gnomes. And then, bit by bit, giant vegetables and fruit also materialised. A boy had created an awesome Green Man, clothed in a costume made of leafy branches. On his head he wore a crown of woven ivy and fresh flowers.

In complete contrast to the other outfits, a boy dressed up as a robot. I loved the different buttons for domestic chores, including one for tiding up teenagers' bedrooms!

'What a cool idea,' said Tania. 'Imagine everyone havin' a personal robot butler.'

'I'd definitely get one,' I said.

The drummers struck three loud gongs.

'Cooee! May I have your attention?' called Chris, trying to be heard over the hubbub of laughter and chattering. 'You've five minutes to complete your preparations and enter the arena. You'll be presenting your handicraft in pairs, and I'm sure you'll love the next bit: Alfie's hounds will guide you.'

Tania and I walked together. Now and then, I raised my arms sideways and moved them up and down like a flying goldfinch. The Border Collies treated us like a flock of sheep, whenever anyone stepped out of line, they herded them back to their place.

'And now,' Chris went on, 'it's time to judge the costumes. Louise Blake, who worked with you tirelessly on your outfits, will help with selecting the best ones. In view of not having an activities organiser at present, Alfie has kindly agreed to be the third judge. Originality and effort are the two main criteria. I can see many great creations and therefore we have a very difficult task ahead of us.'

After a while, Chris said, 'Please stop moving now and face the stage. It wasn't easy, but in the end we were able to agree on the best three. I will start with the third place. Forest spirit, please step forward. We appreciated the effort and time you've invested in making this most captivating and convincing fairy attire.'

I was happy that Tania's hours of embroidery had been acknowledged. She sprinted forward with her dress and hair flowing behind her. The musicians drummed a fast beat and we all clapped along.

'The second place,' Alfie declared, 'goes ... to the robot! We liked the concept of teenagers with tidy bedrooms.

What a novelty this would be, in fact, quite revolutionary!'

The robot walked mechanically forward, waved an arm in an automated fashion and stood next to Tania. Everyone applauded and cheered.

'And now we have come to first place,' Louise declared. 'The best costume is ... the Green Man. I know how much planning and work went into making this outfit. We loved the association with nature, change and renewal.'

A roaring approval broke out. The hounds barked, dancing circles around the three winners.

'The Custodians' Festival is over,' Chris announced, 'but the fun continues. You're now free to enjoy Coriander's scrumptious food and drinks once again. And thank you all for helping to make this such a memorable day.'

'Wow, I really enjoyed myself,' I said to Tania on our way to the food stalls. 'I tell you, this is the most incredible day in the history of ever!'

A number of kids I hardly knew talked to me. At school, I was a weirdo, an outsider looking in rather than taking part. But now I belonged in the Custodians' camp. We were all members of the Nobodies' Club for Kids with Sad Eyes. Chatting freely to those around me, I felt I had discovered my lost tribe.

CHAPTER TWENTY-EIGHT

Breaking Free

After the festival, I often pictured film shows of flying air dragons and galloping dragon horses. Lovely thoughts circulating in my relaxed brain: *It's really great here. I couldn't have found a better place.* I knew I could count on Chris and Lavender and I had Tania and Liam as friends. I let all that good stuff roll inside my head, but at times, a less pleasant thought sneaked in: *Soon I'll be leaving this amazing hangout.*

So sadly, the end of my stay in the camp was fast approaching – to be honest: far too quickly! During the last week we had daily meet-ups in Emerald halls – Chris was preparing us for going back home. And believe me, I needed all the help I could get.

'I'd like the newbies to know,' Chris told us during the last gathering, 'that you'll not be alone after leaving. Everyone will be given a list of Custodians belonging to the Nobodies' Club for Kids with Sad Eyes living in your locality, or attending your school. Those of you who live in rural areas though, may have to travel to befriend another Custodian.'

'Actually, I think I know a few already,' I remarked. 'All you have to do is to look at their eyes.'

'Unfortunately,' said Chris, 'some unloved youngsters manage their unhappiness by being unkind to others, or in other unhelpful ways. All the new arrivals will be given a password to our forum on the internet, which will enable you to keep in touch with other Custodians. I hope that you'll support each other during difficult moments.'

'I'd love to have a friend online,' Ollie stated.

'Our network extends beyond technology,' said Chris, 'we also organise meet-ups and different activities.'

'But will I be allowed to take part?' asked a teenage girl whose name I didn't know. 'My children's home is very strict and very paranoid. They forever talk about safety, especially when it comes to girls. It's so unfair!'

'I'm certain that they've good intentions,' said Chris kindly. 'Elena is in constant contact with your parents, guardians or social workers, and she'll arrange permission for you to attend our gatherings. Let me tell that I plan a meet-up very soon after your return home. As most of you know, we have a network of old houses and buildings that include libraries and museums. One of our best assistants is the Natural History Museum in London, and that's where our first get-together will take place.'

The thought of a well-organised network run by Custodians was both uplifting and calming at the same time. And, what's more, Tania's children's home wasn't very far from where I lived!

* * *

Fleur remained an unwelcome guest in my mind, but my mum's warm words also frequently played in my head. And then, something very special happened; on one occasion, I brushed Fleur aside and got on with writing a poem.

I was looking forward to seeing Lavender – wanting to tell her about getting closer to calling time on Fleur. 'I told you that Fleur has been a squatter in my head since she left the camp, but yesterday I managed to dismiss her for a while. Do you think I'm getting closer to evicting her?'

Lavender gave me a really big smile – it was one of those smiles which make you immediately feel better. 'I do. How motivated are you to fully let go of her?'

'I want it more than anything else.'

'Don't fight any thoughts about Fleur. Sometimes, when we try very hard to get rid of thoughts, they become even more persistent. How about allowing Fleur to be in your mind, but you simply ignore her and get on with whatever you do.'

I laughed, 'That's what I did yesterday.'

'Part of you knows what's best for you. All you've to do now is to trust yourself and accept that now and then, just like everyone else, you'll make a mistake.'

'I'm a mistake,' I mumbled, my good mood disappearing fast.

'No, you are not,' Lavender stated firmly. 'The problem is your mother's inability to love you – there's nothing whatsoever wrong with you.'

'When I'm with you, I can sort of accept what you tell me, but late at night I've lots of doubts about myself. It doesn't take much for me to hate myself.'

'What will help you is to be aware of your good qualities and your plans for the future. Did you think about the things you do well and what you like about yourself?'

'I did, but it was really hard.'

'The good news is that you don't have to do it perfectly. On some days, it might be very difficult or even impossible, and that's alright. So how about trying again?'

'I will, but I'm not sure I can do it well.'

'It's okay for you to do whatever you can. You told me earlier that you like to have choices. So, you can think about your plans to become a vet and look after animals. You can also play with the idea that if you won't get into a veterinary school, you could become an architect and rescue tumble-down buildings from ruin. This way, you'll have two options for the future.'

'I'm telling you, that's so much easier than liking myself. I often day-dream about renovating my Georgian house and I totally love helping animals.'

'What you've just said shows yet again how caring you

are – I'd like you to remember that. Now let's move on to something different. The school summer holidays are nearly over and you'll be going back home soon. Can we talk about your mother?'

'If you want,' I muttered, shrugging my shoulders.

'I think it's important we do that,' said Lavender gently. 'I really hope that your mother won't ever push you away. However, it's unlikely you'll forget the rejecting words you've heard in the past –'

'When something brings back Mum's words, then there's a storm raging in my head. Sometimes, I feel as if my brain is going to be smashed by fierce winds.'

'Rejecting words by a parent can be devastating. Unfortunately, kids can feel flawed and unworthy of anything good. They may also blame themselves for things they weren't responsible for.'

'This is it – you're on the mark. I think that I let my mum down. She deserved a better daughter.'

'Do you believe that you also let down your father and your paternal grandmother?'

'Don't know ... actually, no ... not really.'

'Why not?' asked Lavender, looking me in the eye.

'Because ... they kind of accept me ... The way they talk to me is different.'

'So when you're treated well, you don't let family members down. Am I correct in saying this?'

'Something like that ...'

'But then, you're still the same kid. Are you really letting your mum down? Or is she unable to love you because she was rejected by her own mother and had been brought up by foster families and in a children's home?'

'Not sure ...'

'Would you expect anyone who never studied Chinese to speak that language?'

'No, I guess I wouldn't.'

'I told you that your mother never learned how to be a loving parent because of the early separation from her own mother.'

'But surely, as a psychologist she knows how horrible it is to hear that she never wanted me.' The familiar pressure crept into my head and chest. 'Why does she do it? I don't get it.'

'Theoretical knowledge works when people are calm and they've worked through their problems. But when they're in the grip of strong emotions like anger or hurt, their past experiences can take over. That's when the way they were parented often repeats itself. Can you think about your mother as being unable to love you rather than intentionally pushing you away?'

'I really don't know ... right now, I feel very confused.'

'It might be best to stop now. However, when you feel better, I'd like you to think about our conversation today.'

I left Emerald halls with my head pounding from the inside. My brain felt busted, like a sinking boat. A big wave of sadness surged inside me and poured out of my eyes. I quickly found a quiet spot behind an old oak tree and cried uncontrollably, until the wave ebbed away.

Sprinting forward, I sped to the kennels and invited one of the Border Collies for a run. After a little while, I slowed down and walked, feeling surprised that I was able to cool off so quickly.

As I said already, at first, I didn't want to work with a trust restorer. But despite all my misgivings, Lavender has helped me to face unhappy events and accept them. It was really weird that after talking about dreadful stuff, I felt better. Now that I was going back home, I knew that I'd miss Lavender, our chats and her clarifying things.

'Why do my parents' fights and Mum's mean words get stuck in my head?' I asked Lavender during our last meet-up.

'You naturally want your mother to love you and your parents to get on with each other. When something very distressing happens, we repeatedly think about it in the hope of understanding it, finding a solution or coming to terms with that event.'

'You also told me that I was fixated on Fleur because she took my mum's place.'

'Emotionally similar situations can bring back the feelings we'd experienced during and after the original, unhappy event. Are you beginning to get used to this idea?'

'In a way ... partly because I can't come up with anything else.'

'You're on the right path. Stay with the possibility that your mother can't love you, and because of this you wanted Fleur's acceptance and approval. I'd like to finish today with a saying by a Swiss psychiatrist called Carl Jung, "I am not what happened to me, I am what I choose to become." I genuinely believe that you can transform your unhappy experiences into a strength and achieve your goals. For you to do that, you need to have faith in yourself.'

I looked at Lavender's kind eyes and sensed her goodwill towards me. 'I'll do my best,' I murmured, even though deep down, I still had serious doubts.

Lavender handed me a piece of paper. 'That's my mobile number. Feel free to call me anytime you want. If I can't answer your call, leave a message and I will 'phone you back.'

Immediately after leaving Lavender's room, I entered her number into my mobile. A pleasant feeling spread into my head and body; I wasn't alone – Lavender accepted me with all my faults and blunders.

I walked to Moonstone halls. Tania was in our room, lying on her bed. I noticed how unhappy she looked. 'Are you alright?' I asked.

'I gotta go back,' she sighed. 'My real home is in the sanctuary, I belong here.'

'We'll meet whenever you want. I'm not allowed to bring friends home, but I'll try to persuade my mum to let you visit me.'

'That's cool. What bugs me is returning to a place where I share a room with another girl and there's staff around, yet I feel lonely big-time. I told ya that I like trees, I feel less alone when I'm by myself in a park looking at an old tree. When Elena told me that you'd be my room-mate, I thought that with a name like Willow Ashwood, you'd be a good and solid friend.'

'I didn't disappoint you?'

'Nah, not at all. Havin' you as a friend means an awful lot to me. Here's an idea, when I'm in the dumps I'll think of you. Can I take your picture next to my trees?'

'Sure thing,' I replied. 'Actually, if we could find Billie, it'd be great to include him. After all, he brought us here.'

'And he's my contact with the camp when I'm in the children's home.'

We went to the kennels and received an awful lot of unrestrained canine love. Billie was there and he happily accepted our invite, bounding next to us on our way to the forest. Tania chose a very old oak tree and took snaps of me and Billie on her mobile.

'Now let's have you next to an ash tree,' Tania laughed. 'This would go really well with your surname.' Having found one, she took more photos.

'It's my turn to choose a tree. I love hawthorns.'

We walked in the forest until we came across a large hawthorn tree with ripening orange-red berries – I took a picture of Tania with Billie, and then we took a selfie with all three of us. We accompanied Billie back to the kennels and walked to Pumpkin Hall where Liam was waiting for us.

'Tomorrow we're back home,' he uttered. 'Coriander normally softens the blow with her best cooking.'

Coriander lived up to everyone's expectations. The tables were groaning with delicious food: scrummy vegetable pasties; vegan burgers; slices of savoury lentil loaf; mixed bean and rocket salad; chunky chips; potato crochets; veggie rissoles spilling out of freshly-baked baps and vegetable laden pizzas. No wonder that Liam was licking his lips.

'Eat as much as you can,' Coriander announced, smiling broadly. 'A special invitation to teenage boys: Please eat me out of house and home.'

'I'll do that, I promise,' Liam grinned, piling heaps of food on his plate. 'I'll try every single dish.'

The chattering in the hall stopped when everyone was totally focused on the important business of enjoying Coriander's fare. Liam, true to his word, gorged himself and then, looking contented, stopped eating.

Coriander and her assistants cleared the tables and served a generous selection of desserts: banana split; gooseberry pie; apple, currant and almond crumble; chocolate layer cake; trifle and summer pudding. Liam stopped after two deserts.

'I wish I could eat more,' he laughed, looking longingly at the desserts he didn't have, 'but I'm seriously full.'

'What a yummy ending to our stay,' I murmured.

'I'm telling ya,' Tania said bleakly. 'I wish tomorrow would never ever come.'

Before going to sleep, I thought about Fleur and suddenly realised that she had vacated my head; I no longer cared about her. Then I wondered whether Lavender had replaced Fleur, but thinking some more, I was certain that Lavender was a welcome guest. She never intruded. I invited her into my mind when I chose to do so; if I didn't, she was never there.

CHAPTER TWENTY-NINE

The Homecoming

For the time being, my very last day at the Custodians' Sanctuary had arrived. The sadness of leaving was mingled with a faint hope that things at home might be different. Replaying Mum's warm voice during our last chat – despite all the horrible words she'd said in the past – made me kind of hopeful.

Reminding myself that Tania's children's home was not far away from my house, helped me to feel better. I also loved the thought that I will be keeping in touch with Liam.

Elena drove Tania and me home – looking at the wooden buildings when we were leaving the camp was a downer. I opened the car's window and inhaled deeply the energy of that incredible place where kids, animals and dragons came together. We reached the gates of the sanctuary where Chris was standing – he approached the car with a broad smile on his face.

'Have a safe journey home,' he said in his warm and kind voice. 'I'll see you soon.'

We waved goodbye to Chris as the car drove through the gates. When the gates closed behind us, I slumped back into my seat. This is it, back to my parents' never-ending fights and unfriendly kids at school.

I thought about Sophie but it felt as if the Grand Canyon was separating us now. I knew I couldn't tell her about the sanctuary because she'd never understand. Bubbly Sophie with her caring mum and many friends would find the sanctuary as appealing as a Chihuahua trying to adjust to life in Antarctica.

For a while no one spoke.

'I defo don't wanna go back to the flippin' children's home,' said Tania in a forlorn voice. 'It's gonna be as awful as ever.'

I looked at Tania's sad eyes, feeling uncomfortable that I lived with my parents. 'I'm on my own after school. I told you it'd be great to see you. How about us meeting every day?'

'Oh, yeah, let's do that,' she replied, perking up a little.

'I think it would be good for you to meet as often as you can,' said Elena. 'Also, Willow, join the Custodians' forum and you'll be posted about Fireball's progress and all the other new developments in the sanctuary.'

Tania agreed wholeheartedly. 'The forum is wicked. I've been on it for years.'

'Willow, we're now close to where you live,' said Elena, 'So I'll drop you off first.'

The moment Elena parked her car, Mum got out of the house. She introduced herself and then greeted everyone warmly.

'Pleased to meet you. I'm Elena Howell and this is Tania Eliot. Willow and Tania shared a room. They got on like a house on fire.'

Mum and Elena chatted for a few minutes and then we all said our goodbyes. I got out of the car and Mum embraced me.

'It's so good to have you back home,' she told me. 'The house was strangely empty without you.'

Did she really mean it? Or was she practising her acting skills? I wondered whilst walking indoors with her.

'When you were away,' Mum went on, 'I realised how important you're to me. Things will be different from now on. I promise.'

I wanted to believe her, but I still had lots of doubts. After all, she didn't keep her word in the past and I didn't want to be disappointed again. I decided not to say anything though. 'When will Dad come home?'

'Literally any minute now. I've cooked your favourite food; we'll have a vegetable curry and a chick pea dish for lunch.'

'That's cool. May I ask you something?'

'Go for it.'

'Tania lives quite close by. We plan to meet after school. Can she visit me at home?'

'Well, I'm not sure it's such a good idea, given the state of this house.'

'I Don't think she'd mind. She lives in a children's home, so she won't be too fussed.'

'In that case, do invite her. I know what it's like to grow up without a family.'

I looked at Mum surprised; it was the first time that she'd ever talked about her childhood. 'What's really important for us is to see each other. She is now my best friend.'

'Friendships can mean an awful lot when you grow up in a children's home.'

I heard the front door open – my dad walked in and gave me a big bear hug. 'I missed you terribly,' he said. 'It's wonderful to have my daughter back. At long last we can do things together. Now, Willow, tell me more about your stay in the countryside.'

*   *   *

Having switched on my computer, I joined the Custodians' forum with the password given to me in the camp. It was great to read about the latest news from the sanctuary. Ophelia Leech posted a detailed update about Fireball; he continued to make a steady recovery and started going out of the healing retreat for short walks on a regular basis. Amongst other entries, there was a message from Liam:

Nothing has changed at home. Mum is cooking my favourite food and plenty of it – that, if nothing else, is always good.

I immediately typed:

Hi Liam

Believe it or not, but my mum is being nice to me! The big question is for how long. I think we're going to be chill for a while and then everything will return to normal. I'll be meeting Tania after school.

Liam was apparently glued to the forum because he replied straight away:

That's cool. Let me tell you about my town. I'm certain that you'd love the old buildings in the village nearby, I know what you're like about your architecture. So, you and Tania are invited to Hitchin!

I spent a long time with Liam on the forum. Chatting with him and Tania online made me feel like a dog with two tails.

* * *

The new school year started the following Monday. I had difficulties listening to what the teachers were saying because my mind was taken up with the sanctuary.

Sophie was very happy to see me and I really wanted to tell her about the dragons, especially Fireball, but I knew that she wouldn't get it. I let her chatter away while I was counting down the minutes to the moment I'd see Tania and go on the forum with her.

After the last lesson, I scooted to the agreed meeting point on Hampstead Heath. Tania was waiting for me with her big eyes sadder than ever.

'Are you okay?' I asked.

'I told ya, I'm always in the dumps after leaving the camp. I'm gonna be alright in a couple of weeks.'

'I've chatted with Liam on the forum. He has invited us to visit him in Hitchin.'

'I'll ask, but I ain't holding my breath, the children's home would be suspicious that I might be meeting a creepy perv who's chatted me up online.'

We walked in the park and afterwards I invited Tania to my home. It was a big relief that she didn't mind it being run-down and untidy. My parents were still at work so I called out, 'Hello George, I'd like you to meet Tania from the Custodians' Sanctuary.'

We waited briefly and then George said in his deep, croaky voice, 'I'm privileged to meet you, young lady.'

'Wow,' said Tania, 'I've never talked to a house before. Actually, it's quite spooky.'

'Well,' said George, 'you'll get used to us conversing. I'm heartily glad you made friends with Willow.'

'By now,' said Tania, 'we're practically sisters.'

'In that case,' George laughed, 'I entreat you to be my guest anytime you wish.'

'Thanks, I'll take you up on that.'

'Enjoy your visit. I bid you farewell.'

I prepared beans on toast and Dragon Well Tea. After we'd eaten, I signed into the Custodians' forum. The latest entry was from Chris Light:

Re: A meet-up in the Natural History Museum in London next Sunday.

You're all invited to our gathering at 11am in front of the main entrance of the museum next Sunday.

We'll visit the museum and weather permitting, will have a picnic in Hyde Park. If it rains, we'll find a quiet corner in the museum.

If you can, please bring savoury food to share. Coriander promised to bake desserts for everyone! I'm sure you'll be glad to know that Billie will be joining us.

Tania looked thrilled. 'That's exactly what I need!' she exclaimed.

'I couldn't agree more.' I said, giving her a big hug. 'I can't wait to see them all.'

'I gotta go now, or they won't let me see you tomorrow. Actually, how about you coming with me and meeting the staff?'

'Do you think that'd help?'

'Deffo. They wanna know who we meet. Tell them your mum is a psychologist and your dad a teacher, and then they'll let me visit you after school every day.'

We travelled by bus to Tania's children's home. Tania introduced me to her social worker who asked me one million questions, wrote down my address and mobile number as well as my parents' telephone numbers, and then called my dad. She talked to him for some time and eventually agreed to Tania visiting me every day after school.

* * *

At long last Sunday showed up. Tania and I reached the museum half an hour early. Chris, Billie and a few kids from the camp were already there. The hound sprinted in our direction with his tail wagging furiously and danced circles around us. After he'd calmed down, Tania and I embraced him – he reciprocated by licking our faces.

Even though I'd visited the museum a number of times, I was carried away yet again by the utterly fab design. Standing in front of the building, I got a big buzz out of its cool and, at the same time, playful architecture.

Before coming to the meet-up, I read on the internet about the museum and memorised new architectural words. I practised on my dad and he appeared suitably impressed by my new vocab.

I fully connected with the energy of the building, enjoying the two grand towers and the numerous semi-circular arches around the entrance. High up above the gargoyles and between each of the dormer windows proudly sat various animals – but no dragons. *Honestly!* I thought. *Didn't the designer know about the natural history of dragons?*

The lavish terracotta *façade* invited you to enter and explore the inside of the building, promising lots of architectural beauties as well as exhibits telling the story of the evolution of the natural world.

'Look at the blue sky,' Tania gushed, looking upbeat. 'Not even one cloud, we're gonna 'ave a picnic in Hyde Park today.'

At that moment, Liam joined us. 'I'm so glad you made it,' I said to him.

'I'd not have missed this for the world. That's what keeps me going during term-time. Believe you me, I wish I lived close to you and Tania.'

Having checked the list of kids, Chris called out, 'Now that everyone is here, let's start our ninety minutes' visit. You're free to explore the different parts of the museum, but I'd like everyone to be in front of this entrance by a quarter to one. From here we'll walk to Hyde Park where we'll have our picnic.'

Unfortunately, Billie wasn't allowed inside the museum. He sat on the grass and watched us enter the building, looking somewhat sad.

'I wanna see the dinosaurs!' declared Tania. 'They're soooo cool.'

'Totally,' raved Liam, 'they've here the most intact Stegosaurus fossil ever found.'

We located that awesome dinosaur skeleton and stood there marvelling at its enormous size and completeness. We also checked out other dinosaurs and then spent some time in the company of different mammals, some of which are now extinct.

'I think we'd better make a move now,' said Liam. 'I'm starving. Breakfast was a long, long time ago.'

We left the museum and joined the others. After counting

the number of kids, Chris announced, 'We'll walk to the park as one group. Please stay together.'

Having reached Hyde Park, we found a good spot for our picnic. Chris asked us to sit down in a circle and share the food we'd brought, which turned out to be mostly sandwiches. After the savoury fare was eaten, Chris opened his wicker basket. My mouth watered at the sight of its scrummy contents: a pumpkin cake; an apple pie; pastries; buns and gingerbread – all lovingly prepared by Coriander.

I enjoyed Coriander's superb baking and Billie sitting next to me. The afternoon sunshine opened the door to feelings of ease and laziness.

'It's good to be together again,' said Chris. 'I hope you've all settled down by now at home and at school.'

'Nothing has changed,' said Kayla gloomily. 'I really miss the camp. I'm counting the days when I'm gonna go back.'

'That's one of the reasons why we're having our meet-up today,' Chris went on. 'I'd like to talk now about how you can help each other. So, as well as sharing good things, tell your friends also about unhappy thoughts or feelings.'

'What helps me is reading the posts on the Custodians' forum on my mobile,' said Tania. 'I even do it under the bed covers when I wake up in the middle of the night. They relax me and then it's easier to go back to sleep.'

'I keep checking for new messages all the time,' Liam admitted. 'I think I'm kinda addicted to them.'

'Well,' said Chris, 'moderation is a good thing, but now let me tell you how to manage difficult moments. As you know, you can always contact your trust restorer when something upsetting happens, or if you prefer, you can call me. If possible, join a local Custodians' group. Also, look out for kids who have problems at school or at home and befriend them. If you feel they might benefit from joining us, invite them to one of our gatherings. Those of you who like animals, volunteer for a few hours at an animal rescue centre. Doing things for others can make you feel better.'

Looking at Chris, Billie and the kids in the circle, I felt that they were my second family. A totally lovely sensation of belonging and warmth swept into every cell of my body and head. I noticed how calm and contented Tania's eyes were, and even Liam appeared chilled! I pictured dragons flying in the skies about us, and added their power to the mix of good feelings. Just then, I realised that I was one of the luckiest girls in all of London.

Printed in Great Britain
by Amazon

72340857R00139